Tempest I ... It
was a fool's be ... uer
success depended on an unknown factor—the enemy
Leonard Allred. And Blair had to do nothing. This was
where Tempest would usually negotiate a better deal.
But she *wanted* to do something stupid and rash. And
risky. She calculated risk all day at work—used to
calculate risk. But she didn't take any of the risk
herself. She saved her pennies and walked the careful
path forward, far from the edge. All that had gotten her
was laid off. And not often laid.

Tonight she wanted to fly. To hell if she crashed.

Betting on Love

by

Mary Beesley

Betting on Love

Cover Art by *Jennifer Greeff*

The Wild Rose Press, Inc.
PO Box 708
Adams Basin, NY 14410-0708
Visit us at www.thewildrosepress.com

Publishing History
First Edition, 2021
Trade Paperback ISBN 978-1-5092-3557-5
Digital ISBN 978-1-5092-3558-2

Published in the United States of America

Dedication

To Doug
For going all in with me

Acknowledgments

Thank you to Wild Rose Press, to Josette Arthur and the entire team for believing in my book and being great to work with. Thank you to my husband for being a big nerd and teaching me what an actuary is and for taking me to Dallas. Thank you to Katherine for reading my early drafts. Thanks to Amy for loving the Astros and catching my typos. Thank you to my critique partners. And most importantly, thanks to God for inspiring me to start writing fiction, for gifting me the perseverance to improve, and the creativity to spin a compelling story.

Chapter One
The Bet

The risk was low, the reward potential high. If Tempest talked to him, what was the worst that could happen? Maybe he'd be rude or think she was an annoying groupie gold-digger. The best-case scenario? He'd fall in love with her at first sight. She was maybe a little in love with him already, and she'd only gotten a good look at his backside.

Leonard Allred stood directly in front of her in line at the juice bar. The genius had invented the software program that made her job as an insurance underwriter so much easier. Almost so easy it wasn't fun anymore. Tempest had never seen him in person before, but she recognized his face from previous internet searches. She pulled her phone from her leather tote and googled him quickly to make sure. Definitely the same guy as the image search, but he was even hotter in person. Leonard Allred had moved his billion-dollar company, Red Rocco, from Palo Alto to Dallas two years ago, but to see him right here in Highland Park. At her juice shop. Swoon.

She pretended to look at the menu as she studied him. He was half a head taller than her five foot ten inches. Classically handsome, dark wavy hair, and hooded eyes. Brains and beauty. How annoying. Unless he was into her. But what could she say to him? Tell him she was an underwriter? A beneficiary of his creation?

Before she could decide, he stepped up to the counter and ordered a Protein Lovers smoothie and a Love Your Grains bowl. Someone was hungry. And why was he here getting his own breakfast? Didn't he have an assistant, or three, to do his errands?

He stepped away from the counter, making space for her. Disappointment panged when he didn't look at her. In her fluster, she stammered through her simple order, a green drink for her sick colleague. The juice was already made, so she had no excuse to loiter after her purchase. He stood near the window, his face tilted toward his phone. Her tongue lay heavy in her mouth. No charming ideas on how to talk to him came to mind. Feeling like a major wuss, she left the store. Blair would have said something to him. Her best friend would have spoken the moment she recognized Leonard Allred. Completely disappointed in herself, Tempest drove out of the parking lot. She squinted at the store windows, but she couldn't see him. She'd lost her chance.

****

"And how are we feeling today?" Tempest asked Fred, the coworker who'd been blowing his nose like a disgusting trumpet every three minutes yesterday. She'd timed them like a labor nurse watching contractions. She'd also showered the second she got home from work and had three cups of echinacea tea. She could not live through that again.

"Much better," Fred said. "Thanks for the tip about the honey lemon tea and the Epsom salt bath."

She set the bottle of green juice on his desk. "Don't

think about how it tastes. Just throw it back. The ginger might burn a little going down, but I promise it will help."

He scowled at the brightly colored bottle, but he picked it up anyway. "I trust you. And thanks."

Gratification lightened her step as she strolled to her corner desk. Today was a good day. She hadn't talked to Leonard Allred, but she'd still seen him, the sun had broken through the clouds pestering Dallas all week, her remedies were helping Fred, and in a few hours, she would review her latest fantastic work reports with her boss. Good. Day.

She spent the morning, her best working hours, analyzing the data and risks for new applicants. They'd been using Leonard Allred's software, Red Rocco, for six months now. The program not only took into consideration the applicant's submitted information, it crawled through the internet for hidden risk. Tempest used to double-check all the quotes manually, but when the software proved as good an analyzer as she, she cut out that step. Now she rarely had to do the tedious analytical work herself.

Every ninety minutes, she obeyed the alert she'd set on her watch. She stood, stretched, and did one loop around the office to get the blood moving. Fred gave her a cheerful thumbs-up on her way past. He reminded her a little of her father, large-jawed, honest, and lacking humor.

Standing at her desk, she pulled her hands behind her back, her arm muscles lengthening. As she twisted her torso, the pink macaroni necklace hidden under her shirt shifted between her breasts. She had to wear it until Sunday—the terms of the bet she'd lost. Turned out coins *could* be balanced on their sides. She had no idea why she always agreed to these stupid bets with Blair. Actually, she did know. Blair Stickley was fun. Blair Stickley was the best thing that had ever happened to her.

At twelve thirty, she ate her chickpea and kale salad. It was a little wilted. Typical Friday lunch problems. On Sundays, she made five salads for her weekday lunches, portioning them out into matching glass containers. The quinoa with black beans and orange zest was her favorite. She'd make that next week.

She sat as close to the kitchenette window as she could, letting the sliver of sun caress her face. Her two favorite colleagues ate at the table with her, but she had a hard time listening. She wasn't interested in a nephew's bout of chicken pox. Didn't they have a vaccine for that now? The coworkers didn't need her words anyway. They were both talkers.

Tempest thought about her meeting today at four thirty. Was it weird to have it scheduled just before closing time? She usually did her quarterly reviews on Monday mornings. She'd been working with the company for five years now, since she was twenty-three. The next step was a big one. Actuary. She got a hit of excitement just thinking about it. With this new software, Red Rocco, doing so much of the computing, she was itching for more responsibility, more of a challenge. If she kept on her trajectory, she'd be an actuary by this spring. She grinned at the sunny sky.

Damn, she loved her job.

****

"Fired." Tempest threw her tote bag on the couch

as she stormed into her house. "I got *fired*."

"Okay, honey," Blair said, coming around the island in the kitchen with her hands up in a calming gesture. The apartment smelled like caramel. Pots and bowls littered the counter.

Tempest's chest heaved up and down as she jerked open the buttons on her suit coat. Of course she'd dressed up for her meeting—dressed for success. *Bah.* She tossed the coat on the couch, her pasta necklace coming free and smacking her in the face with the motion.

Blair's brows bunched as she watched the blazer crinkle in a heap.

Tempest usually hung her clothes neatly as soon as she got home, but today she didn't bother with the coat. What did it matter if it wrinkled now? She didn't take out her lunch box and put it in the dishwasher. She didn't need it clean by Sunday. She wouldn't be packing lunch salads for work next week.

"I'm unemployed." Tempest sulked past Blair and slumped onto a counter stool. It sounded so much worse when she said it out loud. She inhaled the inviting scents of vanilla and roasting sugar. An amber liquid simmered on the stove. "What are you making?"

Blair walked back to the pot and stirred. "It's apple cake with—"

"Can I have some?"

Blair opened her mouth, closed it.

Treats before dinner wasn't Tempest's order of things. But screw it. Today had already gone to crap. She made a pass-it-over motion with her fingers.

"It's almost done. Talk while I finish." Blair stirred boiling butter.

"They laid off three underwriters. That's all of us except Fred Burns because he's been with the company the longest. At least that's what they say. And I can't really argue with his years of experience, but just compare our numbers. I'm better than he is. That's a *fact*." She exhaled so hard her cheeks ballooned out. "But he's got a penis and a birthday before 1990."

"That pisses me off," Blair said with the appropriate amount of verve.

Tempest poked at a spill of flour on the granite. "Stupid Red Rocco software took my job."

"I'm sorry, Stormie."

"And you know what's ironic?"

"No. I don't." Blair dumped powdered sugar in a bowl.

"I saw Leonard Allred this morning. I stopped to get Fred some juice for his cold. Last time I ever do something nice for that coughing fart again."

Blair snorted.

"And Leonard Allred was in line in front of me."

"What did you say to him?"

Tempest cringed.

"You didn't even talk to him." Blair whisked the hot caramel into the sugar with pointed aggression.

Tempest flared. "I'm glad I didn't. Can you imagining being all gushy and starry-eyed to someone just hours before they destroy your life?"

The mixture in Blair's bowl turned a fluffy amber. She spooned out a dollop and handed it to Tempest. "What does it need?"

She licked the frosting. Sugar and salty butter hit her tongue like a drug. "A bigger spoon."

Blair grinned, the freckles that dusted her nose and

cheeks crinkling. She cut a piece of cake, put it on a plate, and topped it with a generous layer of frosting.

"You're taking advantage of my weakened state." The forkful of food garbled Tempest's last words.

"I'm healing your soul."

"This is the opposite of health—"

"Let's not talk about nutrition right now." Blair cut herself a piece. "Or ever."

"Oh." Tempest groaned as heaven saturated her tongue. "It tastes so good. So, so good."

"We can always talk more about that."

Blair's dream was to open a treat shop one day. They'd discussed it at length but hadn't decided exactly what she'd specialize in yet. She loved making it all: pies, cakes, candies, cookies, chocolates. She was working for SMU campus catering while she was deciding—and saving up the money. Although Tempest knew the saving part wasn't going as well for Blair as the fantasizing part. Tempest figured she had plenty of time to convince Blair to open up a salad place instead. She hadn't made any progress in that direction so far.

She shoveled the last third of the cake into her mouth—she could get a lot in there at a time if she wanted. Thanks to her dad, she had a long jaw and wide lips. The dessert was gone. And with it, all the brief comfort. "What am I going to do now?" Her voice turned shrill. "This was not part of the plan."

"First step." Frosting flicked onto the counter as Blair held up a spoon. She leaned over and licked it off before focusing back on Tempest. "We're going out tonight. After we finish our first drink, we'll come up with step two."

"Yes. Good. But we're going to the Honor Bar. I

think this cake needs to be followed by a French omelet."

"It can stand on its own," Blair muttered as she took a pile of dishes to the sink.

****

Two hours later they walked into the hip downtown restaurant. Blair wore a short yellow dress that accentuated the richness of her skin, her remarkable curves, and the gold highlights in her riot of curly dark hair. Tempest, in her black mourning clothes, felt like an empty garment bag next to her friend.

Blair got a genuine smile from the bartender as she ordered their drinks. Of course they didn't have a reservation. Of course it was busy.

Loitering near the bar, Tempest sipped her gin and hoped some of these seats would vacate pronto. She drank faster as she replayed the scene with her boss. The compliments that carried the poison. She'd been an asset to the company. She was a great worker, a team player, reliable, and responsible. But they just couldn't keep her on. She hadn't done anything wrong. Red Rocco was to blame. She imagined Leonard Allred at the juice shop this morning, shiny hair, chinos fitted nicely over toned legs. He was so easy to hate right now. Her grudge mixed well with the alcohol warming her belly.

"It's empty."

Blair's voice broke through the fog, and Tempest stopped sucking air from her glass.

Blair took Tempest's drink, trading it for a fresh bee's knees from the bartender. Gin with lemon and honey was Tempest's favorite. There went another fifteen dollars. She should really stop. She didn't have a job. No more paychecks. She had six months' salary in the bank, but that was her savings. Her fingers clutched the glass as her logical mind tried to command her to put the drink down. She lifted it to her lips.

"They're leaving." Blair sauntered to the end of the bar and snagged two stools.

Tempest slid into her seat. "I should probably eat something besides sugar and alcohol."

"We are missing fat." Blair glanced down at the menu. "Crispy chicken sandwich for me."

"Always," Tempest said, because fried chicken was one of the areas Blair was entirely reliable.

Blair checked out the crowd while they waited for their food. She'd been on-again, off-again with DeShawn for a year, but they were off right now. Tempest hadn't had a boyfriend for nineteen months. Hadn't been on a third date in nearly as long. But tonight she didn't even look around. She stared, unseeing, at the TV. Some football team was playing another football team. Usually a little alcohol loosened her up, made her laugh like a hyena and become way more fun than usual. Not tonight. She could feel herself close up, her edges folding in.

"Come on, Stormie," Blair said after swallowing a handful of fries. "It's going to be okay. I would die for your resume and your brains. And your savings account." She gave Tempest a sideways grin. "You'll get a new job in a blink."

"Not with Red Rocco plowing the field."

Blair opened her mouth, but only a puff of air came out.

A drop of condensation ran down Tempest's drink.

Her voice was hollow. "Instead of salivating over Leonard Allred this morning like a pubescent, I should have spit at him."

"That would have been so much more mature."

She ignored the sarcasm. "I can't believe I thought he was attractive."

"I can't either. When I saw him at the event we catered on campus last week, I was not impressed."

Tempest snapped to attention, her defenses flaring. She lifted her phone and pulled up this morning's search of images of Leonard Allred. She clicked on a well-done head shot. "Come on, you can't tell me you don't like this."

Blair plucked the phone from her hands. "Oh. That's him?"

"Who were you picturing?"

Blair zoomed in on the tan face and dark eyes. "I definitely had the wrong guy. I saw this hunk at the event too, but he wasn't acting conceited or famous at all. He even talked to me."

"Don't make him a nice guy. He's not a nice guy. He's destroying American jobs."

Blair tapped the screen with her thumbs. "It says here his company employs twenty-four hundred people."

"Whose side are you on?"

Blair slid the screen back to the picture, stroking the man's smooth cheek with a sparkly gold fingernail. "His side."

Tempest snatched the phone.

"Maybe you should try to work under him."

Tempest rolled her eyes, but she chuckled. "Don't even pretend that wasn't one hundred percent sexual."

"If that's what you want."

"Ew. Never."

Blair grinned, showing her white teeth. Her eyes sparkled as if she knew Tempest was lying. "Work for him. Work with him. Work around him. Whatever works."

"I don't work." She didn't mean to be such a downer, but she was not ready to come out of her dark hole. She looked away from the couple sharing the same side of a single person booth.

Blair and Tempest lapsed into silence, picking at the remains of Parmesan fries and watching the mingling of humans out on the town on a Friday night.

"This guy ruined your carefully drafted life plan," Blair said. "He cost you a job you love. And one I love because you can afford to buy me good presents." Her fingers rested on the gold necklace Tempest had given her last Christmas. It had a tiny donut charm, and the sprinkles were made out of diamond shards. She never took it off. "He should pay."

"I wish he would walk through those doors right now. I would march up to him and tell it to him straight…and slap him."

Blair whooped. "You go, girl."

Tempest sobered. "I do wish I could see the look on his face when he realizes he cost three people their jobs today. How does he feel? How does he sleep at night?"

"Probably quite well atop his piles of gold."

She envisioned a greedy king sleeping atop bumpy bags of coins. "I bet that would be hard and uncomfortable." She winced. Why had she said bet?

Blair's eyes lit up, invoked by the magic of their

little game. Whenever Tempest said that word, Blair thought of one.

Ah, crap.

"I'll take that bet."

"I didn't say that word you think I said." Tempest picked up her fork and pointed in at Blair.

"Are you going to stab me with that?"

She set the tiny trident down and smoothed out her napkin. "What's for dessert?"

"Don't try to change the subject. You said bet, and a bet you shall have."

According to Blair, saying the word was akin to a binding contract. Tempest shook her head vigorously. "I said pet."

"Tell me no more lies."

She scowled at her grinning friend. "There is no bet here. We don't know Leonard Allred."

"There is always a bet to be made."

That was true. Anytime, anywhere, Blair could come up with a wager.

"Besides. I know where your Red Romeo lives."

Tempest let out a laugh at the smug look on Blair's face. "Of course you do."

Blair bit her lip as she nodded. "SMU was sending thank yous to the people who sponsored the big event last week. I might have taken a picture of all the return addresses."

"What were you thinking?"

Blair shrugged. "They were business addresses of people in the community. I thought it might be good for a marketing list when I start my chocolate-ery."

"It's a chocolate-ery now?" Tempest stumbled over the non-word.

"I just tried it, and I don't like it."

Tempest picked up her drink and sucked in the last drop. "I can find Leonard Allred's office online. Or I can just look up when I'm driving down Cole. It says Red Rocco huge on the building."

Blair's eyes gleamed. "But Romeo's address on the list was his home address. I'm sure it was a mistake." She wiggled her phone. "But I got it."

"So what, we're going over there and knocking on the door?"

Blair beamed.

"Yeah. No. And we should probably stop drinking now."

"You're right. That's lame." Blair set the phone down and turned her attention to the football game.

Tempest couldn't stop herself. "Where does he live?" Blair found the address in her photos, and Tempest mapped it. "That's a third of a mile from here."

"Let's go right now."

"No." Tempest didn't dare call bluff. Blair never bluffed. Talking about it was easy, but she balked at the thought of actually knocking on his door at nine p.m. on a Friday night.

Blair's bronze gaze flitted over Tempest's face. "You're not looking your best right now, anyway. Your hair looks like you've been in a convertible...or electrocuted."

"Such flattery." Tempest's hair was shorter than her shoulders, and she had been pulling at it all evening. "But I'm not going to his house ever."

"Here's the bet. You have to get him to take you out on a date before Halloween."

"What? That's impossible." But a flicker of pleasure flared at the thought.

"Oh, stop it. You're a total babe, and he'll love that you're smart. Your legs are as long as Texas. And you can fit a whole maple bar in your mouth." Blair's brows popped up and down. "If you know what I mean."

Heat rushed to Tempest's cheeks. "Now we really need to stop drinking. And talking. No more words."

"After he buys you dinner—order the lobster—and you get your revenge sex, you can ask him how it feels to destroy lives. Or you won't even have to ask him. You'll know from destroying his."

"What if I don't want to sleep with him? Because that would really be a win for him."

Blair's lips curled up like they always did when she had Tempest hooked. "Fine. That's not part of the deal. The deal is you go out with him before the end of the month. That's thirteen days. And on the first date, you must tell him he cost you your job. You don't even have to kiss him. You can be super lame if you want."

Tempest nodded primly. "Thank you. I will."

"Winner gets to pick the paint color for the family room."

It needed new paint so badly they could see faint outlines of the drywall seams through the paint. The landlord had told them they could choose the color if they took care of getting it done. She and Blair had not been able to come to an agreement or find a compromise between pink and cream. Blair kept saying how good pink would look with the gray kitchen cabinets. But really, it would make her so happy. Cream would make Tempest happy. So soothing and normal. So safe.

Tempest had very little chance of winning this. It was a fool's bet. She had to do so much to win, and her success depended on an unknown factor—the enemy Leonard Allred. And Blair had to do nothing. This was where Tempest would usually negotiate a better deal. But she *wanted* to do something stupid and rash. And risky. She calculated risk all day at work—used to calculate risk. But she didn't take any of the risk herself. She saved her pennies and walked the careful path forward, far from the edge. All that had gotten her was laid off. And not often laid.

Tonight she wanted to fly. To hell if she crashed.

Chapter Two
The Accident

Tempest stared at Blair's bike, an old hybrid with peeling handlebars and rust on the gears. How the hell had she agreed to this? In the light of day, this felt beyond preposterous. She should admit defeat now and prepare for pink.

But nope, she would never back out of a bet without a fight. She would battle for the sad remains of her pride. She had twelve days, an address, and a bike.

She picked up Blair's helmet, a hideous thing with long aerodynamic curves—like Blair ever went for speed. Tempest had spent extra time on her hair, washing it with the expensive shampoo and styling it carefully with cream. The dark bob curled around her jaw and danced with her neck. Was it better to be safe and look like a nerd, or if she didn't wear it, would he think she was an idiot with no concern for her brain? She put the helmet on.

"Here goes nothing."

A cool breeze ruffled the orange and yellow trees along her path. The sun had dropped low in the sky. She biked slowly. No good getting sweaty for the big "meet." And she needed time to settle her nerves. It had seemed so easy last night when they made their drunken plans. Just pretend to fall. But that wasn't a thing. She'd either fall or not fall—for reals. She looked down, past her black leather slip-ons to the rocky ground. Adrenaline surged.

Leonard Allred's house wasn't far from hers. One-point-two miles. A high-end community of six condos. Gated. That was probably a huge selling point for him, but it made stalking him so much harder.

She biked past the front entrance, not stopping until she'd rounded the corner a block up. She panted, her face burning. She hadn't even looked through the gates as she zoomed past. *If that is what you call recon, you're fired.* She let out a maniacal laugh. Fired twice in two days. A record. When she finally sobered, she turned her bike around. This was so stupid. Why was she doing this? *He cost me my job.* Jaw hardening, she pedaled. She'd loved her job. All the numbers and data waiting for her to puzzle out. All the digits on the paychecks.

She stopped by a streetlamp a few yards from the pedestrian entrance to the condo development. Through the iron gate, six front doors lined up facing each other in two well-manicured rows. If he wasn't home, she was screwed. If he stayed home for longer than a few minutes, she was screwed. If he left through the garage, she was screwed. Of course he'd leave in his car. Like anyone walked anywhere. This was Texas. She pulled her phone from her pocket and dialed.

Blair picked up on the first ring. "Did you meet him?"

Tempest let out a sharp laugh. "Of course not. I'm standing here creeping on some closed doors. I can't even tell which condo is his. There is no chance I'm going to run into him. Why did we ever think this would work?"

Blair laughed. She laughed so hard Tempest nearly hung up. "We might have been drunker than we thought last night."

"That's helpful. Thank you." Tempest almost said the bet was off, but she bit her tongue. Blair would never let her live it down if she gave up with such little effort. The bet had been made and sealed with spit, wet pinkies intertwined, just like they always did it. She wouldn't give Blair the satisfaction.

"I have to go back to work. You totally got this." Blair was still laughing when she hung up.

Tempest locked her phone. What now? If she got close enough to the gate, she might be able to see into some windows. Maybe catch his house number, 121 according to Blair's stolen contact sheet. But how was she going to fake a bike accident if she had her face pressed against the fence? She could stay down here on the sidewalk and pretend to be looking at her phone. But how long was that acceptable? Two, three minutes? And to stage an accident, she needed to back up so if she saw him, she could get some speed before falling at his feet—literally. She chuckled darkly as she tucked her phone into her back pocket.

Time to go home.

She pulled gum from her pocket. As she was putting it in her mouth, she heard male voices through the gate. Her pulse soared. Was it him? Could she be so lucky? A man came into view through the iron bars.

Leonard Allred.

No freaking way. What were the chances? Well, if he came and went on a Saturday an average of four times, more with good weather... Nope. No time to actually calculate likelihood. This was meant to be. But what was she going to do now? He was nearly to the gate. He hadn't seen her, thank goodness. He stopped and looked down, pulling a phone from his jacket pocket.

Start biking and then crash into that bush by the gate.

Her body seized up. *Abort. Abort.* She couldn't do it. Her heart was beating so hard she couldn't see straight. She needed a new plan. One that did not include self-inflicted pain or injury. Or humiliation. A healthy run-in at the juice stop like last time perhaps. *Go. Go. Go.* She put her left foot on the pedal and jerked the handlebars. The right grip ricocheted off the light post. Oh no. The front wheel twisted. It slid on the loose gravel around the base. This could not actually be happening. Her pulse soared into hyperdrive. She hopped on her right foot to regain balance, and her calf nicked the sharp teeth of the bike's chain ring. "Ow." Reflex had her skipping her leg out, trying with everything to save her balance. Her overreaction caused her already teetering bike to lurch too far to the side. The crossbar knocked into her left thigh. She cursed as she went down with the bike.

Her butt slammed into the cement, and then her spine hit. The back of her foam-wrapped head bounced off the ground before settling. Good thing she wore the helmet. Sharp pain flared from her left ankle and her wrist where she'd tried to catch herself with one hand. "Ouch."

"Are you all right?" a male voice asked.

She closed her eyes. Had she seriously just pulled this off? And by *accident.* That was how accidents worked. She opened her eyes, lifting her head and turning toward the sound. A man crouched at her side, balancing on the balls of his sneakers.

Not Leonard Allred.

Are you effing kidding me?

Pale blueish-gray eyes watched her below a brow knitted in worry. The man looked thirtyish, but with the hair covering half his face, it was hard to tell.

Annoyance surged over the waves of pain and embarrassment. "You're going with the beard?"

He tilted his head back as if she'd flicked his nose.

She widened her eyes at her own incivility. Had she seriously said that out loud to a perfectly nice-seeming stranger?

He leveled his eyes at her the way Tempest's mother used to do when she disapproved, as if to say, *manners!*

"I'm sorry. That was rude. It looks—well…you can do what you want."

His tawny hair was thinning on top, so maybe he was compensating. It didn't help, but he clearly wasn't in the mood to hear that now.

"Thank you for your permission." His voice was deadpan.

She craned to see over the man's shoulder as Leonard Allred exited the gate. He had his phone to his right ear, blocking the accident on the sidewalk from view. *Look up. See me. Help me.* He turned left. And walked away. Just like that. Gone.

She let her head fall back, the helmet smacking into the cement again. "Ion to Camp," she whispered. "Total mission failure."

The man chuckled.

She was not ready to see the humor in her little

stunt. And her ankle was throbbing now. "It's not funny."

"That was a nerdy thing to say."

"You got that phrase?"

"I have read book five in the Ion Biode series."

She tried to ignore the flicker in her core. He liked her "weirdo sci-fi books," as Blair called them. "Now who's the nerd?"

"Guilty for sure, but you can call me Arty."

"Arty?" She failed to keep the skepticism from her tone. She blamed him entirely for ruining her meet-cute, but she gave him a small smile. "Tempest."

One side of his full mouth curved up, the beard quivering in the lip corner. "You don't have the right to look at me like that with the name Tempest."

"I've heard all the jokes."

"That sounds like a challenge."

Now was not the time. She was still lying on her butt with a bike between her legs.

As if he read her thoughts, he glanced down. "Do you need help up?"

She followed the line of his gaze to her sprawled body. Limbs everywhere. She didn't know if she needed help. But it would be nice if he did something besides gawk. Her left ankle was pinned around the pedal and bar. It pulsed. "I think I actually hurt myself."

"That sometimes happens when you crash." He chewed his lips, as if holding back humor.

She scowled. "You saw me fall."

"If it makes you feel better, most bike accidents happen at zero miles per hour."

"If that were even remotely true, then that might help. As it is, I feel worse." She shifted, trying to wiggle out from under the bike. He gripped the middle bar. No wedding ring, she noticed as he lifted the weight off. She hissed as her ankle sparked in pain.

He frowned. "You're hurt."

"Is that not exactly what I just said?"

He studied her face for a second with unconcealed interest before scanning her legs. "It's your ankle?"

She nodded as she sat up, reaching for the unhappy foot. She'd worn black skinny jeans, a terrible choice now that she saw how well the gray cement dust showed up on the fabric. Today could not have been more of a failure if she'd planned it that way.

"Good thing you wore a helmet."

Oh hell, she still had that on? Good thing Leonard Allred was not seeing her like this, or she would never get that date. She unbuckled the chin strap and lifted it off, then fluffed her matted locks.

"You can tell your daughter she did a nice job with that necklace."

She looked down at her chest where the blasted macaroni had come free again. It lay like a clown smile over her blouse. She'd been so careful to tuck it into her bra so Leonard Allred wouldn't see it. She only had to wear it one more day. "I don't have children. Or a husband." Satisfaction flowed through her at the change that came over him. "I have a roommate who likes to mess with me."

Arty looked puzzled, then his brow cleared, and he let the tips of his straight teeth show. "Lost a bet?"

"I certainly didn't win it."

He laughed, his mouth a pink and white crescent moon in a sky of dark beard. It was a good laugh, even if it was at her expense.

"Just help me up already."

"Let's get you some ice. I live just through the gates."

"You live here too?"

"You know someone who lives here?"

"No."

He looked at her sideways as he held out a hand. She set her palm in his. It was dry and clean. A friendly hand. He tugged, and she lifted to her feet, immediately shifting all her weight to her right foot as her left, in an angry strike, refused to do its job. She grimaced.

Arty strung her helmet through the handlebar. With the bike in one hand, he held out the other to her. "Come on, I'll help you."

She eyed his outstretched arm warily. "Don't you have somewhere to be? You were leaving, weren't you? I don't want to be a bother."

"No bother. I'm not busy."

Should she be worried about that? Should she go into this stranger's house? He didn't seem like a serial killer or a rapist. But how would she know? She wasn't familiar with any that she knew of. She wobbled on her right foot and reached out to him, catching her balance.

His arm went around her middle, and a jolt of attraction hit when his palm wrapped her waist. Each of his fingers seemed to burn through the silk of her shirt and send sparks along her nerves. She glanced over at him in surprise. Really? This regular dude? He was partly turned away, focused on the bike. He had thick eyelashes. The small round nose and smooth pale skin made her wonder if he was younger than she'd first thought, but then she noticed a few gray strands hiding in the light brown hair above his ears.

"How old are you?"

He chuckled. "Twenty-nine."

And she was twenty-eight. A nice match. He looked at her sidelong, the return question dancing in his pale eyes. But he didn't ask, so she didn't answer. She guessed he was five eleven, one inch taller than she was. Another good fit. She lifted her arm and rested her hand on his shoulder. Her fingers melted into downy fabric.

"Wow, that's soft."

"I hope you're talking about my sweater and not the iron muscles underneath."

She felt around the ridges of his deltoid. He wasn't a big man, but he was wiry and hard. He turned his hairy jaw her way, his face so close she could see the patterns in his irises, like the sky before rain. His eyelids half closed, and his face dropped into a humorless mask as her fingers continued to prod over his shoulder, feeling the lines of lean muscle. *Very nice indeed.*

She waited another moment before saying, "Cashmere?"

"That's what the store claimed." He took a step forward, and she hopped to keep up. She balanced while he used his key in the gate and held it wide.

"You're just going to let me in?"

"I was, but now you're sounding like a stalker. I do not like stalkers."

He said it like he knew from experience. She hopped forward, steadying a hand on the fence. "Who does?"

He pulled her bike through, closed the gate, and offered her his arm again. "I suppose police like finding them."

"I see. Helpful and funny." She gladly slid under his cashmere wing again.

The date with Leonard Allred would have to wait until tomorrow.

Arty leaned the bike against a planter by the front door. "Are you fine with me leaving this here? It should be safe inside the gate, and it's not like it's..." He looked down at the peeling paint.

Tempest chuckled despite the pain growing louder in her foot. "I'm pretty sure my roommate bought that at a yard sale for fifteen dollars."

"I have a wrench in the garage. I can straighten out the handlebars."

She took note of his generosity. "No. I'm looking forward to giving it back mangled."

He glanced over, as if trying to decide whether she was truly a bad person.

"She deserves it. Trust me."

He looked like he was about to ask, changed his mind, and opened the door.

She stopped on the threshold, leaned against the frame, and inhaled the smell of fresh linen and lemon blossoms. A hall of gleaming white tiles spread out before her. "Do you want me to take my shoes off?" She looked down at her slip-ons. "You'll have to take them off for me."

"It's fine. Come inside." He stepped up and put his arm around her waist as if it were his right. As if they weren't strangers.

She liked it there, the pressure of his fingers against her shifting core. She liked the comfort of being held up. When had someone else supported her last?

She'd moved away from home at eighteen and paid her way since. Thirteen months ago, Mom had lost her battle with lung cancer. Dad lived forty minutes away in Southlake, but it felt like he'd disappeared, swallowed up by his own grief. Dad was usually as attentive as a hollow pumpkin when she saw him once a month at the mandatory family meals her sister, Jo, set up. Maybe she should call him, check in and tell him about her lack of employment. She hadn't even told Jo yet. Merely thinking about having that conversation was exhausting. She'd tell them at next month's family dinner. Crap, that was scheduled for tomorrow. She had one day until she had to face the Swan Family Council.

Arty dropped his keys by a hunk of swirling gray rock that looked like it had smoke trapped inside.

"That's pretty."

"And it's supposed to have healing properties. Don't remember what they are, but maybe you should put your foot next to it."

"I'm not that gullible."

"Plenty of people really believe in those crystals."

Had she offended him? Of course she had. He was obviously one of those people. This was why she didn't have a boyfriend. She sent him an apologetic grimace.

"It was a gift." Amusement lightened his voice. "I'm not one of those people." When he turned to her, he was so close, his blue eyes like the open sky. No one came this close without kissing her. Except Blair sometimes. That girl had no boundaries.

Tempest faced forward, looking over his home. How did someone who had a full beard and wore sneakers paired with a cashmere sweater have such a well-designed house? The walls were pale cream.

Obviously the best color for walls. Through an archway to the right was an office with a sleek gray desk and a huge black-and-white print of a horse. Through the arch on the left was a formal sitting area with four chairs angled toward a grand piano. Did he play or just appreciate the design esthetic? Clinging to him, she hobbled into a kitchen with dark cabinets and white Carrera marble.

"Well, this is lovely." She stated it as fact. It was the truth.

"Thanks."

They moved into the adjoining living room, and he eased her onto a plush fabric couch, facing a massive TV.

She didn't want him to let her go. Maybe today wasn't a total bust after all. He stepped away. Friendly plants waved from the corners. The coffee table looked like an enormous piece of petrified wood coated in a glossy polish. She couldn't get over it. She loved his house. "Did you do all this yourself?"

He answered from the kitchen. "I hired the designer. Does that count?"

"I'll give it to you."

"How generous."

"Do you live here alone?"

"Yes." He returned with a bag of frozen mixed vegetables and a towel. He sat on the petrified wood and gestured for her to lift her foot. Without asking, he eased off her shoe, leaving on her thin ankle sock. Good. She wasn't ready to have her bare feet scrutinized. She went for a pedicure every five weeks, and she was almost due. The inked word "steps" was visible above the low line of the no-show socks. She'd gotten the tattoo in high school with some friends when she was feeling particularly righteous. The words of the psalm wrapped her foot arch. *You enlarge my steps under me, and my feet have not slipped.* That verse didn't feel so true now. Where would her next steps lead? Was God even watching?

She shaved her legs every morning, and Arty's fingers sliding over her smooth skin brought her focus straight to him. He folded back the bottom of her jeans to reveal scratches along her ankle. His touch sent a zing all the way up her leg. Who was this guy again? Did she approve of her growing attraction?

He rolled her ankle gently. "Does this hurt?" He flexed and straightened her foot.

"Not any more than it already does."

"That's good."

"Are you a doctor?"

"Not in the least." He set her foot on the towel on the table and laid the frozen vegetables on top.

"Then how do you know?"

"I don't really. But my guesses are usually very good."

Her mouth hung open.

"And I *guess* it's a bit twisted."

"A bit twisted. How scientific."

That muted smile came back, as if he were trying to be serious but couldn't quite manage it. "Maybe a minor sprain. May I recommend ice, ibuprofen, and rest?"

Tempest chuckled. "Arty's orders."

"You know what free advice is worth…"

She shifted the cold pack more to the throbbing side.

"Nothing." He stood. "I'll drive you to the doctor if you want, though. That's worth something." He padded back to the kitchen. "What can I get you to drink? Water? Or wine?" A pause as a refrigerator door opened. "I have a disturbing amount of drink options in here. You name it. I think I've got it. There's even tomato juice."

How much needier could she get? "Nothing for me. I'll call my roommate and make her come get me. I'm sorry to be such a bother. Thank you for helping me."

A moment's hesitation before he said, "You're welcome."

She'd been hoping he'd disagree, tell her to stay forever. She reluctantly dialed Blair. Her roommate didn't answer. Oh yeah, she was at work tonight. Tempest forced a smile when Arty returned and set a cold bottle of water by her elevated foot. "Thanks."

"Don't bother your friend. I'll drive you home."

She exhaled in defeat. "Again, thank you. It's not far, only one point two miles."

He raised his brows. "Wow. That's precise."

She swallowed a grimace, praying he wouldn't ask her why she knew that. It was time to go. She shifted as if to stand.

He held out a forestalling palm. "We're not leaving until that ices for twenty minutes." He looked at his smart watch. "That's another seventeen minutes."

"Wow. That's precise."

The conspiratorial grin he gave her sent warmth down her veins, the feeling clashing with her freezing foot. He sat at her side, just close enough to not touch.

"So, Tempest."

"Yes, Arty?"

"I was just thinking about this event I have coming up I've agreed to go to."

Her pulse sped. *Please ask me out.* She turned her voice high with mock insult. "*That's* what you're thinking about right now?"

"It's more of a Halloween party." He held his own hands in his lap and didn't look at her as he spoke.

Was he nervous? She found that hard to believe. She certainly didn't feel intimidating at the moment. Or most moments, really.

"That's not exactly accurate either." He forced a weak chuckle. "It's the Thanes' annual masquerade. It's next Saturday night. The twenty-sixth."

She knew about it. *The Thane Masquerade.* Food. Drinks. Music. Glitz. Glamour. At least that's what she'd heard. She'd never been invited. It was an exclusive list. And Bearded Arty here had made the cut. Interesting.

"Would you go with me?" The words came out in a rush.

Blair was going to be so jealous. Tempest thought she might be jealous of herself. Or maybe the slightly sick feeling was just the mixing of too many hormones in her belly.

"You have to dress up, though. Like a serious costume. If that's annoying, then no worries. I think it's a little ridiculous myself, but that's the deal." He finally looked over at her. Gray eyes above a small nose.

"Your sales pitch could use some work."

"Not the first time I've heard that."

"But I'll come with you. Sounds fun."

He had a nice smile. What would it look like without the fur? He pulled out his phone, and she typed in her name and number.

"You're not going to leave me on my own to come up with a costume, are you?" she asked, trying to make light of it, but she was deadly serious. The Thane Masquerade was no neighborhood Halloween party. What were his expectations of her?

"I was hoping you would come up with something for the both of us." He grimaced.

"The truth comes out."

"It always does." A beat of silence struck. An unidentifiable emotion flashed over his face before he brightened. "But I'm teasing. I'll figure out the costumes for us both."

"Phew."

"I thought ladies liked dressing up."

"There's a stereotype if I've ever heard one."

He lifted his hands in surrender. "I retract the comment with apologies."

"Stricken from the minutes."

"Thank you, madam chairman."

"Has it been twenty minutes? Because my foot is halfway dead by now."

"Ah. Then we are halfway to our costume. You can be an amputee."

"How delightful."

He lifted the frozen vegetables. "How does it feel?"

She rolled her ankle. The sharpness had dulled to a low throb. "A lot better. Thank you, Doc Arty."

"But still not well enough to stand."

"Well, I think I can man—"

"More rest, I think. It's a long walk to the car. Dinner first."

She settled back into the couch. She didn't want to

leave anyway. "Okay."

He turned away with the makeshift ice pack, but not before she saw his grin. "What is the patient in the mood for? Thai? Pizza? Chinese? Mexican?"

****

They spent the thirty minutes waiting for dinner connecting over science fiction novels and geeky movies. When the food arrived, Arty insisted she stay on the couch. Tempest refused to eat curry over the cream linen. She hobbled to the table, her limp more pronounced than was strictly honest. Her ankle was hardly throbbing anymore, but she felt weird being suddenly fine after all that hurt foot drama.

She set out the foam containers while he washed his hands and got a bottle of wine and two porcelain plates. When everything was ready, they looked at each other expectantly for a moment. He must have grown up saying grace before meals too.

"What do you want to try first?" he asked.

She scanned the many choices. "Should I be offended that you ordered enough for a basketball team?"

"Are you?"

"No. I'm pretty good at basketball. Please pass the veggie makhani."

They shuffled around dishes. Sitting here in his kitchen with him felt so normal. How was she not freaking out about this guy right now? She felt like he was already *in* her life. For real. Maybe she was calm because he wasn't drop-dead gorgeous. He was regular. And nice. She hadn't enjoyed this level of comfortable companionship with a man in a long time. She put a scoop of rice in her mouth. But she knew nearly nothing about him, except that he kept a sparkling, clean house and over-ordered takeout. And he helped damsels in distress.

"How long have you lived here?"

"I've been in this house about twenty months. What about you?"

"Born and raised. I grew up in Southlake, went to SMU, and now I work just..." The words faded, and she looked down.

"What's wrong?"

Her cheeks burned. Why had she brought that up? "I used to work a few blocks from here, but I lost my job yesterday."

He blinked at her.

"I was an insurance underwriter for Salvo Insurance. I *loved* my job. I have, I mean had, been doing it for five years, and I was really good at it." Why did she feel the need to defend herself? "But the company got this new software that apparently can do my job better than I can." Her voice caught. Hell no, she was not going to cry right now. She swallowed, blinking her lashes at hummingbird wing speed. She spooned lentils into her mouth.

Arty had gone white. "I'm so sorry."

She forced a smile. She did not mean to get so personal and heavy right now. "It's not your fault. It's that prick's—Leonard Allred."

He jolted.

"He developed the software program."

"Yes." His voice was raspy and dry, like he'd choked on some rice. "I've heard of him."

"He might be a genius, but I can still hate him and his shiny hair and pretty face for destroying my life."

33

Chapter Three
The Lie

She hates me.

Leo looked at his plate, trying to avoid those burning blue eyes while he got his bearings. He took a bite of tandoori chicken, his thoughts flying. He knew insurance companies were cutting back on personnel because his software was so efficient. He prided himself on Red Rocco's optimization of underwriting analysis. But to experience the aftershocks of her pain...

It was much easier to read about these people in a report. He felt better seeing the tally of people he was helping dwarf the number of people he was hurting. Clean cut columns on a page. A net positive.

He couldn't look directly at her; she was like the scorching sun. "I'm sorry." His voice was heavy with sincerity.

He finally looked up when she didn't respond. She was studying him, the sharp angles of her face softening. Her anger dissolved now that she was looking at Ardy, or *Arty* as she'd understood it. Giving strangers the ridiculous nickname had become habit. He liked his privacy, and he liked not being recognized as a twenty-nine-year-old billionaire.

"What about you?" she asked. "Tell me something."

He should start by telling her his real name. He liked this woman. A lot. And that was exactly why now he could not fess up. If she hated Leonard Allred, he would remain Arty. Simple. "I like swimming."

"Is this a ploy to get me into a swimsuit?"

He burst out laughing, bringing his napkin to his mouth just in time to catch the spew of half-chewed chicken.

"That was charming."

How did she keep a straight face? He was bent over with laughter, his stomach cramping, and she had let loose the barest hint of a curved lip. She took a controlled bite of curry, the picture of poise.

He wanted to know everything about her. Starting with what was tattooed on her foot. He'd been so close to taking off her sock, but he wasn't sure he would have been able to stop there. She was all lean length. The kind of body that looked good in a fashion magazine. Or strutting down a catwalk in lingerie. Or naked. *Keep it soft, man.* This whole date…was this a date? Whatever it was, it was better than any date he'd been on in a long time. And he'd been on quite a few. Why did everyone assume a single man with a good job was obviously seeking a wife? A least now that his mom was having a little romance of her own, she was leaving him alone for the moment. He didn't expect that to last long, though.

"Are you going to tell me more about your love of swimming?" Tempest asked. "Is it lap swimming you like? Or lounging poolside? Or paddling around the filthy Texas lakes?"

"I do not swim in the Texas lakes." He shuddered at the thought of all the possible diseases in that warm brown liquid. He swam in chlorinated pools or saltwater. "I picked it up when I started training for a triathlon, and I really like it. I go three or four times a week. I can pound it out in under thirty minutes."

At his choice of words, she raised a seductive eyebrow that sent a flare down his core.

He bit back a grin. "It is a great workout."

When she chewed her bottom lip, he decided he'd better steer the conversation to safer waters.

"Swimming laps is great cardio, and I feel like my lung capacity has improved. Good for the joints." He tilted his head to look at her foot under the table. "Maybe you should try it."

"I don't like getting my hair wet."

"Look at you living up to stereotypes."

She pursed her lips. "Fine. I'll consider it…for medicinal purposes. But we don't have a pool, and I don't go to the gym."

"Don't go to the gym?" That surprised him. Was she seriously born with those legs?

She pulled a face, as if she had read his mind. "I didn't say I didn't work out."

"Runner. No, dancer."

"I'm going to be flattered, but no. Yoga mostly. But sometimes I'm known to bike."

"Ha."

Her face was tilted down, but she glanced up at him, her smile sly and a little hesitant. Attraction sparked, and he couldn't stop the returning grin.

She had an intriguing face. He hoped she hadn't noticed him staring. And drooling. Her jaw was so long it was almost masculine, but the way it tapered to a point at her chin and the height of her cheekbones made it work so well. The thick brown hair falling around her face further softened the angles. He envied her sharp nose. His was small and round, cute on newborns, but not commanding on a man.

Tempest. It was a bold name. A hot lady's name—*she* made it an attractive name. Ardy was a loser's name. He wished again he hadn't said it, but if he had told her the truth, they wouldn't be here, eating at his kitchen table like old marrieds.

The benevolent universe had literally dropped her at his door. If he learned anything with Red Rocco, it was to seize opportunity when it came. *Don't count on second chances.*

****

After dinner, they stayed at the table and talked for nearly two hours before Leo drove Tempest home. He'd taken his pickup. He didn't need to flash his Aston Martin. She might ask questions. And what did he buy the truck for if not to haul old bikes? Within minutes, he pulled up to her curb. They were practically neighbors. Her place looked nice from the outside, a single level with twin square windows flanking a brown front door. She said goodbye at the car and hobbled up her front walk unassisted. Not even a goodbye hug. *Two can play this game.*

Now he had her name, phone number, and address. Not like a creeper or anything. He felt a little like a creeper when he got home and pulled out his computer. He searched *Tempest Swan.*

What people put out there on the public domain always blew his mind. He should talk to her about security. Another day, though. Maybe after he told her the truth—although that was probably going to be the end date of this relationship, or whatever it was that had just happened. He clicked through her social media accounts. She didn't post often; he liked that. She'd had long hair last year. She was cute that way too. He pretended not to be disappointed she hadn't uploaded any swimsuit photos. Didn't every attractive woman have those? Now he really felt like a creeper. He had to remind himself that he thought it was super cool she wasn't putting herself out there like that for people to ogle. But it was inconvenient when he felt like ogling.

Blair looked like a fun friend—she posted plenty of swimsuit photos. Tempest had an older sister and two nephews and a niece. He halted. Her mother had died thirteen months ago from lung cancer. *That's horrible.* Leo quit the screen, feeling dirty and wrong. Just because all the information was there didn't mean he should rob her of her stories. He'd have to earn the telling.

He typed in *Leonard Allred.* The Red Rocco website populated first. Good. The rest of page one listed articles about his company. He had no social media accounts. Wikipedia was short and sparse. No photograph. He clicked the images tab. Photos of his assistant, Dean Anders, filled the screen. He had to click through to page two before an image of himself popped up. Few people ever went to page two. Tagging Dean in the search engines as Leonard Allred had been a fairly simple task. He'd paid Dean for the use of the photographs. He would have paid a lot more for his anonymity and privacy. And it worked—strangers didn't know who he was. Neither did Tempest. Her comment about Dean's shiny hair and pretty face stung, but he'd dodged a bullet today.

She was hunting the wrong man.

****

Tempest rolled over in bed at the sound of her phone vibrating. How? She'd turned notifications off last night before falling asleep. She lifted the phone from the end table. *Dad.* Since Mom's diagnosis, Tempest had made the settings so Dad's calls always came through. A jolt of adrenaline had her sitting straight up. Why was he calling before eight a.m.? She was seeing him in just a few hours.

"Dad?"

"Good morning, honey," Dad said. "I'm looking forward to this evening."

She couldn't be sure over the phone connection, but he sounded weird, strained. Fear swelled. "What's going on? Did something happen?"

"No. No. I'm sorry if I made you nervous." He chuckled. "I suppose I don't call too often, do I?"

She sucked in a calming breath. She'd stayed up way too late last night supposedly trying to plan how to meet Leonard Allred, but really thinking about Arty. She didn't have to get up for two more hours, but she wouldn't be sleeping anymore now that her heart was cranked to sprinting speed.

"It's just I'm excited about a surprise I'm bringing to dinner."

"That's why you called?" Her voice came out a little too harshly. She'd made a promise to herself, her mother, and God that she'd be patient with her old man. She'd sworn to have compassion for his grief, loneliness, and eccentricities. It was a work in progress.

"I wanted to make sure you'll be at dinner tonight."

"I'll be there."

"Dress nicely."

"Why?"

"Surprise."

"But—"

"Until tonight." He hung up.

She hated surprises. Almost as much as she hated being woken up for no reason on Sunday morning. Her left ankle complained when she stood. Bruising darkened the outside, but the swelling was minimal. She'd ice it while eating breakfast. What had she been thinking yesterday? The bike accident had been the worst idea ever. Arty's face flashed in her mind. That had been weird. And good. She couldn't wait to see him again. Would he call before their masquerade date? Would he flake? Did she really trust him to pick out a costume? What if he went along the lines of Princess Leia in the gold bikini?

One problem at a time.

As she staggered to the bathroom, she called her sister. Jo was thirty-two, four years older. She lived in Plano with her husband, Benji, and their three children. She'd probably been awake for hours. Hopefully she hadn't had a bad night with the baby. Harrison was five months and not sleeping as he should be. Tempest got to hear all about it.

"You're up early," Jo said.

Tempest closed the door so she wouldn't wake up Blair down the hall. "So are you."

"Harrison was such a little angel last night. He slept eight hours straight, ate at five thirty, then went back to sleep. Still hasn't woken up. Such a sweetie." Her voice went from gooey to grim. "It's Hunter who was up at six a.m. wanting waffles."

Tempest rubbed the skin between her brows. "Dad called to make sure I'm coming to dinner. Have I ever missed? And then he wanted to put me in a bad mood by telling me he has a surprise."

"Yeah. He's bringing a woman."

"Like a girlfriend?"

"Yup. He met her last month, but I'm pretty sure they've spent every day together since."

"Why am I the last to know everything?" Tempest dropped her panties.

"Do you call Dad ever?"

She bristled. "Have you met her?" She sat on the toilet.

"We went to lunch." Jo's voice muffled. "Hannah, wash your hands first. No, you can't have that."

"Thanks for the invite," Tempest said, tone sarcastic.

"Are you peeing right now? It's echoing so loud."

"Don't change the subject."

"It was last Wednesday. I knew you were at work. I didn't think you'd want to come anyway. It's not a big deal. You didn't miss anything."

Jo only said that when Tempest had missed something.

"Dad's excited for you to meet her," Jo said. "Act surprised."

She should tell Jo she got laid off. "I hate surprises."

"Hunter, help your sister." Jo's voice got louder. "She's nice. You'll like her."

That seemed unlikely, but she kept her mouth shut. Letting this bother her was immature. So what that she hadn't met the woman yet—hadn't been invited to lunch. Her dad starting to date was good news. Why was she being so sour about it? This woman would take the attention away from Tempest's lack of work. "I have the salad for tonight."

"Oh, I meant to text you. Dad's girlfriend—her name's Silvia—said she really wants to help with the dinner, so I told her she could make the salad since I'd already gotten everything else for the meal."

Tempest had already picked up everything for the salad too.

"That means you're off the hook. I've got to go. See you tonight."

"See ya." She set the phone by the sink. Still sitting on the toilet, she dropped her head in her hands. *I will meet this woman with an open mind. I will be happy for my dad. I will not resent my sister.*

I love you, Mom. I wish you were here.

****

When Tempest pulled up to Jo's house in Plano, Dad's Mercedes was already there. *Here we go.* Salad not in hand, she let herself in the front door. They were all in the kitchen. Jo, Benji, Dad, and *Silvia.* She was a little thing, but she didn't make a small impression. Big blond hair, fake boobs, lip filler, lots of makeup. The woman made it all work, though.

"Hello," Tempest said.

"There's my baby." Dad's voice was too loud, his hug too tight. "Tempest, meet Silvia."

Next to the petite woman, Tempest felt like she stood on stilts. Silvia looked years younger than Dad. Maybe it was the plastics and makeup and the tight little jeans, but Tempest could see the attraction. Silvia had big friendly blue eyes and a welcoming smile.

"It's so nice to meet you." Silvia held out a small hand.

"Thanks. You too. I love your shoes."

Silvia glanced down at the patent leather pumps, then beamed at her.

Tempest turned to her dad. "So what's the surprise?"

Dad's face fell, but Silvia chuckled. "He told me you had a dry sense of humor."

"Don't believe everything he tells you," Tempest said.

Jo sashayed around the island, swinging her wide hips away from the sharp corner. "You look nice, T."

"Thanks. Smells good in here." Tempest inhaled melting cheese and garlic. Jo's food was not light, but it tasted good. Tempest was always in charge of the salad. But now Silvia was here, and Tempest didn't know if anything healthy would be on the table. Did her family know that she considered this her cheat meal for the week?

Benji handed Tempest a glass of sparkling water with a lemon slice, her usual.

"Thank you." She took a sip, startling as vodka heated her tongue.

Benji winked. "Thought you might need that today."

She'd always liked him. He was mellow and slow to temper. He had a thick head of curly brown hair and a happy round face. Jo had gotten lucky. Ten years, three kids, and forty pounds heavier, and he still treated Jo like a queen.

"Tempest," Silvia said, "tell me all about yourself."

Tempest took a big gulp of her drink. Should she

lead with the job loss or the new bet she'd made with Blair? Or Beardy Guy? Crying crackled through the baby monitor, drawing everyone's attention away from her muteness. *Thank you, baby Harrison.*

Silvia turned to Jo, face aglow. "Oh, let me get him." She held her hands to her chest. "Please."

How could anyone deny that earnest face anything? Jo didn't. "That would be so nice, thank you."

Dad put a hand on the small of Silvia's back. "This way, darling. I'll show you."

Tempest mouthed the word *darling* as she, Jo, and Benji looked at each other in silence.

They waited long enough for Dad and Silvia to have gotten out of overhearing range before Jo said, "What do you think?"

Benji held his hand out in front of his chest like he was holding melons.

Jo hit him with a dish towel. "Don't make fun. You know I'm getting some as soon as the baby finishes sucking me dry."

Benji leaned in and kissed her mouth. "You're beautiful no matter what."

Jo blushed and rolled her eyes.

She was a softened, shorter version of Tempest, as if all the angles and colors had been buffed and muted. Jo's eyes were grayer, her hair a light brown. But where Tempest was even-keeled, Jo was the storm, a vacillating wave of highs and lows.

Tempest was about to speak when Silvia's voice came through the monitor again. "Tempest is beautiful."

Jo pursed her lips.

Dad's voice was garbled. "She looks like her

44

momma."

Pain flared in Tempest's chest. *Momma.*

"Your daughters are wonderful, Christopher. I like them already."

"And I can tell they like you too."

Silvia's voice turned high-pitched. "Hello, handsome. Aren't you just the sweetest little man?"

"She'd better be talking to the baby," Jo said.

"Stop snooping," Benji said. "Turn that off."

Jo curled her lower lip but flicked off the baby monitor. "Help me take this food out."

Tempest lifted the rolls while Benji hefted the macaroni and cheese from the oven.

"Hunter and Hannah," Jo yelled. "Time for dinner. Get in here and wash up."

****

The kids were a good distraction. Hunter loved to talk in detail about his favorite movies, and Hannah could be counted on to discuss school. They were nearly to dessert before the adults had to talk about themselves.

"Do you have family in the area?" Tempest asked Silvia.

"I have two children. I lost them to California for a while, but they both moved back recently." Silvia's blue eyes sparkled with delight.

Tempest missed her mom. She had taken for granted that Mom always lived close by. Now she was gone.

"I've been divorced twice." Silvia looked sheepish but brightened when Dad reached over and touched her leg under the table.

Whoa. So Dad was serious about this woman.

Tempest didn't know what to think. Her insides swirled with conflicting emotions.

"Harvey is the father of my two children," Silvia said. "He left me fifteen years ago for another man."

"Oh!" Jo blurted the word out.

Dad gave her a stern look.

Jo's face turned pink.

Silvia smiled. "It wasn't easy, but it's for the best now. He lives with his new partner in San Francisco. It's the second marriage that I regret. I was only married to Robert eight months. It was a pity rebound, and I should have known better."

Silence hit as Tempest failed to think of a follow-up comment to that remark. Even Jo stayed quiet.

"Maybe third time's a charm," Dad said.

Jo's jaw dropped, but Dad didn't seem to notice. He only had eyes for Silvia, and she was looking back at him with just as much love.

Chapter Four
The Game

"Here's your costume." Dean set a wide box on the side of Leo's desk.

Leo lifted his head, his mind still on the email he was composing.

"The Count of Monte Cristo getup for Saturday," Dean said.

Leo's thoughts shifted gears with reluctance. *The Thanes' party. Saturday. Costumes. Tempest.* "Oh no. That won't work anymore."

"Good. I was hoping you'd say that."

Leo blinked at his assistant.

"Can I use it?" Dean flashed his charming smile.

Tempest's voice saying the words *shiny hair and pretty face* cut through Leo's good mood like a razor blade. "You're going to the Thanes' party?" Leo didn't mean to sound so annoyed.

Dean's face fell. "I was invited, but..."

Aw, crap. Leo stood up, thoughts a jumble. He would have to figure out how to keep Tempest away from Dean, the man she thought she hated. It was a big party; it shouldn't be a problem. He handed Dean the box. "Take it. And I don't want to hear a word about you pretending the cloak will be too short for you."

"Pretending?"

"Help me come up with a costume that will work

for a couple."

Dean raised thick eyebrows.

"Yes. I'm bringing a date. You don't have to look so shocked."

Dean grinned.

"Any ideas?"

"Leia and Han."

"You're fired."

Dean chuckled. "Kidding. Give me a minute. I'll come back with a list." He walked out of Leo's office, closing the glass doors behind him. Leo turned to his screen, but he couldn't see the words over the image of a pretty brunette filling his thoughts. She would look very good in Leia's gold bikini.

****

"Ketchup and mustard?" Leo looked up from the list to spear Dean with a sharp gaze he hoped came off as incredulous.

"I was just warming up."

"George the monkey and the man with the yellow hat. That's at least better." Leo sighed. "Why did I think this was a good idea? Who wants to look like an idiot on their second date?"

"Take her out tonight. Then you're good. Anything goes by the third date."

"Should I be taking advice from the man who's never been on a third date?"

"Hardy har har." Dean took the paper out of Leo's hand. "What about you be the miner, and she's the diamonds? You could have her wear a dress all made of gemstones. That would dazzle her." He chuckled. He was always laughing at his own jokes. The opposite of Tempest.

Leo sank to his seat. Should he cancel? But he couldn't wait to see her again. He had to force himself not to text her every second. Maybe he should call her tonight. She wouldn't be working late. Thanks to him. He slumped lower. He could take her to that little Italian place no one knew about. Nope. The owner always called him Mr. Allred, even after Leo had insisted otherwise. He'd have to take her somewhere where paying in cash and wearing a baseball cap was normal. Baseball. No one would recognize him at a sporting event. It was baseball season, right? He hadn't been to a Rangers game since Grandpa Duke had last taken him and Zena twelve years ago.

Leo clicked open his internet browser. Rangers had a home game tonight. It felt like fate. He looked up at his assistant, who was still listing off famous couples he'd clearly copied from a Google search.

"Get me two tickets to tonight's Rangers game."

Dean looked momentarily caught off guard. Then he smiled. "Perfect second date. I give such good advice."

Leo pulled a face.

"Behind home plate? Or commissioner's box seats?"

"Hmm." Both of those sounded fancy enough that she might ask pointed questions about work. "What tickets would you buy for a date?"

Dean scrunched his lips. "I'd scalp or look at discount sites."

"Seriously?"

"You don't pay me enough."

"Those designer shoes beg to differ."

"You testing this woman's motives or something?"

49

Leo let out a dark laugh. "Just get us something in the middle-ish section."

"Middle-ish. That's exactly what I'll ask the ticket office."

"Also get me a Rangers hat."

"Will do." Dean turned to leave, then twisted back and lifted the paper in his hand. "So do you want me to get the Caesar and Cleopatra costumes?"

Leo shrugged. "That's not bad, but not good. Seems a little cliché." He closed his eyes and took a deep breath. What would Tempest not hate? "I have an idea."

****

Parked outside the Red Rocco office building, Tempest and Blair sat in Tempest's Audi A3. They'd been "scouting" for nearly an hour, a.k.a. watching strangers go in and out of the front doors. No Leonard Allred sightings. Blair popped another potato chip into her mouth. *Crunch. Crunch.* Tempest gave her the side-eye.

"I'm not spilling." Blair lifted the bag, showing her clean thighs, the short shorts scrunched so they'd nearly disappeared into the bend of her hips. "I promise."

"You can't eat that whole bag without getting grease crumbs on the seat."

Blair crunched another chip. "Wanna bet?"

Tempest chuckled. "No. I'm still regretting this bet."

"Aw. Is little Stormie giving up? Maybe we should put this sucker in gear and head for the paint store right now."

"Um. I still have nine days. Hold your horses, Sticks." She didn't use the nickname much, usually only when Blair was being a big *stick*.

Blair leaned back and put her foot—socks, no shoes—on the dashboard. "Holding them." *Crunch. Crunch.*

The bravado drained from Tempest. It wouldn't have mattered if she had ninety days. She wasn't going to find Leonard Allred and get him to ask her out.

Today was Tuesday, her second weekday of unemployment. It didn't suit her. She'd done all the laundry yesterday, including Blair's bedding. This morning after her daily yoga flow, she'd gone to a movie. A movie. In the morning. She and a geriatric couple had been the only ones in the theater. She'd left feeling nauseous and slightly hungover. Blair didn't work tonight—no one catered parties on Tuesdays. So here they were, at five twenty-two p.m., sitting in a parked car outside her enemy's office.

I am such a loser.

Her phone vibrated with a new text message from Arty. She flickered back to life. Something good from this dreadful day.

—*What size pants do you wear?*—

She giggled.

"What is it?" Blair asked.

Another text from Arty appeared. —*So that sounded super sketch, didn't it?*—

Tempest chewed on her lips as she replied. —*I'm just glad to hear I'll have pants to wear.*—

Blair leaned over the console, and Tempest shifted the screen so she could see. Blair made the sound of a rubber ducky being squeezed. "The mystery man?"

Tempest nodded.

"You could have thought of a better reply than

that."

"But I actually want to wear pants, not some themed lingerie."

"I'm so sad I don't get to wear a costume." Yesterday, her boss had asked her and a few others from her crew to work the Thanes' event.

"You get to dress up as a caterer."

"I'm considering dropping a chip in the seat crack right now."

"You wouldn't dare."

Blair looked through the window to the tall building. "Maybe you should ask Arty to set you up with Leonard Allred. They live in the same place. You said they were talking to each other before you crashed my bike. They must know each other."

Tempest didn't dignify that with a response. She turned the engine on and drove away, hating that she was giving Leonard Allred another thought.

"Eek," Blair said, looking at Tempest's phone. "And you've got a date tonight."

Heart pitter-pattering, Tempest reached over, groping for the phone.

Blair held it out of range. "Nope. No texting and driving. Safety first."

Tempest's eyebrows lowered. "You're not even wearing a seatbelt."

"I'll take care of this." Blair's greasy fingers flew over the screen. "Come over, and I'll let you get a good look at the size of my pants."

"Stop. What are you saying? Blair!" Tempest pulled over and snatched the phone from her giggling friend.

Arty had written —*I have two tickets to the*

Rangers game tonight. Can I pick you up at six thirty?—

Blair had responded *—Is that baseball?—*

Tempest exhaled relief. "You're such a butthead." Three dots showed Arty was responding. She typed out a quick *—Just kidding.—*

They both sat watching the waving dots.

"He's trying to think of something clever," Blair said.

Finally Arty's next text came through. *—LOL. I'm mostly in it for the Belgium beer and hot dog.—*

"Please tell him you're mostly in it for the players' tight pants."

Tempest rolled her eyes at Blair.

"Come on. It's funny, and we've got to see if he's cool."

"Fine." Tempest relinquished her phone back to her bossy friend. She bit her tongue as she looked out the window, giddiness swelling.

"Oh yes, now *I'm* in love with him too," Blair said.

Tempest snapped back to face Blair, who held up the phone.

"He said he'll bring binoculars."

****

At home, Tempest double-checked the Rangers' colors. Blue and red. Blue jeans were an easy choice, but she didn't wear a lot of red, so she went for a simple white V-neck. She cranked up pop music as she did her face and hair and readied her jacket and purse.

Blair poked her head through the bedroom door and sighed wistfully. "Ah, young love."

"Stop it," Tempest said, failing to sound sincere.

"I wish I could stay and meet Beardy, but I'm

meeting up with peeps, so I'm out. Have fun."

"Love ya."

Blair ducked out, and Tempest turned down the music so she wouldn't worry about missing the doorbell.

She was ready twelve minutes early, and Arty was a cool thirteen minutes late.

"Hey," he said at the door, looking adorable with his blue Rangers hat brightening his eyes. He pointed to her white T-shirt and jeans and then his own. "Costume party's not until Saturday, but I see we're getting a jump on the matching theme."

"If Blair were here, she'd tell us who wore it best."

"I don't need her to tell me the answer to that." He stepped over the threshold and drew her into a warm hug before stepping back and motioning her out to the pickup truck at the curb. "You look beautiful."

It was such an obvious compliment, but still it warmed her core nearly as much as his hug had.

"How's your ankle?"

"It's fine. Just a little bruising at this point." She glanced over at him as they walked. "Must have been the top-notch post-accident treatment I received."

"Obviously." Steely blue eyes flashed sidelong at her. "Thanks for coming with me last minute."

"Your other date bailed?"

He opened the passenger door for her. "I'm trying to decide if I'd sound cooler if I said yes."

The side of her lip curved up.

"But no. I just thought it sounded like fun. I needed to get out of the office today." He cringed.

"Trouble at work?" She didn't even know what he did.

His eyes went wide. "Oh no. Everything is good." He shut the door so hard she startled. "Sorry," he said, his voice muffled by the window and his face panicked.

She grimaced. Clearly work was a touchy subject. *Do not bring that up tonight.* As he climbed into the driver's seat, she lifted binoculars from the center cupholder and raised an eyebrow.

He grinned. "I've got to make sure my date is satisfied at the end of the evening."

Her brows rose to their highest position.

He winked. "And it's been a long time since I've been to a baseball game. I'm hoping they took my suggestion letter seriously and got themselves some cheerleaders." He pulled away from the curb.

"You didn't."

He smiled. It was aimed at the windshield, but that almost made it easier to enjoy. He had a very nice mouth hidden in that beard. His side teeth were as white as the front ones—a sign of good hygiene and proper personal care. He glanced over at her, and her skin heated at the realization he'd surely caught her staring.

"I did. I was fourteen. My grandpa took me and my sister to games once in a while. I loved going, but the games dragged on too long. In the fifth inning of a boring game against the Mariners, I started to whine. Where were the runs? Where was the band? Where were the dancing girls? Why weren't the players at least getting in fights? My grandpa had shrugged and told me if I wanted to complain, to do it to someone who might at least have a chance to do something about it, but harping to him was poor manners and frankly rude."

"Whoa. Go, Grandpa."

Arty nodded, making a left turn. "He was the best.

I miss him. But at the time, I was insulted. So I decided to show him. I went up to the shops and got a piece of paper from customer service. For the rest of the game, I crafted a letter to Major League Baseball outlining how the NFL was outdoing them in so many ways and they needed to step it up. Naturally adding cheerleaders was my chief argument."

"Naturally," she said, voice dry, but inside she was thinking he sounded like a pretty interesting kid.

"I mean there is so much downtime for them to entertain between innings."

"Beer sales might go down because people don't want to get up from their seats."

"Not if the cheerleaders were selling the drinks."

"Did you include that in your letter?"

His face fell. "No. I thought of that later."

"Probably better. Not sure Major League Baseball wants to turn into Hooters."

He laughed. "Oh man, I sound like I was the creepiest kid ever."

"Nah. I started it when I said I was only coming to check out the baseball players' butts."

She decided right there that she really liked the sound of his low rolling chuckle.

"At least I can blame it on being a hormonal teenager. What's your excuse?"

"I was joking."

"I see," he said, voice drawn out and sarcastic.

Conversation stalled as they neared the stadium, and Arty's focus shifted to following the cone-marked lanes and finding the parking lot that matched his pass. Tempest half expected him to leave the binoculars, but he put them in his jacket pocket before closing the door and locking the truck. They met at the front of the car.

"I don't think our seats are very good."

"Seems like something that should have been disclosed upon invitation." She put on her jacket.

He looked her over, his eyes dancing. "You are…"

Her core heated. When he didn't finish, she couldn't help asking, "What?"

Pink lips turned up. "Just perfect."

Fire licked along her nerves. Sweet tea, that was the sexiest thing anyone had ever said to her. She bit her lip, and his warm gaze dropped to her mouth.

"I think the game is about to start." He took her hand as if it were the most natural thing in the world, and together they walked across the parking lot.

They didn't talk. She didn't think she could have heard his voice over the blare of his touch anyway. Tingles skittered over her hand and up her arm. She was seriously twenty-eight going on twelve right now. *Get a grip.* But it felt so good. He felt so good. Who was this guy, and how had he hijacked her senses so quickly?

They found their seats halfway up the lower bowl behind first base.

"These seats are great," she said, hoping he knew she really didn't care where they sat. "Best place to catch a foul ball."

"We definitely want to do that."

She eyed the many hopeful fans holding mitts in their laps. "Highly unlikely."

"Good. I don't want to get hit by a baseball." He sat down.

She sat next to him, disappointed he didn't immediately try to hold her hand again. The game was in the bottom of the fourth. Rangers were up on the Astros five to two. "I see you solved the problem of the games being too long."

"If only all problems were so easily solved."

She chuckled. "Or is it that you didn't want to commit to nine whole innings on a first date?"

"Um, I bought you dinner on Saturday. This is date number two."

"Important distinction, Your Honor."

He nodded and turned to the game, never answering her question. She wouldn't have minded sitting for twelve innings with this guy, enjoying the fluttering in her belly and rush of pleasure through her veins. Strike three. End of the inning.

He stood. "Well, that's made me hungry. What can I get you?"

"I'll have whatever you're having."

"The pressure is on." He turned and wormed back down the row.

Her attention drifted from texting Blair, to people watching, to following the game.

Arty returned with a beer, a soda, a water, nachos, kettle corn, a hot dog, sunflower seeds, and licorice. "The gunshot approach." He carefully sat down with his balancing act.

"Mitigate the risk. Smart." She took a sip from the soda straw as he started shuffling things over. "Thanks for dinner…again."

"Not exactly what my mom would call a real meal." He stuck a red licorice between his teeth.

"Calories don't count at baseball games."

"I think I saw a sign up there that said the same thing."

"In that case, pass the popcorn."

After they'd picked at the treats for a while, Arty pulled out the binoculars. He didn't spend much time with them aimed at the diamond. Was he stargazing? With so much ambient light, she could see only a few twinkles in the dark sky.

"What are you looking at?"

He passed the binoculars to her and pointed to the sponsor signs. "Look just above the O in *Cola*."

The sleek binoculars were so small she couldn't imagine they would be any good, but when she put them to her eyes and focused the knob, the faraway world came into stark detail. These were really nice. Like sneaky fancy. Who was this guy? She really wanted to ask him what he did for work, but she bit her tongue. If he'd had a rough day at the office, she wasn't going to blight the date with it. She scanned the billboards, surprised to see cracks and bird-poop splatters.

"These binoculars are amazing."

"Do you see the nest?"

She lifted the scope to the cola sign, and there it was, a bird's nest housing four brown birds with yellow beaks sitting in it. She let out a whispered chuckle. "They're watching the game."

"Pretty cool, right?"

"Very rad." She lowered the focus to the players, getting a major close-up on sweaty faces, mouths bulging with chew, and dirt-stained jerseys. "It's like watching in high definition."

"Yeah. Except you aren't home on your comfy couch, and you can't follow the action watching through a pinhole."

"What action?"

He chuckled as they watched the next hitter amble to the plate. She traded him the binoculars for his bag of sunflower seeds and settled against her seatback, completely content. The Astros came back to tie it in the eighth. They were sitting by a large vocal group from Houston. As the ninth inning started, Arty and Tempest found themselves suddenly super Rangers fans, standing up and cheering for their hometown heroes. The Rangers lost. She was shockingly disappointed, but by the time she was back in his truck, she'd shaken off the inconsequential loss. She turned giddy with the thought of closing her date more successfully than the Rangers had ended their game.

He drove slowly, as if he didn't want to get to her place too soon. He didn't hold her hand. Why didn't he reach over and put his palm on her thigh? Why didn't he lean over and kiss her at the red lights? She bit her lip as she looked out her window at the inky sky. So she was ridiculously into this random guy she barely knew and kinda loving it. She hadn't thought about losing her job or Leonard Allred the entire night. Until now. She brushed the annoying thoughts away again and focused on the man at her side. He looked over, eying her smile.

"I think you were bad luck for the Rangers tonight."

Before she could think of a clever retort, his phone rang through the car, cutting off the soft music he'd been playing.

"Sorry." He pressed a button on the dash.

"It's okay, you can take it."

"No, I don't—"

"Hello?" A female voice came through the car

speakers.

"Zena?" Surprise sharpened his voice as his fingers jumped back up to the dash.

"Yeah. So get this, L—"

"Whoops." He hit another button, cutting off the woman mid-word.

"Ahh. Did you just hang up on her?"

She couldn't read his face in the dim light, but his gaze darted over the windshield.

"Yeah. But I answered by accident, so it doesn't count."

"I did not know that rule."

He relinquished a half smile. "It was just my sister. I'll call her back later." He pulled up to the curb in front of Tempest's house, his shoulders tense. "Thanks again for coming with me. I had fun."

"Me too." Why wasn't he getting out? And why did he look so nervous and shy all of a sudden? Was she seriously not getting any love tonight?

"Will you still come with me Saturday?"

"Yes." She hesitated. Why wasn't he walking her to the house? Or all the way to her bedroom right now? He didn't get out. She opened the door. "See you later." She closed the door and hurried up the walk. She had a pretty good idea how those poor Dallas baseball players were feeling tonight.

Chapter Five
The Party

Saturday evening Leo parked in front of Tempest's condo. Hopefully she didn't hate the costume because he'd left zero room for error, not the usual way he operated. But all the parts hadn't come together until yesterday afternoon, and he'd gotten busy at work, and he couldn't have Dean deliver the costume for her to try on. And he didn't want to send anyone else, lest they slipped up and told Tempest anything important—like his name. Lying was super annoying and way too much work.

Tuesday had been a disaster. Well, the game had been amazing, and he'd been halfway blind with infatuation by the end. But then Zena had called. After she'd almost outed him by saying his name, he hadn't even had the balls to walk the poor woman to her door. No kiss. No nothing. He was so ashamed, and yet the thought of admitting the truth had him wanting to glue his mouth shut. If only he didn't like her so much. He could almost feel his heart bracing itself against the incoming explosion.

He hefted the garment bag and stalked up the path to her door. At least he imagined he was stalking. He planned to stalk all night. Came with the costume. He knocked. After thirteen seconds, Tempest opened the door.

Still beautiful.

She wore yoga pants and a loose tee, but her makeup was done so her blue eyes popped. She looked him over, her gaze betraying nothing. "Don't tell me you're Romeo."

He laughed. It was a joke, right? He wasn't quite sure; she said it with a face as straight as a ruler. "I regret not thinking of that."

"A peasant?"

"Really? That's where you went next?" He looked down at his brown vest, made from real leather. The canvas pants. The supple boots. Nothing a peasant could afford. "I shouldn't have left my bow and arrow in the car."

"Ah. Cupid."

"Just stop, okay. You're killing my confidence."

She finally smiled, that wide mouth curving. She stepped back, allowing him inside.

The place was neat, but not *clean* clean. Sneakers lay on their sides by the doormat. Junk mail splattered the kitchen counter, and dust frosted the lamp. But still, much better than most, and she had a roommate. Was the half-empty coffee cup hers or Blair's? *Stop doing that. It doesn't matter.* The place smelled fresh, and he got a clean vibe from Tempest. He would have no hesitation putting his mouth on this female—once he worked up the courage. The thought gave him a little thrill. Hopefully he'd end tonight better than last time. "Nice place. Is your roommate here?"

"No. She's already at the Thanes' party."

Leo stopped in surprise.

"She's a caterer. They called her in to help with the serving. Hopefully you'll get to meet her there."

He could only hope Blair didn't know who he really was. This lie was giving him an ulcer. *Come clean, man. Now is always the time.* He turned with a grin and a flourish of his arm. "I am Robin of the Hood."

She gave him an appreciative nod. "Outlaw, thief, and murderer."

"The murderer part is up for question."

"No. It's not. How do you think he became an outlaw in the first place? Sometimes Hollywood gets the facts wrong."

"He's fictional."

She huffed as if insulted. "As long as he's still a good date."

He chuckled because he couldn't think of anything to say. He hadn't sparred like this since Ivan moved into his dorm freshman year, and that man didn't have Tempest's sense of humor.

"But," she said, "I've never been out with a criminal before, at least that I know of. 'Twill be an adventure." She paused, her face going serious. Her shoulders dropped, and her voice came out low. "I'm Maid Marian."

If she was trying to cover her disappointment, she was doing a terrible job. He'd never been happier to say, "No."

Her eyes brightened. "Little John?"

"Also no. I didn't bring you an enormous man outfit."

She opened her mouth, but he held up a forestalling hand.

"I can't take any more guesses. I'm going to tell you, and hopefully you'll act like it's acceptable." He pulled a delicate mask out of a box. It was painted tan and gold, with white dots on the cheekbones and a dark brown bar over the nose. Fine shimmering antlers curled from the top. "You are a forest fawn."

She giggled and clapped her hands to her chest. "Oh, I love it."

"Wow. That was really good acting."

She rolled her eyes and held out her hands. "I'm being serious. It's perfect."

"Phew, because you really stressed me out with how anti-Lady Marian you were." He set the mask in her long fingers.

Her voice was quiet. "It's beautiful."

And she would never know how much it cost to have that rush custom made.

She settled it over her eyes, the bottom of the mask ending just over her cheekbones. She blinked her big eyes.

Yup. Super sexy.

"Is there more to this costume?" she asked.

"I'm pretty sure deer go naked." He bit his tongue. What a creepy thing to say.

"You think I look like a deer under here?" She lifted the hem of her shirt, exposing a curved waist and flat stomach. The shirt kept going up. Pale ribs. The bottom edge of a black bra.

What's happening? He jerked his gaze down to the bag in his hand. "No. You don't look like any kind of antelope I've ever seen." He sensed her drop her shirt, but he didn't dare look up. Unless...what if they just skipped the party...?

She chuckled. "Just checking."

Face hot, he pulled out brown suede leggings and a

65

long-sleeve button-down tunic, printed with fawn spots on the back. He handed them over, and she disappeared into a room down the hall. She was not going to actually strip in front of him. A little disappointing at this point, but good. Call him old-fashioned. He wanted her naked all right, but he wanted to *earn* every bare inch. And after failing to kiss her goodnight Tuesday, he had a long way to go. Not to mention the identity situation.

She reappeared, smile coy under that alluring mask. She wore brown booties that worked well with the tight pants. She held her hands out to her sides and twirled, the silk shirt flowing over her narrow curves. "How do I look?"

"I'd shoot you." A flash of pleasure hit at the smile his words provoked.

"We shall see how good your aim is, Sir Robin."

"I'll be sad when you stop calling me that."

She slipped her arm into his. "You want the sir to stay? Sir Arty perhaps? Take me to the party, Sir Arty."

He suddenly didn't want to go. He didn't want to risk seeing anyone who would call him Leonard. He wanted it to stay just the two of them, together, flaming this ember that was so fragile and new and full of potential.

When they stepped outside, Tempest's gaze snapped to the black Aston Martin Vantage gleaming under the streetlamp. "Whoooaaa, Sir Robin. What rich bloke did you steal this from?"

"Leonard Allred." It just popped out.

She stopped. Her face turned, her eyes unreadable in the shadow of the deer mask.

Figure it out. Don't figure it out. Do figure it out.

Or just shoot me now. "Leo lives where I live. I thought it would only be fair. A little payback for what he cost you. You want to drive it? You want to drive it into a ditch?"

Her jaw slackened. "You're serious."

"Not really about the ditch part. I'd be the one paying for that."

Her face lit up. "Heck yeah, I want to drive it." She skipped to the driver's door, and Leo hoped he wouldn't regret this. She slid into the car, shifting her backside against the fine leather, her fingers caressing the steering wheel. "Oh, that guy has it so good."

He salivated at the sight of her nearly making love to his car. "Not as good as I do."

She grinned, a white moon under the animal mask. "Get in, you big charmer. Let's see what she can do."

"She can do a lot. So no sudden movements."

Her grin only grew.

But she made no sudden movements. Despite a tiny bit of speeding, she obeyed every traffic law and avoided coming within ten feet of another vehicle. She kept her hands at ten and two. He chuckled as they pulled in the valet line at the party.

"If you're laughing because I'm a safe driver, you can get out and walk," she said. "This car is pretty, but she makes me very nervous."

"I can relate." He wasn't looking at the car; he was looking at her, but she didn't see.

She walked her fingers over the gear shift. "I can't believe this is Leonard Allred's car."

He hated how she said it, *Leonard Allred.* The full name every time, the awe and anger. "It's not a big deal. He's just a regular guy."

She pursed her lips but didn't say anything as she pulled up to the waiting valet.

The young man opened the door. "Welcome, ma'am."

Leo hurried out his door, coming around the hood to talk to the valet.

"What's the name?"

"Robin Hood."

"Very good, sir." The man handed him a valet tag.

Leo pulled his old-fashioned bow and quiver from the trunk and settled his green felt hat on his head. He'd considered shaving his beard after Tempest's reaction when they first met, but that felt like giving in too easily. And he was harder to recognize with the low hat and facial hair. She really was on a date with a criminal—on the run from his own identity. He took her hand, her fingers soft against his palm. His pulse rose as they walked the dim path toward the looming mansion. *Tell her now before you get to the door.* Outside the entrance, a photographer took glamour shots of the guests. Leo steered right past the setup.

"Welcome." A woman greeted them at the house entrance. "May I take anything? Jacket? Weapons?"

"No, thank you."

Past the spiral staircases and through the archway, they stepped into a massive ballroom. The silver cast of the lights and the plush velvet draperies made it feel not like Halloween, but like a real vampire lair. Adults wore an array of costumes ranging from Queen Victoria to super heroes to prima ballerinas—which was a tough one to pull off. Candelabras dotted the long dining table spread with food and drinks. A string quartet played in the corner, the music heavy with minor chords and eerie modulations.

"How ghastly," Tempest said.

"So glad you love it." He kept his voice as flat as hers.

She turned to him, her face close and her eyes silvery. She winked, and his stomach flipped.

"Something to eat? I can ask about fresh grass or flower petals."

"I'd like to see that."

They weaved through the crowd toward the tables.

"Blair!" Tempest called over the pulsing music.

A short woman with a cloud of curly hair turned, her face jolly as an elf. "Stormie!"

He would definitely have to remember that nickname.

Blair finished stacking the last couple of bread twists from her bakery bag and sauntered over. She looked "Stormie" up and down. She turned her friend around. She touched the antlers and ran a hand against Tempest's suede thigh. He could get some tips in confidence from this woman.

"A-mazing," Blair said. "All of it." She turned to Leo and held out a hand. "You've already won me over."

"Well, you're easy."

"I'm not that easy."

His cheeks warmed.

The woman laughed. "I'm Blair."

"Robin Hood."

"No shooting in here. I have to help with cleanup."

He put a hand to his heart and pinched his voice. "Upon my word as an outlaw."

She frowned. "I don't think that accent works on

you."

He could only laugh. "You two are a tough crowd."

"I'm passing out sweet chili fried shrimp in a minute. They are unreal. I've already snuck like seven. Come try one." Blair took Tempest's hand and pulled her through a side door.

Leo nearly knocked a man in the head with his bow as he tried to follow. The brightness of the serving area was a shock after the party dim. They leaned against the wall, out of the way of the black-and-white-clad workers. Blair brought them red wine and the promised shrimp. Then she brought cheese puffs and smoked sausage bits.

"Don't forget to tip your server." Blair took away his empty plastic plate.

"Wha—?"

"I'm kidding…mostly."

"Thanks for the treats." Tempest finished off her glass of red.

"I like these chefs." Blair looked around the kitchen. "Everything has been well done."

"I'll come find you again." Tempest slid toward the door.

Leo held it open, and Blair waltzed out first with a tray of appetizers. She went to the big ballroom. He didn't follow. He wasn't ready to run into the hosts or anyone else he knew. So, like a coward, he turned left with Tempest. They found half a dozen more rooms with lounging guests and low light. Leo skipped the one that smelled like a high school gym and the one with the pot smoke and the one with the heavy metal music. Down a set of stairs, he led the way into another large room. The only light came from the lit-up bowling alley, the neon dart boards, glowing bowls of candy and popcorn, and the silvery light strips marking the ground and furniture. Only a few figures dotted the room. Most guest probably hadn't found this little gem of a spot yet. But Dean had.

Leo shifted, stepping to block Tempest's view. He could not let them meet. His heart thumped. He whirled to face her. "Let's try somewhere else."

She bobbed, trying to see around him. "But this looks cool. Is that bowling?"

He glanced over his shoulder. Dean was heading for the door, straight at them. "It's kinda hot in here. Let's get some air and then come back."

She looked at him with a disappointed gaze that made him go still all over. This was it. The end of the relationship. No, it couldn't end with him being lame on purpose.

His focus dropped to her lips. He took a step forward, fear making him bold. The free hand that wasn't holding the stupid bow found her silky waist. She gasped, her lips parting slightly as she looked up at him. He took the spark in her eyes as invitation enough and pressed his mouth to hers. His body awoke with a jolt as her soft lips shifted under his. He took another step, their bodies coming flush together. Her hands found his neck. He took another step, forcing her back against the wall. He stifled a groan. The bottom edge of her mask bumped his nose. He considered taking it off. But no, they were in public. He found it hard to remember that with the darkness, with her mouth opening, her tongue tasting of grapes and salt. A wave of heat flared down his body. He gripped her ribs, forcing his hand not to move higher. This was *not* the place to do this. He pulled away, breath coming fast. Weak light shone off her eyes, dark as night, as she stared up at him. He couldn't speak, couldn't move. He was the prey, caught in her trap. His body was warm and throbbing, screaming for more.

"What do you bet I beat you in a game of bowling?" Her voice was low and husky.

He wanted to kiss her pale throat. "I'll bet a date. I win, you buy. You win, I buy."

She pulled a face. "Blair would be so disappointed in that uncreative wager." Her mouth softened. "But I'm in."

When he turned, he thought of Dean again, but his assistant/fake identity had left the room. As he stepped up to the narrow lane, he thanked his lucky star for both the save and the sizzling-hot kiss.

Leo won the first game, so Tempest begged for best out of three. She still lost, two games to one.

"Where are you going to take me?" He threw his arm over her shoulder as they left the room. "Somewhere with lobster, I hope."

"I am unemployed, remember?"

She said it with a teasing tone, but it turned him cold. He did remember. He should have let her win that last game.

But that wouldn't have solved the real problem here.

****

Tempest was flying high as they climbed the stairs from the bowling alley. She could almost still taste his kiss on her tongue, sweet chili and male. His beard had been so soft, like feathers. She didn't hate it like she thought she would. After his shyness on Tuesday, the shock of his sudden kiss had melted her middle. He'd been bold, confident. Hungry. No waiting until that awkward moment on the doorstep or until they were half drunk. She felt half drunk now, her veins tingling pleasantly.

"Hey," Arty said. "It's getting pretty late. Are you ready to head out?"

Absolutely she was. "Sure. Let me just find the little girl's room and say goodbye to Blair."

"I should probably say thank you to the Thanes. I'll meet you over by the serving kitchen."

They split ways at the landing. After a quick pee, she worked her way through the dissipating crowd. The food trays were picked over, and the bread mountain now resembled an anthill. She didn't see Blair in the main hall. She opened the door to the butler's kitchen and stopped on the threshold. As fluorescent light illuminated the couple, her body flooded with heat.

Leonard Allred leaned against the counter, his full attention on Blair, who stood close to his chest, in the shadow of his broad shoulders. Blair was ignoring the stacks of dirty platters and piles of used napkins. Leonard Allred said something too quietly for Tempest to pick out, but Blair's responding giggle could have been heard a state away. Tempest plastered on a stiff smile and strode forward.

"There you are, Blair."

Blair jolted, guilt flushing over her face. "Tempest, come meet my new friend."

Leonard Allred turned. His rich brown eyes seemed to dance in amusement as he took her in. "Nice costume."

She bristled. How dare he make fun of her? "And I

suppose you're Scrooge."

His brow furrowed at her cold tone.

Blair's eyes widened. "Tempest, darling. Can I talk to you for one quick second?" She handed Leonard Allred a slice of lemon meringue. "Be right back."

Tempest's belly churned as she followed Blair behind where a large man handwashed dishes with steaming water.

"What are you doing?" Blair asked.

"What are *you* doing?" It came out as a hiss.

"I'm talking to Leonard Allred for you. This is your chance."

Tempest pursed her lips. "Don't tell me you're doing this for me. I know you. I saw the look in your eyes when I walked in here."

Blair stood straighter. "Fine. I'm totally into him."

"He's the enemy."

"Not my enemy. Not if I can get him to fund my Blair-kery."

"That's the keeper right there."

"Shut up." Blair said it in jest.

"You're sabotaging the bet."

"That's an added bonus." Blair smiled. "All in the name of pink walls."

Tempest exhaled with a scowl.

"I know it's basically impossible for you to win now that he's got a whiff of the good stuff." Blair traced the sides of her ample curves with her hands. "But I have to go bring back another tray before I get in trouble. You go over there and talk to him. Get that date, girl." Blair pushed Tempest in the direction of the very handsome man and then slipped through a side door.

Tempest walked slowly, calculating risk. This man was a mountain of risk. And for what reward? Cream walls? She didn't want a date with this man. She wanted to leave right now with Arty. But she would tell Leonard Allred how much he'd cost her before she left. Therapy. Closure. Revenge. Justice.

He looked up when she approached. He glanced behind her, clearly looking for someone else, a shorter, curly haired someone else.

"Blair had to go help clear for a minute. It's almost like they expect her to work for pay."

He sent her an utterly charming smile as he set down the half-eaten slice of pie.

"I'm sorry I called you Scrooge. I didn't mean it, and it's far from true."

"Forgiven."

Why was he looking at her as if she were a joke? "You look very nice. What's your costume?"

"The Count of Monte Cristo."

"Ah, rich guy who ruins everyone's lives." Her tone was cold. "How fitting."

He narrowed his eyes and blinked.

She opened her mouth to tell him exactly how well he fit that description, but no words came out. He looked so young, hardly even twenty-five. And innocent, with wide welcoming brown eyes. She had a hard time imagining a genius mind behind those clear eyes. She thought of Arty suddenly—he could totally have hidden layers. She exhaled, her anger releasing. She didn't want to hurt this nice man. That wouldn't get her job back. That would just make her feel small and wretched. The sweet touch of forgiveness lightened her chest. She closed her mouth and smiled, a genuinely kind smile. He rocked back slightly at the sight of it.

****

Leo opened the door to the serving area and froze on the threshold. *Shit.* Tempest and Dean stood against the far counter, talking. A tête-à-tête. *Double shit.* She smiled up at Dean, a seductive smile that practically sucked all the oxygen from the air. *What the hell?* Fury flared. She leaned in and whispered something that made Dean's whole face light up. Dean slid closer to her. *Maybe I really should fire your sorry ass, you traitor.* She chuckled, putting a hand on her hip, her shirt pulling tight over her breast.

Either she knew the truth, and she was done with "Arty" because he lied, and she was now hitting on Dean harder than a wrecking ball on demo day, or she still thought Dean was Leo and she didn't hate Leonard Allred after all; she was a gold-digging little liar. Leo didn't know which was worse.

He wasn't going to wait around to find out. He turned and walked away, the door swinging shut behind him.

"What happened to the deer-lady?" the valet asked when Leo went to climb into the driver's seat.

"Missed my shot." The car smelled faintly of her perfume. *Damn it.*

"I'm glad to know even Sir Robin strikes out sometimes."

He did not tip the young punk, and he violated seventeen traffic laws on his way home.

****

Leo told himself he would let it go. He'd been out with her all of three dates. And one kiss—one spectacular kiss, but still, not much excuse for him to feel all hurt and vicious. He swore he wouldn't say a word to Dean. They worked together well, even becoming close friends these last two years, hanging out plenty outside of work. But on Monday morning when that little weasel walked through his office door with green tea and a Love Your Grains bowl for Leo's breakfast, Leo's voice came out sharp. "Had a good time at the party on Saturday, huh?"

Dean halted, his eyebrows pinching in. "Good morning, boss." He put the food down slowly, as if not wanting to poke the sleeping dragon.

This dragon was awake. "I saw you talking to my date."

Dean beamed. "That deer costume looked hot on her. Well done."

Acid washed over Leo's tongue.

"She seemed super rad too. Best woman you've found in a long time."

Leo's nostrils flared.

"I approve."

"Do you?"

Dean balked at Leo's deadly tone.

"Is that why you're trying to cock-block me now?"

Dean's hands flew up. "What are you talking about, bro?"

"Don't bro me. I saw you two in the kitchen, one joke away from making out right on the leftovers." Leo bit his tongue, heat rising to his cheeks. He could not believe he'd just said that. Any of it. Was he twenty-nine or nineteen? He waved a hand. "Forget it. It's none of my business. Make sure everyone's ready for the nine-thirty meeting."

Dean didn't leave. An arrogant smile spread over

his tan face. "You really like her."

"Get out."

"You're being such a pig that you don't deserve me telling you this, but I can't let you screw up again."

Leo opened his mouth to argue the *again* comment.

"We weren't flirting," Dean said. "I was hitting on her roommate, Blair. Tempest was giving me a leg up. She gave me Blair's number and told me a sure way to win Blair over would be to take her out for fried chicken on our first date."

Aw, hell's bells. Leo sank into his chair as reality hit like a punch to the gut. And he'd abandoned Tempest at the party. Just left her there without a word or text. *Shhhiiiitttt.* Why was he such an anxious spaz when it came to women? "Did you introduce yourself as Dean?"

Dean's forehead crinkled. "It never came up. I guess I never told her my name. Why?" His eyes went as wide as a dinner plate. "You're kidding me, Leo."

Leo looked down in shame.

"Who does she think you are, then?"

"Ardy. Although she says it like Ar-tee. I didn't correct her."

Dean plopped down in a leather chair.

Leo hissed out a pent-up breath. "I royally screwed it up."

"Yup."

"I'm an epic idiot."

"Yup."

"You can't take Blair out."

"Nope. I'm definitely taking her out."

"Does she know you're Dean and not Leo?"

Dean paused. "I never told her my name either.

How weird is that? It's like she already knew it." He glared at Leo, his voice turning sharp. "Because she also thinks I'm you."

"Sorry."

"If you're sorry, you'll fix this."

"I will. Give me a week."

"I'm taking Blair out on Thursday night. You have until then before I tell them."

****

It was Thursday night. Five days since Arty had left Tempest at the party, *abandoned* her in the middle of their date. No words. No explanation. No apology. Tempest looked up from her Ion Biode novel when the door opened. She heard Blair grunting before the curly dark hair came into view. Blair swung the paint cans inside and set them on the mat with a *thud.*

"Don't help me," she said, voice sarcastic.

Tempest didn't get up.

Blair disappeared, returning again with more pink paint. The third time she carried in a tarp, roller brush, and blue tape. "I think that's everything. At least that's what the guy at Home Depot said."

"Great." She dragged out the word to make it clear she meant the opposite.

"You're going to love it. Pink is so happy. It'll be fun."

"Great." She managed even less enthusiasm.

"And I take it you're not going to help me get ready for my date tonight."

She set the paperback down. "I'm grumpy, but not that grumpy." She followed Blair down the hall to the messy bedroom.

Blair had food magazines stacked on her desk,

clothes hanging over the chair back and across the bed, and lipstick tubes spread out like Easter eggs.

"Did he say what you're doing tonight?"

"Nothing fancy. I think just dinner." Blair pulled a seductive face. "Unless we go somewhere for *dessert*." She stretched the last word suggestively.

"Just don't come here for it."

Blair glanced at the pile of unfolded laundry on her love seat. "Definitely not here." She winked as she looked at Tempest. Blair didn't seem to have any hesitations about bringing a man home to her "delightfully lived-in room," as she called it, but she was kind enough not to rub Leonard Allred in Tempest's face tonight. "And I'm dying to see his place. I wonder if he has jets installed in his bathtub."

"It won't be nicer than Art..." Her voice died as Blair gave her a compassionate frown. Tempest turned away.

Blair pulled out a tunic that made her torso look longer and wouldn't show grease if Leonard Allred came through with the fried chicken. She put on a final sweep of mascara when a knock came at the door. The women froze. Blair let out a nervous little squeal, then she sobered. "Are you sure it's okay if I go out with him? I'll get rid of him faster than moldy potatoes if you say the word."

Tempest took Blair's hand. "Like I've told you fifty thousand times this week, I am more than fine with it. I don't think I could have handled going out with him even if I had managed to talk him into it. And I'll get a much better, much cooler job when this is over, I'm sure." She tried to believe it but couldn't. Her job search so far had been dee-pressss-ing. "I think you should fall wildly in love and open the fanciest dessert parlor and have really cute, really smart babies." That was true. She only wished good things for Blair.

"Thank you, Stormie." Blair kissed her on the nose. "Are you going to hide in here until we leave?"

"Yup."

Blair flounced out. Tempest heard her say, "Hello, handsome." Seconds later the front door closed.

Tempest made one of her regular weeknight meals, veggies roasted on a sheet pan with a few slices of organic chicken sausage. Prepared, consumed, and cleaned up in under forty minutes. After dinner, she sat down with her book. It was the third in the Ion Biode series, the one where everything went to crap. It seemed fitting at the moment, but it only made her think of Arty all the more. That first day they met, he'd actually defended Malcom Tribone's behavior. She should have known he was trouble when he sided with the book's epic villain. She snapped the spine shut. She couldn't focus on the words, not with Arty in her head and those paint cans over there practically screaming the word *loser.*

She put on a blue-and-white T-shirt she'd been given at a charity walk for lung cancer. It was a men's XL. She didn't have pants to sacrifice to paint, so she only wore the shirt-dress, bra, and panties. Thursday night par-tay. She turned on music, pushed back the furniture, spread out the tarp, and taped along the baseboards. She pried open the first can of paint.

"Congratulations. It's a girl!"

She poured the amoxicillin-colored goo into the tin and started rolling. At least it was probably better than the taupe brown there now. The *slick, slick, slick* of the roller relaxed her thoughts, took her away from her troubles. She didn't think about work, Arty, or Leonard Allred. Paint fumes, pink, and pop music consumed her whole world.

She'd almost finished with the first of two walls when she heard the knock at the door. She jumped down from her step stool and flicked off her music. She did not answer the door. She wasn't home right now. She stepped up on her stool again and kept painting. She was reaching for the top corner when the door cracked open. She looked over her shoulder with a sharp inhale. Arty stood in the doorway like a stone statue, his eyes wide and staring at the backs of her bare legs. What was he doing here? Fire rushed through her veins, and her voice came out hot.

"Hey. I didn't say you could come in."

He blinked, his gaze now going to her face. "I know. You didn't open the door, but you left it unlocked, so…"

She climbed down the ladder and dropped the paint roller in the pan. She put her hands on her hips. "That won't hold up in court." Her jaw tightened against the warring thoughts in her head. By the look of the little blue box in his hand and the regret on his face, he came here to apologize, but it was too late for that. She wouldn't give him the chance to burn her again. But her heart betrayed her, giving a little flutter at the size of his sad steel-blue eyes.

"Tempest." The word was a plea, a prayer.

She held tight to her hurt. "You left me. Abandoned me at the party."

He flinched. "I am so sorry. I have no excuse. Well, I have excuses, but you don't want to hear them."

"You're right, I don't." She picked up her roller brush and started spreading more cheery pink.

"Bold choice," he said, looking over the wall.

"I lost a bet. Again."

"What was it?"

Don't talk to him. "The dumbest bet I've ever made. And I've made plenty. When I lost my job, I made a half-drunken bet with Blair that I could get Leonard Allred to take me out just so I could tell him how his precious Red Rocco had ruined my life."

Arty's face was doing something weird, the skin mottling red and white above his beard.

She pointed with her brush. "You don't have any right to get all judgey on me after your stellar performance on our date." She sighed, her tone loosening. "And I didn't go through with it anyway. So now the front room is pink, and ironically, Blair is out with Leonard Allred right now."

"No, she's not."

Tempest turned, the brush drooping at the low tone of his voice.

"I'm Leonard Allred." The words were soft, but they cut like knives.

She just stood there, not breathing, seeing the truth written everywhere. The house, the car, the cashmere, the intelligence. Yes, he was definitely Leonard Allred. And she was definitely an idiot.

"So." His pale eyes flashed. "It seems you actually won your little wager, including telling me how much you hated me the first time we met. Congratulations."

Sweat prickled in her pits at the surge of resentment. "No one is winning here. Least of all me. Not only did you ditch me on our date, but you've been lying to me this entire time. That's messed up—*Arty*."

"I didn't mean to." His empty hand flipped up as if emphasizing his earnestness. "Sometimes I give strangers the old nickname my sister made up when we were little. Ardy. I would have told you that first night to call me Leo instead, but after you said I ruined your life, I was too ashamed to admit who I am."

"You just decided you would ruin my life more instead?" Her fingers dug into her waist. "You pretended to like me long enough take me out, kiss me without consent, and then leave me at a party."

"You kissed me back!"

"I liked it at the time!"

He balked, then his face softened. Hers did not.

"I wasn't pretending. I did like you. I *do* like you." Arty—*Leo* looked at her with a face stricken with regret. "I saw you talking to my assistant Dean in the catering kitchen. I guessed that you thought he was me. It looked like you were hitting on him for his money, and I overreacted."

Her body tensed, and her jaw hardened so much it was hard to spit out the words. "You should leave now."

"Please let me start over. Give me a second chance."

"I don't want to go through this a second time." It wouldn't hurt so much if she hadn't been so dang into him.

"Please."

"Don't come back."

He set the tiny box on the end table.

"Take that crap with you."

He didn't pick it up. "I'm sorry." He left, closing

the door behind him.

She darted forward and engaged the lock before crumpling to the welcome mat. Her shoulders curved inward against the pain. Angry tears mixed with the pink splattered on her shirt.

****

Leo stood on Tempest's doorstep. The deadbolt slammed into place. He wanted to find some justified indignation in the fact that when they met she'd been hunting him just to win a bet, but the delusion wasn't working. What she'd done was nothing compared to his lies. And leaving her at the party was unforgivable. She'd made that plenty clear. He didn't blame her.

This was why his sister, Zena, never set him up with her friends. This was why he would be sad and alone forever, with nothing but money and regret to keep him company.

Gutted, he slunk down the walkway. Dean's car pulled up to the curb. *Triple crap.* He could not catch a break. Dean honked and waved, his ridiculous grin indicating his night was going the opposite of Leo's. Blair glared at Leo from the front seat. As soon as the wheels stopped, she hopped out and then marched straight at him.

So he wasn't going to be able to avoid them.

"What're you doing here, Leonard Allred?" Blair spit his full name like a curse and put her hands on her round hips. "Here to hurt my best friend even more?"

He flinched. "I'm just leaving."

Dean came around the car, stopping well behind Blair, clearly wanting to stay out of this. Leo wanted out too.

"Good," Blair said. "Don't come back. You should

be ashamed you cost a smart woman a job she loved."

Leo's defenses rose with a flash of heat. "You should be ashamed of yourself. You manipulated your best friend into painting her house that hideous color."

She leaned back as if slapped.

He was not sorry.

"What kind of arrogant prick uses his assistant as a fake identity?"

He exhaled, his temper cooling. He was too tired for this. "Glad we had this chat."

She whirled so fast on Dean standing behind her that he leaned back, his eyes widening and his hands lifting in surrender. "I'm glad you're not a stuck-up billionaire."

Dean didn't have a chance to answer before she grabbed his neck and pulled him a foot down to meet her mouth. She kissed him hard, her hand burying into his hair. Leo had hoped his evening would end in a kiss. How wrong he'd been. She let Dean go, landing back on her heels. Dean blinked at her like a besotted idiot.

"Call me later," she said.

"Yes, ma'am."

She flounced up the path. When she passed Leo, she said, "By the way, that beard is hideous."

"Damn." Dean's eyes glittered as he watched the little tyrant try to open the locked door.

"Stormie," she called. "It's just me. Let me in." She glared over her shoulder. "The asshole is leaving."

Leo's teeth clamped together hard. The door cracked open. He craned to see inside, but Tempest was hidden from view. Blair went in and slammed the door shut. Dean and Leo looked at each other in the sudden silence.

Dean opened his lipstick-smeared mouth.

Leo held up a hand. "Don't."

Dean closed his lips and wordlessly walked over and got in his car.

Leo sighed against the pain in his breast, suddenly too tired to even move. Until the sprinklers turned on, spraying his face and soaking his leather shoes. From the safety of his car, Dean's palm covered his mouth, and his eyes bugged out like saucers. Leo ran to his truck, not daring to glance back at the house for fear he would see Blair's triumphant face in the window.

Chapter Six
The Family Dinner

Tempest sat in the reception of Martin Mortgage, waiting for her interview. Her phone buzzed with another text from *LA—Lying Asshole* as she'd changed his name in her phone. Her heart pinched as she read it.

—*Let me make it up to you. Dinner this weekend?*—

She scanned up through the last three weeks of apology texts from Arty. He'd sent one text every morning. Yesterday's had read —*I'll never lie to you again.*— The day's before had read —*I was wrong and stupid. Forgive me.*— And before that —*Tempest, I'm sorry. I should never have lied. I should never have left you at the party.*—

She had not responded yet, but she felt his words and his persistence hacking away at her fear and her hurt. She wasn't unforgiving; she was afraid. She wanted to go back to the beginning and have a do-over. Deep inside, she still hoped he was the good guy she'd met at first. She'd thought their connection had been a thing of epic poems—obviously she'd been wrong. She shouldn't have felt so much for him after only a few dates. Her rational mind knew that after what he'd done, she shouldn't still care for him, think about him, or want him. But she did.

Her thumbs hovered over the phone, considering.

But how could she risk further heartbreak? She'd walked around that Halloween party for an hour looking for him, alone and confused. She'd called his phone, and he'd *ignored* her. Finally, she'd slunk back to the serving kitchen and helped Blair finish with cleanup. She'd been mortified to the point of tears. Just thinking about it again made her breathless with pain and resentment.

She tucked her phone into her bag as a grinning, middle-aged man approached her chair and held out his hand.

****

Tempest tapped her foot on the ground with the speed of hummingbird wings. She should stop; her interviewer kept looking at it, but it was partly revenge for his making her sit in this dismal office. Seriously, what was that smell? And partly a channel for her building frustration. This was the fourth interview she'd had in the last three weeks, and this was the worst of the lot. She felt juked. Martin Mortgages had posted the listing for a *mortgage underwriter*, but once they'll lured her here, it changed to a job that sounded a lot more like a secretary. With a forty-three-thousand-dollar salary to match. She was not interested, and she was pissed about the false advertising.

Red Rocco was hiring an account manager. With all the success they'd had taking over insurance companies, they needed more soldiers. She could *not* apply for that. Unfortunately. And it had annoyingly good benefits. She hated Leonard Allred—*Leo*—especially how much she didn't hate him. How had he managed to wreck so many facets of her life within a month? It was impressive in the most morbid sense.

How long would he keep texting before giving up? She was afraid he would stop.

"Well, Tempest," Mr. Martin said, "it's been great talking to you. You seem to fit right in here with the Martin Mortgage community. Well, we're more like a family, really."

She grimaced but hoped it looked friendly.

"When can you start?"

"That's really nice, but I was expecting more responsibility and more pay."

His round face fell. "Well, you're just getting started here. You'll need time for training. I'm sure you'll be moving right up fast."

"I'm not so sure." She stood, brushing out the creases in her pencil skirt. "I think I'm better suited at a place that values me more."

"Well…"

"*Well*, thanks. Goodbye."

Her phone rang as she walked out the door. She let it ring until she'd moved past reception and into the shared entrance hall. The smell was stronger here. Like egg salad. She answered the phone, said, "Hello," then held her breath past the open doors of the deli.

"How's my little lady?"

"Fine, Daddy." Was now the time to finally tell him about the job situation? She kept meaning to tell him, but she wasn't in the mood. Ever.

"Change of plans for Thanksgiving. Silvia's invited us to come to her house. We want to bring our families together. She's eager for our children to meet."

She braced her forearms against the hood of her car. She had really been looking forward to wearing sweats to Jo's, eating her sister's buttery rolls, drinking her brother-in-law's *give-thanks-and-gin*, and watching the Cowboys.

"It'll be fun," Dad said when she didn't respond. "Silvia's a great cook, and we want to spend the holiday with all the people we love."

Love. Dad had fallen in love again. She exhaled. "Of course, Dad. If that's what you want."

"Thank you." His relief was audible.

"I'm glad you've found someone that makes you happy."

"She's wonderful. I can't wait for you and Jo to get to know her better."

"Text me the address for Thursday."

"She wants us there at two p.m. Don't worry about bringing anything. The two of us have got it covered."

The two of us. Why was it so weird? How could her sixty-five-year-old dad find love easier than she? Her phone buzzed. Jo was calling. "It'll be fun, Dad. Can't wait for Thursday. I've got to go."

"All right."

She clicked over to Jo. "Hey."

"Did you talk to Dad yet?"

"Just now."

"On a scale of one to super annoyed, I'm a nine point nine. Thanksgiving is in three days. You can't just spring something like this on people. I already bought a fucking turkey."

Tempest breathed deeply, getting another whiff of eggy sulfur. Things were not good when Jo started swearing. Time for damage control. "I hear you. Way late on the invite. But Dad's so excited, and I'm super curious to see her house and meet her kids." That was a stretch, but Tempest knew Jo would be. Her sister loved checking people out.

"I know. I really wonder. They seem fancy. Do you think the son is gay like his dad? Is that genetic?"

Tempest rolled her eyes. "Like you'd even be able to tell."

Jo sounded affronted. "I am very good at judging people's orientation."

She was certainly good at judging, just not necessarily with justice or accurate information.

"I just hope the food is good," Jo said. "I don't get to bring my sweet potatoes and marshmallows because *her* daughter wants to make *her* sweet potatoes." Jo's sweet potatoes were a heart attack in a dish. "I can't handle a bad Thanksgiving. It's the most important meal of the year!" Her voice went high.

"How about Blair and I come over Sunday? She'll help cook, and we'll whip up the traditional Swan Thanksgiving. We can talk about how much better our food is than Silvia's."

Tempest could hear the smile in Jo's voice when she said, "Do you think Blair would be willing to make those pumpkin maple bars?"

"I'll ask her."

"Thanks, T. That's really nice of you."

"It'll be fun."

"Love you."

"Love you too." Tempest hung up. She sighed grandly. And then sighed again.

Feeling sorry for herself, she pulled out her phone and scrolled through LA's unanswered texts. They seemed so nice and genuine. She wanted to curl into his arms and have him kiss everything better. Before she could think too much about it, she texted —*Coffee on*

Saturday morning.—

He responded immediately. *—I'll pick you up at ten.—*

Her heart betrayed her, swelling and marching onward like a ticker-tape parade.

****

Tempest opened the door to her house and stopped.

Blair turned, holding out her paint brush with a flourish. "Ta-da!"

"You repainted it cream." Her voice was soft with surprise. The sudden heat behind her eyes startled her.

"You won the bet. I *always* pay up."

She smiled at Blair, her eyes watering. It had been such a long month. And now to not only feel like things might work out with Leo, but to also come home to this. It felt so good. "Thank you, Blair."

Blair's voice was gentle. "I want you to be happy, Stormie."

Had she been that obvious? She thought she'd been doing just fine. She had kept busy: extra yoga, catching up on her reading list, reconnecting with old friends, deep cleaning, testing out new recipes, job applications. But she hadn't fooled Blair. She hadn't fooled herself. She felt bored and useless. And alone.

"You make me happy, Blair." And it was true. She loved her roommate. Loved coming home to her, loved how their differences brought them closer. She liked who she was around Blair, more relaxed and spontaneous. "I told Leo I'd go for coffee with him on Saturday. Is that the dumbest thing ever?" She braced herself against Blair's disapproval, suddenly realizing how truly eager she was to see him.

"No." Blair set down her paint brush. "I think you

should."

Tempest relaxed. "Really?"

"Are you kidding? That bugger has apologized more times than any man in history."

Tempest chuckled.

"I would have given in long ago."

"Why didn't you say anything?"

"Because it wasn't my place. And who am I to give relationship advice?" Blair picked at paint on her fingers. "And I don't want you to get hurt again."

Tempest didn't want to think about that possibility. "I'm having Thanksgiving dinner at my dad's girlfriend's house."

"Whoa. That's getting serious."

"Seriously." She started unzipping her skirt as she walked down the hall to her room. "She has a son and daughter we're meeting."

"Maybe the son will be a hottie. A backup plan if Leo take two is a bust, if you know what I mean."

Tempest walked into her room without answering. She always knew what Blair meant. And she didn't want to think about the girlfriend's son. She wanted to think about Leo.

****

Leo finished tightening the shelf in his mother's garage. He replaced her rain boots on the now secure rack and returned the power drill to its place among her nice set of hardly used tools. He swiped the bottoms of his shoes on her welcome mat and walked into the kitchen. He inhaled the happy smell of rosemary and garlic. In two days, he'd get to take Tempest out again. He wasn't going to screw it up this time.

"They're here," Mom called, her voice eager.

He found her at the front entry, checking her teeth and fluffing her mane of platinum hair in the mirror she'd installed by the door for that very purpose. Zena slunk over from the couch, not looking up.

"Put that away," Mom said.

Zena slipped her phone into the back pocket of her blue jeans.

"Best behavior." Mom's voice was stern as she looked them both in the eyes. "I really like this man, and this is important to me. I want you to get along with his daughters."

Mom turned to the door, and Zena rolled her eyes like, *who cares about your boyfriend's spawn?* She looked a lot like Mom. The blue eyes, blond hair, and affinity for beauty products. Leo looked more like his dad, with the same gray-blue eyes and perpetually young face. During his senior year of high school, Leo could never be sure if his friends were coming over to hang with him or to hit on his freshman sister. It was still like that. Especially since they hung out together most weekends. Zena made the plans, and Leo tagged along. He liked that she had lots of cute friends, and she liked his black card.

Mom opened the double doors and stepped into the murky November sunlight. "Welcome, welcome."

Leo walked out behind his sister. His gaze drifted past where his mom embraced her new boyfriend. A woman held hands with two children dressed in church clothes. His mom would love their little outfits, but they didn't look comfortable. Following her, a friendly looking man with ruddy cheeks and thick dark hair carried a baby. Leo liked him immediately. Good, he'd have someone to hang with today. The younger daughter came into view at the back of the line, and his veins turned to liquid nitrogen. *No, no, no.* This could not be happening. Not when he'd finally gotten her to go out with him again.

"Leo, Zena." Mom held out an arm to them, her voice high with nervous excitement. "Come meet Christopher Swan and his family."

That was the moment Tempest saw him. He could tell because she almost missed a step and fell into the square-shaped holly bush. The blood drained from her face. Her gaze was like a laser beam.

Christopher motioned to his oldest. "This is Josette Marie."

"Just Jo, please."

The resemblance between the sisters was there, but he couldn't have been less attracted to Jo or more attracted to Tempest.

"And her husband, Benji," Christopher said. He named the children, but Leo couldn't hear over the pounding in his ears.

Tempest looked good. A little tired around the eyes, maybe. Was that partly his fault? The sight of her lit him up. She wore a simple red sweater and tight black pants. Her short hair framed her face in loose curls. Zena was smiling and saying something. Then Tempest stepped up and shook Zena's hand. Leo squinted when Tempest turned to him. She was harder to look at than the muted November sun. She didn't offer him her hand as she looked over him in dismay.

"Nice to meet you," Leo said.

It was the wrong thing to say. As if she'd been teetering between hostility or civility, and that had decided it. Her teeth clenched. Her eyes narrowed.

"We've met." Her voice was cold.

Dread pooled in his belly.

"You remember. Just after I got laid off because your software took over my job."

Leo opened his mouth, but it was too dry to form words. She had clearly not forgiven him. Had she agreed to Saturday coffee not to get back together but so she could yell at him some more? Anger burned through Leo's veins. Good to know now; he'd save himself the heartache. He didn't want to be with someone so unforgiving.

Jo's attention snapped to Tempest. "You lost your job?"

Mom looked stricken. Zena looked interested for the first time.

"Yeah." All the acid had drained from Tempest's voice. "Three of the four underwriters at Salvo were laid off. Happened last month."

"Why didn't you tell us?" Jo asked.

Christopher put an arm around Tempest, but she stepped out after one second. "It's fine. I'll find something else soon." Her gaze darted at Leo, just long enough to strike.

She hadn't found another job yet. His stomach turned. This was an epic disaster.

"I'm sorry I brought it up." Tempest smiled at the silent group. "Let's go enjoy Thanksgiving." Her voice was as bright and fake as neon green. "What a beautiful home." She stepped toward the door. "And it smells divine."

Mom's face flipped to happy mode. "Oh, thank you. I hope so. Come in. Come in. Leo will get everyone drinks."

Definitely drinks.

Mom motioned the group inside and then turned on Leo with a glare that could have stopped Genghis Khan's raids.

Sorry, he mouthed.

"Fix this," she hissed.

He nodded dutifully, knowing she asked for the impossible.

****

Dad was dating Leo's mom. Dad was *in love* with his mother.

"Yup. He's definitely gay," Jo whispered in Tempest's ear as they invaded the house. "Too bad for you, he's cute."

"No, he's not," Tempest said, realizing that it was unclear which statement she was responding to. She slowed her step, going warm at the sudden memory of his kiss, of his hands on her waist, his chest pressing her against the wall.

"He'd make a great stepbrother," Jo said.

"No, he would not." Tempest swallowed down a gag. She could think of nothing worse than Leo becoming her *brother.* But what about coffee Saturday? Should they still go out? Was it too weird now? Practically incestuous.

Silvia motioned to Jo. "Let me show you where I keep the toys."

"How delightful." Jo stepped away from Tempest. "Thank you."

Tempest didn't register more than glimpses of the traditional Texan interior: dark wood, damask drapes, cowhide rug. While Jo, Benji, and the kids went with Silvia, Tempest stared at swirling wallpaper.

"What can I get you?" Leo's voice made it real. They were having family Thanksgiving together.

She blinked the room into focus.

He stood at a built-in bar off to the side of the kitchen, near a dining table heavy laden with fine china and fall foliage. He waited, a slight smirk on his face.

She scowled.

"May I recommend the cinnamon maple whiskey sour or the apple pie sangria? House specials today."

"Vodka cranberry," Zena said, walking through a rounded entry and joining her brother at the bar. She picked up a glass. She had her mother's blond hair and heavy eyeliner. Tempest hated that she felt slightly intimidated by this younger woman. Tempest wondered if she should have worn more makeup, maybe added a bracelet. Zena had five gold bangles climbing up her arm.

"I already tried the apple thing. You definitely shouldn't make that again."

Leo frowned at his sister, but his face held no malice.

"Zena, dear." Silvia's sing-song voice carried from across the room where she stacked an assortment of dinner rolls in a basket. "Come help with the jams, would you?"

When his sister walked away, Leo's focus returned to Tempest. "And what about you? Are you brave enough to take a chance?"

"On you?" Her voice came out harsh. "I already did that. It didn't go well." His face fell, and guilt struck her chest. She hadn't meant to be cruel. Her defenses had reacted for her. This family dinner was not part of the plan, and the shock of it was sending her reeling. "But I'll try the whiskey sour."

They didn't speak as he poured the bourbon and squeezed the lemon. He sprinkled cinnamon and drizzled maple, then dumped an added glug of the amber syrup in her glass at the end. "A little extra to sweeten you up."

"Charming as always." She tried to sound sarcastic, but it didn't deliver well, because, *dammit,* she was charmed. She took the drink, feeling a jolt as his fingers brushed hers.

He frowned, looking down as he polished droplets off the counter. "I thought maybe you were forgiving me. I thought Saturday was going to be fun."

She was forgiving him. Before she could correct his misunderstanding, he kept talking.

"But since clearly you still resent me for everything bad in your life, I think I'm busy this weekend."

Her ribs squeezed as pain and anger flared. Why had she ever thought it would be a good idea to see him again? "Fine."

He looked up at her, his fiery gaze searing over her skin. "Nice earrings."

She startled, clutching the cup. How had she forgotten she'd worn those this morning? Although she'd worn the sapphires every day since she'd finally opened the little blue box. "I told you not to leave them. I told you I didn't want them. But you didn't listen."

"No, I didn't." His lips twitched in the middle of his beard.

She had the sense he was holding back amusement. How insufferable. "I saw no reason such beautiful earrings should go to waste because of my injured pride and hurt feelings." Which wounds he'd managed to reopen today.

He opened his mouth, closed it, opened it. "Well, that's honest."

"You should try it sometime."

His chin lowered, and his voice came out soft, but his gaze cut like a blade. "Tempest, I've said I'm sorry. It's your turn to believe it or not."

The chill of regret curled down her body. Her heart wanted to forgive him. She wanted to touch him, feel if that sweater was also made from baby alpacas, feel how smooth the skin on his clean-shaven neck was. Her mind sent warning after warning. He'd just cancelled their date. She sipped her drink, stomach churning. "This is pretty good, Arty."

A threatening glint darkened his eyes. He did not like her calling him that. *Good to know.*

Silvia's voice rang out. "Dinner is served."

****

Tempest sat by her seven-year-old nephew Hunter and Zena. At least she didn't have to rub elbows with Leo. He sat directly across the table. That was worse. Every time their gazes locked, it was like a flick against her heart. She tried to ignore him, but her wants betrayed her. She wasn't sure what she felt for him, whether she veered more toward hate or love, but whatever the emotion was, it was too high. *Feel nothing. Think about the turkey that died for you.*

She usually didn't like turkey, but nothing about this meal was usual. According to Silvia, this free-range bird had been smoked since an ungodly hour. It practically melted into the mash potatoes and gravy. Jo wasn't going to be thrilled that Silvia's turkey was

101

better than hers. Tempest would never admit she liked Zena's yams better than Jo's too. Zena's side dish didn't give her an immediate sugar headache.

After all the dishes had gone around the table clockwise once, and sufficient compliments to the chef had been given and received with exceptional elegance, Dad spoke. "Zena, how does it feel to be back in Texas? Do you miss California?"

"I miss the weather."

Everyone nodded in understanding.

"But it's good to be home," Zena said. "I missed my friends here. Nowhere is better than Dallas."

Everyone nodded in agreement.

"And you're working with Leo at Red Rocco?" Dad asked.

Zena grinned at her sibling. "Yes, sir. Big brother takes good care of me."

Tempest put a large bite of Brussels sprouts in her mouth. Hopefully no one would notice that her face was hot or the way her teeth crushed the poor little cabbages to smithereens. Jo was probably the only one who would notice, besides Leo, and Jo's attention was fixed on baby Harrison. Leo was too busy smiling at his sister.

"And she does a little work sometimes too," Leo said, his voice playful. "If only we could get her into the office before noon."

"He's joking," Silvia said.

"Thank you for pointing that out, Mother." Leo set down his fork. "It was a joke. I never check what time people come in."

"Silvia was telling me about the new culture you've built." Dad leaned forward, annoyingly eager.

"I'm focused on creating an office space that fosters teamwork, creativity, and joy." He was looking at her dad with such focus it seemed he was purposefully not looking at her. "I had the opportunity to watch a lot of start-ups form in the Bay Area, and I tried to take the bits and pieces that I meshed with and bring them here."

"Best place I've ever worked," Zena said. "For reals."

"Thanks," Leo said.

Tempest picked up her wine glass and held it high. "To Red Rocco."

Silence fell as every head turned to her. Leo's face went white. She grinned, showing sharp teeth.

Dad scrambled to pick up his glass. "Cheers!" He clinked the crystal to Tempest's flute as the rest of the table belatedly followed suit.

Hunter, in his haste, spilled his cranberry soda all down the front of his cream sweater. He blinked puppy-dog eyes up at Tempest. She set her drink down without taking a sip and picked up his napkin and dabbed.

"Oh, Hunter." Jo rose from her seat with an embarrassed frown.

"Sorry, Mommy. I didn't mean to."

"It's okay," Tempest whispered. The starched linen napkin didn't draw any liquid from his sweater. The red had seeped deep into the wool fibers.

"It happens to all of us," Silvia said to the worried boy.

"Come with me, young sir." Leo rose and motioned for Jo to sit back down. "I'll find you something fun to wear."

"Oh, thank you, Leo." Jo's voice gushed with

appreciation.

Surprise, surprise…Jo liked Leo. Tempest did not like that.

Hunter tilted his head down shyly, but he followed Leo out of the room. They left awkwardness in their wake.

Silvia looked over the table as if viewing a train wreck. Her gaze found Tempest. "I'm sorry about your job."

Guilt punched Tempest in the gut. She should not have brought that up before dinner. Or made it worse with her petty toast. She forced a smile. "No, please don't be. It's just fine. It was time for me to move on anyway."

Silvia wrung her hands. "I was really hoping our children would get along." She sent a meaningful look toward Dad.

What was that about? "Of course we do," Tempest said. What did it really manner anyway? Not like they would have to spend much time together in the future. How long were Dad and Silvia going to last?

Silvia looked as though she appreciated the gesture but didn't believe Tempest. They discussed the recent cold spell until Leo returned with a happy Hunter. The seven-year-old wore a black T-shirt with a glow-in-the-dark Yoda face. The shirt went down to his knees.

"He said I could keep it, Mom!"

Jo nearly swooned at Leo. "Are you sure? That's really nice of you."

"Of course." Leo picked up his napkin and slid into his seat.

"It looks like a dress." Hannah pointed a mocking finger at her brother.

"It does not." Hunter looked appalled.

"It's a Jedi *tunic*," Leo said.

Hunter turned his proud nose up and sauntered back to his seat.

The conversation stayed well away from Red Rocco—and all jobs. They didn't talk about dead wives or ex-husbands. They talked a lot more about sports than the Swan family usually did, and based on the lack of knowledge all around, sports didn't look to be a usual topic in the Allred-Steele household either. Benji, a huge sports fan, carried the conversation, happy to spout his opinion on every Dallas area team without the threat of any pushback from the rest of the table.

"It sounds like we should have the game on," Leo said when Benji stopped talking about the Cowboys' new wide receiver long enough to take a bite. "When does it start?"

Benji didn't look at his watch. "Thirteen minutes ago."

Jo chuckled. "He's been watching it on his phone under the table."

"Honey!" Benji's brown curls bounced over his forehead as he swiveled toward his tattletale of a wife.

Silvia half stood. "Oh, Benji. I'm so sorry."

"It's fine." Benji glared at Jo. "I was just checking the score. I don't need to watch." Benji wasn't a good liar.

Leo strode into the family room, making a path between a stuffed chair and a leather couch. He turned on a large TV and found the game. Hunter tried to wiggle from his seat.

"Finish your plate," Jo said. "Then you can go."

The little boy and his father both angled their

chairs slightly and ate as fast as starving hogs.

Leo returned to the table, and Benji whispered a grateful, "Thank you."

"The Dallas Cowboys are white, aren't they?" Silvia squinted at the screen.

"Yes," Christopher said. "They're on offense now."

Tempest asked Zena her favorite local places to eat. She asked Silvia for the salad dressing recipe. She tried to be charming, she really did, but she could feel herself closing up, going quiet and dark.

After second and third helpings all around, the group dispersed. Tempest cleared the dishes while Leo played a ring toss game with Hunter and Hannah in the hallway. Was he doing that just to look like a hero? He couldn't actually enjoy playing with random children, could he? She barely enjoyed playing games with them, and they were blood. She turned away as one of Hannah's high-pitched squeals of joy rang out. How long did Tempest have to stay here? At least through dessert. When was that going to be?

"Those pies look amazing," Tempest said to Silvia. *Hint, hint.*

Silvia glanced at the four pies displayed on the kitchen island like trophies.

Zena patted her stomach and moaned. "I forgot to leave room for dessert."

"Plenty of time for that," Silvia said. "We'll make our Christmas wreaths first." She looked at Tempest. "You can make one for your door too."

Crap.

"It's tradition," Zena said. "We make the wreaths, and Leo takes the dogs for a walk."

106

He appeared in the kitchen as if pulled by the sound of his name. "Ladies' crafting time?" He cocked his brows at Tempest.

She hated crafting. Judging by the amusement on his face, he seemed to sense that.

"It's not just for ladies," Silvia said. "You are always welcome to join."

"I cannot think of anything worse." Leo smiled with all his white teeth.

Zena rolled her eyes. "That's obviously not true."

"Obviously." Leo looked around. "Where are those disgusting animals you insist on keeping?"

"Probably huddled in their doghouse against the cold, as if they weren't wearing fur coats," Silvia said. "Thanks for taking them. Oh, and watch out for Port's poop. He ate something that gave him diarrhea last week. I think it's over, but…" She shrugged.

Leo blinked at his mother, horror flashing over his face. "I'm going to pretend you didn't say any of *that*."

Tempest bit her lips. Leo turned to her, his face brightening as he took in her suppressed grin.

"So are you coming with me and the shitty monsters, or will it be homemaking 101 here at the house?"

He'd invited her. She nearly leapt at the chance to get away from the box of fake pine and holly sitting ominously in the corner. Obviously she would much, much rather go for a walk outside with Leo, even if she was supposed to be closing off her heart. She opened her mouth.

"You go, Leo," Silvia said. "I want to get to know Tempest a little better."

Tempest enjoyed a blip of satisfaction at Leo's

disappointment as she tried to hide her own displeasure. Was Silvia trying to cover for Tempest? Did she think she was doing Tempest a favor?

"Alrighty, then." Leo's voice was a little awkward. "I'm off." He strode out.

Crafting was just as horrible as Tempest had feared: the hot glue, the glitter, the tediousness of securing one sprig at a time to a foam donut. In the end, Zena and Silvia had made something beautiful. Tempest had not. At least Blair would get a good laugh at this when she got home. Added bonus.

Leo came in the back door, kicked off his boots, and shrugged out of his jacket. The cold had colored his nose red and brightened his gray eyes. She hated that she was glad he was back, hated how while he was gone she'd watched the forty minutes tick slowly by on the rooster clock above the stack of cookbooks. He padded up in his stocking feet and glanced down at the four wreaths; Silvia had managed to make two already. Her creations were dynamic and full of spraying foliage, a tasteful ribbon tucked in here and there. Leo chewed on his lip as he looked at the circle in Tempest's hand. White foam peeked through at the bare spots, and the pine, holly, and winterberry were matted flat with too much glue. She hadn't attempted any ribbon yet.

"That," Leo said, "might scare Santa away."

"Leonard!" Silvia's disapproving voice rang out as Tempest whacked him in the chest with her creation, a spray of glitter pluming in his face. He closed his eyes and mouth and waited for the dust to settle. He blinked, his lashes sparkling gold.

Eyes popping, Zena looked at Tempest, then she let

out a snorting chuckle.

Silvia frowned. "What a terrible thing to say to our guest."

Leo cocked his head at his mother, as if her reaction was the odd thing here. "I'm only teasing."

Silvia looked down at Tempest's dismal wreath. She didn't say anything, but Tempest guessed she wanted to tell her son he couldn't tease about things that were true. He shouldn't mock a zitty person about acne or a scaly person about dry skin. But Silvia couldn't say any of that because then she'd be insulting Tempest too. When Silvia stayed quiet, looking sad and discouraged, Leo turned to Tempest.

"Don't worry, Santa doesn't see the door; he goes down the chimney."

Tempest managed to keep a straight face but barely. She knew Leo could see the humor in her eyes. How could he not? His gaze was locked on hers. The corners of his mouth curled, and Tempest had a sudden flash of memory. Those confident lips on her mouth. His hand holding hers. The smell of expensive cologne on his neck.

His brows rose a fraction, as if reading her want. His eyes dilated. Tempest forced a scowl, jerking her gaze away. Her anger landed on Silvia, who reeled back.

Silvia dropped her wreath and stood. "Please excuse my ill-mannered son."

Tempest took a deep breath, then exhaled the heavy emotions. "It's fine! Please don't worry. I'm not much for crafting, and I'm not about to pretend this is anything but garbage."

Silvia looked like she was about to cry.

"I think it's time for pie," Zena said.

Silvia nodded, her face down-turned. "I'll go get the ice cream from the back freezer."

Leo looked sorry. "I'll get it."

"No." Silvia darted out of the room.

Zena lowered her brows at her brother. "Why'd you have to make her cry?"

Leo lifted his hands. "I didn't mean to. It was not a big deal. Tempest doesn't feel bad. Mom's being super sensitive."

"This meal was important to her. She really wanted us to get along and all be friends."

"We're friends," Leo said, voice exasperated.

Zena looked from Tempest to Leo, clearly not believing it.

"But I don't get why she's making such a big thing of this," Leo said.

Dad walked into the kitchen. "Halftime." He looked over the tight faces at the craft table. "Where's Silvia?"

"I'm here." She scurried in and dropped her armful of ice cream containers on the counter. She reached out and caught the rocky road before it plummeted to the floor.

"Ready for *pie*?" Dad emphasized the last word, making Tempest think of something sexual instead of food. She curled her lip in disgust. Silvia saw it. Tempest switched to a quick smile, but Silvia's eyes pinched in, her face portraying distress.

"Maybe not *that* today," Silvia said. "I don't think it's the right time." Her gaze slid to Tempest and Leo for a nanosecond.

Dad cocked his chin in confusion. "But—"

"Time for what?" Jo asked, coming into the kitchen with her husband and baby.

"*Pie.*" Zena echoed the weird way Dad has said it.

"What's going on?" Jo's keen gaze seemed to gobble up the different expressions on everyone's faces.

That's when the chill of dread started in Tempest's lower belly.

Dad's smile lit up his face as he stepped to Silvia's side and put an arm around her shoulders. Silvia looked a little shy, but mostly she seemed giddy.

Oh no. Not that. No way.

"We have a little announcement," Dad said.

All the air sucked out of the room.

"We're getting married." Silvia's voice was an eager squeak.

Dad laid a kiss on Silvia before his glittering gaze traveled over the gathered children, all shocked to stone. "We love each other, and we can't wait to join our families."

Tempest looked at Leo. He looked at her. If their parents married, what did that make them?

Brother and sister.

Chapter Seven
The Run-In

The rock-climbing gym was busy. Leo was annoyed. Why weren't all these people home nursing their Thanksgiving hangovers? Maybe he should build his own climbing wall. It would be private. And it would be sanitary. He wanted to use the blue hold to the left, but another man's shoe was jammed in there like he wasn't moving on for a good long while. Sweat dripped down the gray-haired man's temples and pooled in giant swaths on his shirt. The man lifted his arm, and one of the climbing holds went right into the wet armpit. *Gross.* Leo's fingers curled on his gritty hold, and his stomach clenched. Why had he agreed to do this?

"To the right." Zena called up to him from where she belayed on the ground. "There's one just over that lip."

He considered letting go, but now that he'd started this, he *had* to finish. He tried not to think about all the dirty bodies that had rubbed up against this wall. "I hope you're holding on," he said to his sister. He grunted as he swung, reaching for the next hold. And the next. He went faster than he could think. He leapt long before he looked. But it worked out. That's the thing about risk sometimes. And this time he made it to the top in less than twenty-four seconds. "Coming

112

down." He thrust away from the wall without waiting.

Zena responded with a grunt as her body jerked forward. She adjusted and slowed his rapid rappel. He landed on the balls of his feet.

"How are you so good at this?" she asked.

"Sheer determination." He rubbed his grimy hands together. "And fear."

"You hate this." Her face fell.

"I like climbing." He didn't add that he liked it outside. On sun-sanitized rocks and without random people. "Your turn." He needed a shower. Right now. "See if you can beat my time."

"That's a fun game." Her voice dripped sarcasm.

After they switched the ropes, she stepped close to the wall and stared up.

"Ready, go." His hands felt disgusting. "And climb."

She touched a hold, then changed her mind and moved to another.

Before Leo could pressure her anymore, a young man approached. "Your boyfriend giving you a hard time?"

She looked the guy over, assessing. She must have liked what she saw because she nodded her head toward Leo. "He's my brother. And yes, he's giving me a very hard time."

Then the flirting began.

When the guy seemed to think he needed to touch Zena's spandex-clad legs in order to help her, Leo zoned out. He should have gone to Barbados like he'd originally planned—until his mom begged him to stay for her *special* Thanksgiving with the new boyfriend. Yesterday had been a horror movie. He could not have been a worse host. Tempest had invaded his unprotected heart like an army, and he wasn't thrilled to discover how *not* over her he turned out to be. And she could not have been more difficult. Not to mention she'd been wearing *his* earrings. Did that mean anything? She'd played it off well, as if men routinely sent her apology sapphires. But the real problem was his mom was engaged to marry Tempest's dad. And Mom seemed so happy. Well, not happy with Leo at the moment. He would need to apologize to her. He was so sick of saying sorry. He'd thought all his texts to Tempest were romantic; now he realized how stupid and needy he must have sounded. At least he'd cancelled their date Saturday in time to salvage the remains of his pride. He needed to forget her.

"Let me down!"

He looked up to where Zena swung at the top of the room, kicking out from the wall and glaring at him. How long had she been up there? He let out the rope, and she descended. She was smiling again by the time her feet hit the floor. "That was majorly fun. Want to go again?"

"No."

She pouted.

"That dude will be your partner as long as you want." He glanced at the guy across the room who kept peeking back at her.

"Do we think he's cute?"

"I wouldn't do him."

She rubbed at the chalk on her palms.

"Decide fast because if you're riding with me, I'm outta here."

"Yeah, you're right. Let's go."

He partook liberally of the hand sanitizer by the door.

"Thanks for doing this with me," she said.

And just like that, he didn't regret coming. He put his arm around her shoulders as he steered her toward the car. "I'd do anything for you."

"Or Mom?" She looked at him with a bit of a grimace.

He exhaled. "I ruined her big announcement."

"I don't think it's the announcement she cares about. It's that she really wants us to get along with the Swan women. They're going to be our stepsisters."

A bit of barf wormed up his esophagus. He let go of her.

"It's not your fault Tempest lost her job, but you could have been more sensitive about it."

He didn't want to get into an argument about that. "You think this wedding is for real?"

"Yes." She nodded with certainty. "You know how much I talk to Mom. And she's been so careful since Robert. She's serious this time."

He scowled.

She pointed a finger. "See that. Why can't you just be happy for her? Christopher seems like a truly good man. A little weird, but he worships her."

They arrived at his car, and Leo got in the driver's seat. He took three deep breaths while he waited for Zena to go around to the passenger side. He switched on her seat heater and turned down the music volume. He didn't put the car in gear. "I've got to make it up to her, don't I?"

"Mom or Tempest?"

He'd definitely been thinking of his mom.

"I think that Tempest was a bit of a prig, so you can skip her, but Mom could really use some cheering up."

"Tempest wasn't being a prig."

Zena raised her eyebrows.

He clamped his lips. Why was he defending her? Tempest was being a prig. He put the car in drive and started toward home and a hot shower.

"We don't have to like the stepsisters. We just have play nice until we get through this wedding. For Mom."

****

Leo, hair still damp from his shower, let himself into his mom's house. Her voice echoed through the halls, calling him into the kitchen. She smiled when he came into view. She always had a smile for him. Even when he'd come home late for curfew in high school or when he insulted her dogs. He'd gotten acute lymphocytic leukemia when he was nine years old. Sick for months. Treatment. Chemotherapy. The works. They hadn't expected him to live. And now, no matter what he did, she was always glad to see him.

Thanksgiving dinner two point oh was spread over the counter in various glass containers. She held out a plate. He took it and picked up the mashed-potato spoon. Wordlessly they filled their plates and took turns with the microwave. She got him a linen napkin, and they sat together at the counter.

"This might be even better today," Leo said, taking another bite of yams.

"Don't tell me it's because the Swans aren't here."

That was probably exactly why. He set down his fork. "I'm sorry about yesterday."

"You were nice to the grandchildren. I appreciated

that." She sent him a smile that did not reach her eyes.

"You caught us by surprise. We just need a bit more time to get to know each other."

Mom burst into tears. "This is all my fault."

He put a hand on her thin shoulder. "That is not what I meant. It's my fault. Let me make it up to you. And I've got an idea. Call it an early Christmas present."

She dabbed at her cheeks with her napkin, her eyes brightening.

"We'll go on a family trip." He cringed at the word *family*. Tempest was not his sister. "You, me, Zena, and all the Swans. Bonding time." He tried not to think about the only kind of bonding he was interested in doing with Tempest.

He really needed to get over that.

Maybe he'd call Michelle this weekend, and Dean would have some ladies at his party tonight. Hopefully he'd find someone new and fun.

But the nagging little voice inside his head wouldn't let him forget that Tempest would never actually be his sister. No matter what.

"It's a good idea," Mom said. "But nothing fancy. I don't want them to feel like we're lording over them."

"So Turks and Caicos is out?"

She rolled her eyes. "What about camping?"

"Too far the other direction."

"Do you think Jo could get away? I'm sure they're busy with all the children's activities."

"Anyone can get away for one night."

"One night?"

"If we're camping. One night is plenty. Baby steps."

Mom pursed her lips before it turned into a smile. She picked up her phone. "Where can we go?"

"California." He spooned stuffing into his mouth.

"That's way too far."

"Everywhere close by is too cold. I'll take care of transportation. It'll be quick and painless to pop over to sunny San Diego."

"So much for not putting on airs." Mom stood, eagerness in her step as she retrieved a notepad and put on her readers.

"I'll leave the planning to the expert." He wiped his mouth with his napkin. "Just let me know what you want from me."

She tugged her glasses down the bridge of her nose and leveled blue eyes on him. "I want you to be a complete gentleman to those women. Treat them like you do Zena."

That was impossible. He forced his lip not to curl in disgust. "Gentleman, got it." He kissed her forehead. "I have to run. Haircut appointment. Thanks for lunch."

She turned to her plotting as he put his plate in the dishwasher and strolled out.

He'd fixed things with Mom, so why did he feel the chill of doom spreading through his chest?

Twenty minutes later he settled into the barber's chair. He didn't look in the mirror, didn't want to be reminded how his hair was thinner on top than it used to be or how Tempest had said Dean had such shiny hair. "Just a trim."

The man draped a cloak over Leo's shoulders as he nodded. "And what about the beard?"

****

Tempest leaned against the kitchen counter, nearly

touching the cute man's leg. Tyson sat on the granite slab, his back against the cabinets, big hands holding a plastic red cup in the space between his thighs. She imagined stepping between his knees and sliding her hands up his blue jeans, feeling the long muscles underneath. His hands cradling her instead of that drink. Maybe later she'd get to do more than imagine it...

So far this party was the best decision she'd made in weeks. Tyson was attractive. And hitting on her hard. He made her feel all those good feelings she'd been missing. And the cherry on top—Leo wasn't here. She'd been so worried, when she agreed to come with Blair to Dean's house, that she would see him. Thanksgiving with Leo and his family yesterday was still way too fresh in her mind. She was here tonight to move on. And so far, the next thing looked *good*.

"So how do you know Dean?" Tempest asked.

Tyson leaned down, bringing his dark eyes and buzzed head closer. His breath smelled like peppermint gum and booze. "This is going to sound so cheesy, but we met at the gym."

She giggled, taking a sip from her plastic cup. Only a sip. She didn't love the beer, and she wanted to feel every single butterfly wing brushing her ribs. No reason to dull the heat snaking down her core. "Maybe I should go to the gym more often."

"You should go Monday, Tuesday, and Thursday between six thirty and seven thirty a.m."

Organized and dedicated. A routine nerd like her. She was into that. She gave him a coy smile that had his focus dropping to her mouth. He looked long enough for her legs to weaken before his gaze flickered across the room to where Dean was yelling over the music to three women coming in his front door.

Dark eyes found her again. "How do you know Dean?"

She hesitated before saying, "He's dating my roommate, Blair."

Blair stepped into the kitchen, her face flushed from drink and dance. She tugged down the short skirt that had worked its way to the top of her thighs. She sent Tempest a quick head nod before opening the freezer and leaning into the chill. Electric cold tickled over Tempest for long seconds before Blair filled her cup with ice. When Blair finally closed the freezer, Tempest pulled her friend against her side.

"This little lady is Blair."

"Ah," Tyson said. "The goddess Dean won't stop talking about."

Blair batted her eyelashes and beamed at him. "You are invited back anytime."

His focus shifted from Blair to Tempest. "I'm sure hoping I get to do this again."

Blair let out a little *ooweeeh* squeal. "Oh, he is smooooth."

Yeah, that last line had come out a little too glossy. Tempest chided herself. She should give him a break, at least until she knew him longer than fifteen minutes. He hadn't asked her where she worked yet, which made him her favorite person at this party.

The front door opened again. A familiar man and his sister entered along with a gust of cold wind that rushed across the room and straight into her blood.

"Oh, shit," Blair said.

"Why are we shitting?" Tyson looked from Tempest to Blair to the newcomers at the door.

Zena waved to Tempest with an exaggerated smile, but Tempest was frozen in place.

He'd shaved.

That was totally against the rules.

He had a jaw. Straight cheeks. The cup in her hand crinkled, complaining against the sudden squeeze of her fingers.

Leo hadn't seen her yet, his focus on bro-hugging Dean and smiling at the women on the couch.

"Strong move, Red Romeo," Blair said.

"I'm missing something," Tyson said.

Tempest glanced up at him. He suddenly seemed to be missing a lot of things. The biggest being that he wasn't the man across the room pulling at her with invisible ropes. "It's nothing. Just got warm in here." She fanned her face. "I might step out for some fresh air."

"It's freezing out there." Tyson's face crinkled with the distress that came from knowing his catch might be slipping away.

Tempest turned. "I'll be right back."

"Please do."

Blair grabbed Tempest's elbow and steered her down the hall and into Dean's bedroom. She flicked on the light and shut the door.

Tempest gulped down air. "He looks good without a beard."

"He looks okay."

Her defenses flared. "Stop acting like he's ugly. He's a good-looking guy."

"Whoa, girl."

Her faced flamed. "Sorry."

Blair chuckled. "I see we are *not* over him."

Blair's sweatshirt was draped over Dean's chair. Tempest moved it and sat down, crossing her legs. She wore dark jeans and a V-neck sweater. She stood again, took off her sweater, and started fanning her overheating torso with it. She didn't want to sweat in it. It was a wool blend, handwash only. Blair sat in the seat Tempest vacated.

"I need to leave," Tempest said.

"No. Then he wins. It will look like you're running away from him."

"I am."

"Take Tyson with you. Then it's like you left with a man."

"I don't want Tyson—" Her words cut off as the door opened.

Dean led Leo into the bedroom. "I got it at a flea market," Dean said. "It's super dope. You're going to love—" The men stopped, both gazes landing on Tempest's bra...well, more accurately the cleavage pillowing out of it.

Tempest lifted her sweater to cover her front.

"Woohoo. Looks like we're just in time for the strip show," Dean said with a slightly drunken drawl, taking another step forward.

"Not funny," Blair said.

"I'm kidding, babe." But Dean hadn't taken his gaze off Tempest's partly covered torso.

"Get out." Blair's eyes turned to coal chips.

Leo, face stony but pink, turned and pulled his friend into the hallway. The door closed.

Blair, bless her terrible soul, burst out laughing. "You definitely win this round."

Tempest flopped over the bed, her arms up to air

out her sweaty armpits. "Everyone is losing." One of the recessed lights in the ceiling had burned out. "Except you and Dean. And my dad and Silvia."

"You and Leo…soon to be siblings." Blair laughed harder.

Tempest threw a pillow, hitting Blair in the side of the head.

With visible effort, Blair reined in her mockery. She stood. "While you're deciding the fate of the world, I'm going to pee." She disappeared into the bathroom.

When Tempest was alone, she sat up with a jolt, realizing she didn't want to be lying anywhere near Dean's bed. Blair's perfume drifted up from the blanket. Tempest put her sweater on and checked her face on her phone. A little flushed, but the light was dim enough in the front room no one would likely notice. She cracked open the bathroom door and spoke over the sound of tinkling.

"Thanks for bringing me tonight. I'm heading home. You okay here?"

"Yes. Sorry about Leo. Dean didn't think he was coming."

"It's fine. I had fun."

"See you tomorrow. Love you, Stormie."

"Love you too, Sticks."

Tempest crept down the hall as quietly as she could in her heels. Leo stood where the hall spilled into the main room, his back to her as he talked to a pretty blond. The twelve inches between his shoulder and the wall looked like enough room to slip behind him without touching him. Tempest sped up to pass, but he turned at the wrong second, spearing her side with an elbow. She exhaled a small grunt.

He reached out on reflex and steadied her with a hand on her upper arm. She hadn't needed steadying until he touched her, sending a spark through her system.

"Excuse me, I'm so sor…" He looked up and saw her. He dropped his hand as if she were hot lava.

"Hi," she said.

He didn't smile. Neither did she. But she didn't look away. Couldn't look anywhere but the smooth planes of his face, his unearthed lips, plump and flushed and calling to her. Was he so sexy because he was off limits now? Or was it the new face? Or maybe the devil was paying her a visit tonight, but she wanted him like a flame wanted air. She brought her fingers to his jaw. He stilled, his breath catching. She ran her thumb along his cheekbone.

"It's so soft." Her voice was smoke and velvet.

His pupils popped wide as the night sky. His voice came out hoarse. "The barber does this hot-towel thing that gets a super-close shave."

She nearly gave in, fell headlong into that glimmering gaze, discovered what kissing that smooth pine-scented skin would taste like. She might have if she had finished that drink; as it was, she was thinking too clearly. This could only end badly. Mitigating her risk, she dropped her hand. "Okay. Have a great night." She stepped to the side of him.

He stuck his arm in front of her and caught her around the waist. His fingers burned hot all the way through the fabric. Her abs tightened, but her insides melted.

"Tempest, wait."

Hormones surged, serving up two choices in her

mind—battle or embrace. She gritted her teeth and spun, pushing his arm away. "Why can't you just leave me alone?"

Regret tugged at her heart at the look of shocked injury in his wide gaze.

"I don't think she wants you to touch her, dude." Tyson appeared at her side.

Crap. She'd said that last sentence way too loudly.

"Who are you?" Leo asked, voice hard and annoyed.

"I'm the guy who's not going to let you get away with disrespecting women."

Leo's nostrils flared.

"And who are you?" Tyson's tone turned challenging. Pectoral muscles flexed beneath his shirt.

Leo looked to Tempest. She waited for him to make up some bullshit name. His jaw twitched like he'd been caught, like he knew her thoughts. He turned on Tyson. "You need to butt out. I'm not some random jerk *disrespecting* Tempest. I'm her br—"

"Don't you dare say brother." She pointed a stiff finger at his chest, her worst fear bubbling up.

He swallowed, his face tensing as he seemed to recognize his monumental mistake.

And she had almost kissed him two seconds ago.

Tyson's whole demeanor changed, a goofy grin appearing. "Her brother! Oh. That makes so much sense. Sorry, man."

"No. I'm not..." Leo stopped talking. His face went white with dismay.

Zena approached, throwing an arm over Leo and another over Tempest. "Family meeting?" She chuckled at her own joke. "What did I miss?"

125

Blair appeared. She looked over the trio of soon-to-be siblings and turned right back around. She walked over to Dean and slipped under his arm. His hand drifted down Blair's side. Tempest wanted Leo's hands on her hips.

"I think I'm going to take off." Tempest stepped out from under Zena.

Leo opened his mouth, but before he could speak, Tyson said, "I'll come with you."

Leo's jaw rippled, and as much as Tempest wanted the satisfaction of him watching her leave with another man, she didn't want to leave with Tyson anymore.

She sent Tyson an apologetic smile. "No. You should stay. I'm not feeling well, and I'm heading straight home."

His face drooped. "Are you sure? Let me at least walk you out."

Leo's voice was cold. "She said she doesn't want you to. Maybe you should *respect* what she said."

Zena's jaw came unhinged as she looked from her brother to Tyson and back again.

"Bye, y'all." Tempest marched out the front door without looking back.

****

Leo felt as if he were being dragged through the fourth level of hell. His insides froze and his skin boiled as he watched Tempest walk out that door.

The family camping trip was a terrible idea—*his* terrible idea. But not worse than saying he was Tempest's *brother* just to one-up that guy.

That guy turned on Leo. "Dude, I'm a nice guy. You didn't have to do me wrong like that."

"You can't seriously be wanting to pick a fight

with me right now."

"Just give me her number."

Leo felt as if he'd been doused with cold water.

"She was going to before you got all weird about us and made her leave."

Satisfaction clashed with fury, but only a hint of his simmering emotions came out in his cold voice. "There is no way in hell I would give her number to you. And I had nothing to do with her wanting to get away from you."

Zena stood between the two men, wide eyes darting back and forth.

"What is your problem?"

"At the moment, you." Leo had no idea what he was saying, but the words felt good.

The guy had inches on Leo and arms the size of saplings. A dangerous gleam darkened his face. Big hands fisted at his sides. Leo stared back, his own heartbreak making him bold. He almost wanted the stranger to hit him—a distraction from the pain inside. For maybe the first time in his life, this computer nerd wanted to brawl. The big man finally shook his head and lumbered away, muttering curses under his breath.

"Did that just happen?" Zena coughed out a stunned laugh.

"That guy was a dick."

"Seriously, who are you right now?"

He glared at her, still steaming from the confrontation, still seeing the image of Tempest without her sweater on.

Zena laughed. "Already acting the protective older brother to your new baby sis?" She thumped him on the shoulder. "You do it so well."

Horrors.

She dropped her arm. "Although I don't think Tempest appreciates it as much as I do."

He hissed out a heavy sigh. "I guess I should apologize to her again."

She pursed red lips. "No. It's so not a big deal. That woman needs to chill."

He bristled but swallowed the arguments that rushed to his tongue. He was not talking to Zena about Tempest. The whole point of this party was to move on, but his face still tingled where Tempest had laid claim to his jaw and cheek with her velvet touch, and his blood still boiled in anticipation of fighting over her.

"Come on," Zena said. "There's Tasha and Jill."

He didn't follow his sister over to the group of ladies gathered near the dining table. He went to the bar. Dean and Blair cornered him in the kitchen. *Please not the roommate right now.*

"Arty." Blair's voice was colder than the ice in his plastic cup.

He refused to respond to that name.

"Thanks for scaring Tempest off."

He turned. "I did not..." He stopped talking. He wouldn't win this argument with Blair. He exhaled and looked into her dark eyes. "I'm sorry, Blair. I didn't mean to lie to Tempest, or cost her her job, or hurt her. After I found out about your hideous bet, I was afraid she wouldn't give me a chance once she knew who I was. I really liked her." His voice dropped, and he looked down at his cup. "I still like her. I'm a mess at relationships."

"That's true, he is," Dean said.

Leo did not appreciate the support.

Blair softened. "I believe you." She sighed grandly. "Well, are you going to remain a coward, or are you going to go fix this?"

Leo blinked, wishing it were that easy but fearing starting over was impossible. He'd ruined his opportunity with Tempest. He washed down the terrible tang of regret with a swallow of cheap beer. "You're not going to tell me to stay far away from her?"

Blair shrugged. "Is that what I should be saying? Besides, seems futile to try and keep a brother and sister apart." She grinned with pure wicked delight.

"You've got one sexy sister," Dean said. Clearly, he'd had too many drinks tonight, and by the red-tinged look Blair speared him with, he was going to have to pay for that comment. And Leo didn't think she would let the strip-show joke slide either. At least Leo wasn't the only idiot here tonight.

Leo spoke, drawing her scowl away from Dean. "Oh, I see. This little conversation wasn't to make friends. It was to continue the torture."

She dropped the mockery and held out a hand. Her tone turned serious. "Friends."

Leo accepted it. "Friends."

Dean kissed her brow and grinned. "Look at us all getting along like one big happy family."

Leo's voice came out low and threatening. "Never use that word again."

****

At nine thirty-six on Saturday morning, Blair stormed into the house and slammed the door. Her hair was a riot of tangled curls. Last night's makeup ringed her eyes. She wore sweats and flip flops, her arms full of stuff.

Tempest dropped the fork she was using to whisk her eggs and slipped around the kitchen island. "What happened?"

Blair flung clothes and cosmetics cases over the couch. "Why are men such disgusting pigs?"

Tempest floundered for a clever response.

"I could have forgiven him for his insensitive comments while drinking." Blair looked up and pointed a finger. "Although he needs to filter that too." She slumped onto her clothes and slung a leg over the back of the couch, the picture of drama. "But this morning I woke up to him taking the nastiest dump—with the door wide open!"

Tempest burst out laughing.

Blair's thick lips turned up. "I told him to shut the door and put some water on it. And do you know what he said?"

Tempest shook her head.

"He looked up, his eyes all red and his face waxy. I mean, I was right there on his bed, five feet away, and he goes, 'You're still here?' With that exact tone, all unpleasant surprise."

Tempest's eyes widened. "Oh no, Dean."

Blair tried to run her hand through her hair, but it got stuck. She jerked her fingers free. "I honestly think he was just being a hungover idiot, but I'm not okay with that." Her bravado failed, and Tempest could see true sadness underneath.

"I'm sorry, babe."

Blair's eyes pinkened. "Yeah. I had liked him. At least the cool attractive him I first met, not the dumbass I went to bed with last night."

Tempest knew just how her friend felt. And she

didn't admit she was a little glad it was over with Blair and Dean—one less connection to Leo. "I can make you some eggs."

Blair laughed. "Eggs." Her voice was incredulous. "Those are not going to cut it this morning." She stood. "I'm showering, and then we are going to the grocery. Get ready for some serious culinary therapy."

Tempest braced herself.

****

The gray sky reflected Tempest's mood as she and Blair walked up to Jo's house the next morning. Jo swung her front door wide and beamed. "Welcome to Fake Thanksgiving. Fakesgiving."

Blair held up a baker's box and nodded her head to indicate the two bags Tempest carried. "Pumpkin maple bars, as requested. And garlic rolls, mille-feuille, and coconut rice with pomegranates and pine nuts, because I felt like it." This morning, as Blair packaged everything up to give away, she'd said all her comfort cooking had to go somewhere besides her own ass.

Jo clapped her hands. "Sounds amazing. Thank you so much." Blair was the only one whose food was always welcome. Jo hustled them into the house and out of the damp cold. "Turkey's got another fifteen minutes. We have hors d'oeuvres in the kitchen."

"Auntie Blair!" Hannah ran up and hugged Blair's legs, nearly knocking her over.

Jo snatched the box away from her before the precious maple bars met with disaster. "Hannah." Jo's voice was short, her brows drawn.

Blair leaned over and stroked Hannah's brown curls. The start of a real smile brightened Blair's face. "Hello, my tiny princess. What have you been up to?"

"I made you a painting. Come see." Hannah took Blair's hand and led her away.

"It's like she didn't even see me. I'm invisible," Tempest said, her voice teasing. Blair had magic, and Tempest did not. And that was fine.

"I wouldn't mind your superpower once in a while," Jo said. "Or on the daily."

"Ha." Tempest followed her sister into the kitchen. Benji's head appeared in the window, wreathed in a cloud of smoke from the grill on the patio. He waved at her with his tongs. Tempest set out Jo's cutting board and sharpened a paring knife. Jo did not sharpen her knives enough. Tempest pulled the salad fixings from one of the bags she'd brought and got to work chopping the pears.

"So," Jo said, picking up a fussing baby Harrison from the swing and patting him against her shoulder, "how have we not talked about Thursday? Dad's engaged! How do we even feel about this?"

Tempest was not about to untangle that answer. "He seems really happy, doesn't he?"

"Yeah. I mean, I know he's been so lonely. And I want him to be happy, but I feel weird. Mom *just* died."

"It was over a year ago."

Jo pursed her lips and snitched a slice of pear from Tempest's pile.

"Is she going to be good for him?"

"Two divorces isn't a good track record."

Tempest sprinkled the pears over the mixed greens and added glazed walnuts. "Do they have a date for the wedding?"

"Dad wants March."

Tempest jolted. "That's so soon."

"It's whatever." Jo waved a hand. "As long as we don't have to plan it."

"It seems like Silvia would really enjoy doing all that. She was certainly good at making wreaths."

"I bet it will be fancy. She's fancy. But don't get me wrong. I like her. I'm kind of really impressed that Dad snagged her. I mean, she's got a great bod. She's young and peppy. She's pretty and hip. And he's just Dad. Is that mean?"

Yes, it was mean. But Tempest had also thought it. "He's steady and kind, and maybe she's finally realizing how much that's worth."

"She seems like a great mom. I really like her kids." Jo wiped spit off Harrison's mouth. "Do you think they like us? Leo seemed a little closed off. I bet people hit him up for money all the time. That would be so annoying. But if we're family, do you think we'll get in on that gravy train?" Jo giggled at her own candor. "I hope he gives good presents."

Tempest resisted the urge to touch the sapphires on her ears.

"He had Hunter's sweater cleaned and delivered."

"How pretentious."

"How polite." Jo wrinkled her nose and checked the baby's diaper. "Just gas." She rubbed her nose against Harrison's and put him back on her shoulder. "Zena is pretty. I mean if I had all the time and money in the world to get my hair and face and nails—" Her voice cut off when her phone rang. She picked it up and snorted, tilting the screen toward Tempest.

Silvia Steele.

"Do you think she felt us talking about her? Like ESP or something?" Jo answered and put the phone to her ear. "Hello. Great, thanks. And you? We had a great time. We are so excited for you and Dad. And Leo and Zena are really wonderful." She bounced Harrison on her hip, her forehead crinkling as she listened for a long time. Then the confusion on her face turned to pure excitement.

Anxiety coiled in Tempest as Jo looked at her with eager eyes.

"That sounds amazing. And I'm here with my sister. I'll tell her about it. She'll be thrilled too. Yes. She can go anytime. She not working right now."

Tempest tossed the salad too hard, and lettuce flew onto the counter.

"Oh, New Year's makes it easy. Thanks for doing this, Silvia. Let me know how we can help. It's going to be so fun. Okay. Talk soon. Bye." Jo set the phone down and smiled grandly.

Blair came in, Hunter and Hannah in her wake. She picked up a chunk of cheese and popped it in her mouth.

Tempest didn't need to ask Jo what the call was about. Her sister was already taking a massive inhale in preparation for some big reveal.

Benji walked in the back door. "Two-minute warning."

"We're going on a trip with the stepfamily."

"What?" Benji asked.

Tempest stilled, her mind and heart warring.

"Silvia just called," Jo said to Benji. "They're planning everything. She wants to start the new year off right, together as a new family. On the thirtieth, we'll spend one night camping outside San Diego, and then we'll move to a hotel on the beach for New Year's

Eve."

"I'm not buying four tickets for our family to fly to California for the holiday weekend," Benji said. "That's a long flight too."

"I'm sure it will be just fine on Leo's private jet." Jo actually squeaked.

Tempest thought her sister might turn to a puddle of drool right here on her kitchen floor. Tempest caught Blair's raised eyebrow and her best friend's sly grin.

"How romantic," Blair said, her gaze trained on Tempest.

"Oh, gross," Jo said. "The parents better not try any funny business while we're together."

The parents. How had Jo accepted all of this so quickly?

Blair grinned as she lifted an olive to her mouth. "And New Year's together. That's powerful stuff right there. But who is Tempest going to kiss at midnight? It's only the most defining moment of the year."

Tempest rolled her eyes.

"Too bad Leo is gay," Jo said.

Blair's eyes nearly popped out of her head. Tempest stifled a laugh.

"But he's family now. Would have been off-limits anyway." Jo moved the knife away from the edge when Hannah reached for a piece of cheese.

"He's not blood," Blair said.

"They are *not* family yet." Tempest's tone came out sharper than she intended.

"Better hurry, then." Blair winked.

Tempest almost threw a mini pumpkin at Blair's smug face.

"A   private   jet!"   Jo   turned   dreamy,

uncharacteristically oblivious to the subtle drama right under her nose.

"I'm not a big camper." Tempest folded her arms.

"What a great opportunity for you to get to *know* Leo." Blair picked up an olive. "And Zena—of course."

"That's what Silvia said." Jo opened the oven and pulled out a tray of stuffing. "She wants us kids to bond."

"Interesting." Blair managed to make her voice even lower and more seductive. "*Bonding* sounds so fun."

Blood warmed Tempest's cheeks. She narrowed her eyes at her friend, but she couldn't stop her lips curving up slightly at the thought of a weekend with Leo.

****

Mom answered her phone after the first ring.

"New Year's?" Leo's voice rose in pitch, and Dean looked up from his desk just beyond the glass doors. Leo swiveled to face the back windows of his office and lowered his voice. "We did not discuss New Year's."

"I'm sorry, honey. I thought it was perfect because it's a holiday for everyone. No one would have to adjust their schedule. Did you have something planned? Do you have a special woman I don't know about?"

He rubbed the space between his eyebrows. "No. It's fine. But I thought we agreed on one night camping, nothing fancy or showy...the Fairmont?"

Through the phone, her voice came out soft. "I changed my mind. I want it to be a nice trip. I think they'll enjoy the Fairmont."

"Who doesn't?"

"We're still going camping one night like you suggested."

He didn't want to go camping. How had that become his idea?

"Is this hesitation because of the Swan women? Are they that hard to be around?"

"No, Mom," he lied, feeling guilty for again being rude and strangling her joy. "It sounds like a great trip. I'll schedule the plane. Anything else?"

"Do you want to golf while we're there?"

He loved golfing, and that course was awesome, but he didn't want to spend five hours alone with anyone in their party. Except Tempest. The chance she'd magically end up in his twosome was zero. Maybe Benji would golf with him. But he had three kids to take care of. Could he get away that long? Leo did not want to go with Christopher. "No, thanks, I'm good. It's only one night, and with the young kids, they'll probably want to hang at the pool."

"Zena made a spa appointment for right after check-in."

Of course she did.

"I'm going to stay with Christopher's family the whole time. I don't want to ditch them. Seems a bit rude. But do you want a massage?" Mom asked.

"When you put it like that."

"Maybe I should book Tempest and Jo a treatment."

"I don't know, Mom."

"Yeah. Maybe too complicated. How should we do the rooms?"

"I don't know, Mom."

"Should I put Zena and Tempest together? Is that

too much too soon?"

All of this was much too much, much too soon.

"And you don't think his daughters will feel weird about Christopher and me sharing a room, do you?"

Leo felt weird. He itched at his chest. His collar felt like it was choking him. "I don't know, Mom."

"Okay, thanks, honey. Love you."

"Love you." He disconnected the call and sank into his chair, the custom contours failing to bring their usual comfort. He cursed for a while, and when that didn't help, he stood and walked out the doors to Dean's desk. "Schedule the plane on December thirtieth at ten thirty a.m. to fly to San Diego."

Dean jotted down notes.

"There will be nine passengers and an infant."

Dean cocked a questioning brow.

"Have Rachelle come to my office in fifteen minutes to talk about her Kentucky issue. If Travis still wants me to look over his new marketing plan, I can meet with him after that. Actually, go ahead and open up my entire evening to anyone who wants to meet with me…about anything."

Dean's jaw loosened.

"I can stay late." Leo would work until he couldn't see straight. That's how he'd solved his problems before.

"Are you okay?"

Leo turned back to his office. "Never ask me that again."

Chapter Eight
The Christmas Season

Southern Methodist University Catering hired Tempest for the holiday season. Tonight was her third event. It wasn't a terrible job—well, the pay was—and she didn't like having to small talk with strangers and replace napkins and refill drinks and clean up spills. Were people always this sloppy? But she loved working with Blair. Her friend smiled, laughed, and sampled this and that as she worked.

Tonight's event was for the Lyle School of Engineering alumni. Maybe Tempest should have studied engineering instead of math. These people looked prosperous and employable. The event was certainly costly. Twelve decorated pine trees dotted the expansive hall. Each table had fresh flowers and glittery ribbon. The entree tonight was prime rib. They'd hired four caterers whose sole purpose was to serve alcohol. Engineering was where it was at. Who knew?

"What have you got there?" A man in a red sweater blocked her path.

"Good evening, sir," she said.

He looked like he'd just graduated high school, but his name tag boasted of much greater accomplishments. It read *Ethan Hillberg, Founder of Hillberg Robotics.*

"I have bacon-wrapped dates. Would you like one?" She held the tray steady at he took two. She barely refrained from asking if he was hiring. She had the same problem with the next two guests—the CEO of Hector Labs and the vice president of Alloquil. The lighter her tray, the heavier her heart. She couldn't let all this potential slip away, could she? This was an opportunity, but she wasn't sure how to grab it. She was working as a servant here. She couldn't strike up a conversation as if she were a guest. Shoulders drooping, she headed for the kitchens to restock.

"One left, lucky me."

His voice stopped her just before the service door. She glanced up through her lashes, dread and excitement clashing. Leo looked from the lonely appetizer on the tray to her face. His eyes went wide. His jaw tensed as he scanned her black-and-white catering uniform. He wore a tailored blue suit with a white shirt unbuttoned at the collar. No nametag. He looked older in his suit. Sophisticated and smart. His light-brown hair was brushed and styled off his forehead, making it appear thicker on top. He looked like he belonged at this party. At any party. She lowered the tray and held it out.

"It's all yours, sir."

"Sir?" He frowned and didn't reach for the appetizer.

"You look nice." Her voice came out slightly on the warm side of professional.

He blinked, looking her over again. Her hair was in a short pony to keep it out of the food, but chunks had fallen loose around her face, and a remnant of frosting smeared her waist from the piping incident during setup.

"What are you doing here?"

"Working."

"Why?"

Her eyes tightened, and she opened her mouth, but he held up a hand.

"No. I know. I did not mean it like that. You don't need to remind me I cost you your other job. Just hold up."

"There is nothing wrong with working as a server."

"I know that. You surprised me is all."

"The feeling is mutual. What are you doing here? You didn't go to this school."

"And yet they still invited me." He said it with an arrogance that sent her blood boiling.

She was not in the mood. Face set in hard lines, she turned on a heel and took a step away.

"Tempest, wait."

Against her better judgment and all the warning bells in her head, she stopped and turned.

He smiled. "You still owe me that date."

Was he trying to be cute? He was definitely trying to be cute. She had forgotten about their bowling bet. She owed him a date, and she always paid her debts. She picked up the last bacon-wrapped Medjool date and handed it to him. "Perfect. Because here is your date."

He chuckled. Her frown remained. He sobered and popped the bite in his mouth.

She watched him chew it. Why was she still standing here with him?

He swallowed. "That was weirdly good."

"I didn't make it."

A silent pause. "Well, congratulations on your new job."

"Thank you."

"If you ever want to consider another career path, I know some people at Red Rocco, and they're always looking for hires with your potential."

She froze. He froze. Had he meant to say that? By the tension in his face, she guessed not. Could she work at his company? Why not? He had destroyed her last job. It was cosmic balance. Karma coming back around. "Are you serious?"

He hesitated, and his next words came out a bit strained. "Yes, of course. You'd be a great fit at Red Rocco." He tugged at his collar.

Working with him *and* joining families. It was too much, and that didn't include any of that other stuff she wanted to be doing with him.

After she'd stared at him for several long seconds, he said, "Come to the office on Monday, and we'll talk."

A beautiful woman approached. She had long blond hair and a tight dress that left no doubt of the voluptuousness of her body. Her neck was bare, revealing tanned skin. "Leo, there you are." She draped an arm over his shoulder. In her heels, she was inches taller than he. Like a super-model praying mantis.

The cold bite of rejection ate through Tempest's belly. Leo had moved on, and the next thing was *this*. Heat prickled behind her eyes. She welcomed the pain—*may it help me move forward.*

"You are in big trouble for leaving me with that stodgy woman," his date said. "I don't know a thing about soil technology."

He looked her in the face and said, "Oh."

She chuckled as if he'd made a charming joke, but it was a little forced. She looked at Tempest and over the empty tray.

"Sorry, ma'am." Tempest took satisfaction in the woman's tiny flinch at the word *ma'am*. She didn't look older than twenty-five. "Nothing left for you here."

Leo sent Tempest a warning glare. She returned it with a syrupy sweet smile.

The woman put a hand on her waist. "I can't really eat in this dress anyway."

"What fun," Tempest said.

The woman looked confused, as if she weren't sure whether Tempest was insulting her or complimenting her. It didn't help that Leo tried to stifle a laugh but ended up snorting. The woman looked appalled. He sucked his lips in, forcing a straight face. Her nostrils flared as she turned back to Tempest.

"Could you at least bring me a drink?"

"Yes, ma'am," Tempest said at the same time Leo said, "No."

He and his date shared another heated glance. Tempest bit down hard on her tongue. She didn't usually have this much trouble controlling her amusement. This woman really did need to loosen her corset. Or unclench a few areas.

"What can I get you?" Tempest asked with another saccharine grin.

She opened her lacquered red lips, but Leo said, "I'll get it from the bar." He pointed to the setup along the other wall, then looked at Tempest. "I'm sure you have another round of *dates* to give out to poor unsuspecting fellows."

"You clearly don't need one." Hopefully the cutting edge to her voice was sharp enough to hide her hurt.

The woman put her hands on her cinched waist. "Do you two know each other?"

"No," Tempest said.

"Yes," Leo said.

Tempest cocked her chin and tilted her mouth into a casual smile. "He knows me, but I've only just met him."

Leo flinched.

"I don't see." The woman looked between them, clearly not liking what she did see.

"Interesting." Tempest voice was deadpan.

The woman's mouth dropped open. She must have figured out Tempest wasn't complimenting her.

Leo bit his lips, but the corners of his mouth rose, and Tempest flushed with satisfaction at the sight. He might be on a date with Sexy Spandex, but he was still talking to the caterer in the corner and looking at Tempest like she was dessert.

She reeled in the thoughts. Oh no, she could not wander down that fantasy. Clearly he was over her. She bowed slightly. It felt like the thing to do in the moment. "I've got to get back to work. They don't pay me to stand and chitchat. Enjoy your evening. I'm sure you'll be crowned king and queen."

She showed them her back before they could respond, but she heard the woman ask, "Like prom? Do they do that here?"

Leo's low chuckle chased Tempest through the service door.

****

He got to work early on Monday. Was Tempest going to show up, or was she going to spare them all and pretend like he hadn't invited her in for a job interview? Or had he already offered her a job?

Saturday had been a fiasco. Michelle had been mostly sweet, except for the weird conversation with Tempest, and exceptionally sexy, until she decided to consume only alcohol for three hours. No food. She'd barely made it through her front door before she passed out on his shoulder. He'd dragged her to her bed. She was heavier than she looked. He wasn't even sure he'd put her in the right room. It could have been her roommate's. He'd dated Michelle for three months last year and never been inside her house before. He couldn't ignore the dirty kitchen, laundry on the floor, or water marks on the mirror. This was why he always had women over to his house. After he heaved her onto the bed, her breathing had turned squeaky and shallow. He'd been so afraid of her suffocating in her sleep that he partly unzipped the back of her skintight dress before leaving. That flash of back flesh was the most action he'd gotten in weeks. But it hadn't been Michelle he thought about when he went home horny.

He rubbed the skin between his eyes. How had he run into Tempest with Michelle on his arm? He was *trying* to move on. Trying to forget the pleasure of kissing Tempest. Forget how well she could deliver a joke, her jaw straight but her eyes twinkling. He was trying to forget how much he liked eating Indian food at his kitchen table with her. Forget how she looked in only a T-shirt. Or just in her bra. He nearly groaned out loud.

Tempest had looked so betrayed when Michelle put her arm over his shoulder like a territorial animal. But it was nothing compared to what he'd felt seeing her working as a part-time server after he'd cost her not only a great job, but a career.

He had eighty-two emails to respond to this morning. He didn't get to a single one. He looked through the company department directories. Where would be a good place for her? He'd already spent all yesterday thinking about this and had decided to put her with Steven Lith in research and development. Who better to have testing the product than a skilled underwriter? Assuming she was skilled. Which he very much did. She had that vibe.

He stayed in the office at lunch. Just in case. But it wasn't until four thirteen in the afternoon that he looked up and saw through the glass her stunning face on the far side of the office. His heart lurched. She'd come.

Dean's head popped through the door, his face full of surprise and the rush that came from a little office drama. "Were you expecting Tempest?"

That seemed like a loaded question.

Dean had had what sounded like a very fun, very short ride with Blair. He was still recovering. "Should I let her in?"

As if Leo might kick her out of the building. He'd never turned anyone away. Anyone that got past security on the ground floor at least. That was the tightly controlled gate. Leo stood up and walked through his private office's double doors. Dean's desk was to the right, and in front was an open space with a cluster of tables and chairs for collaborations and meals. A few heads looked up, tracking the beautiful woman's progress. She wore slacks and a sweater and a tilted-down face, as if she were trying to hide.

"Welcome." Leo held his office doors open for her.

She waltzed in, her subtle perfume clouding his

focus. The swing of her hips destroyed it entirely.

"Nice to see you." He closed the doors and gave Dean a look through the glass that meant *get back to work*.

Dean grinned.

Leo turned his back on his assistant. He was the one that needed to get back to work.

Her gaze traveled over the custom furniture and panoramic view. "This is nice."

"Thanks." He sat in his ergonomic chair.

She perched on the edge of the seat across the desk from him. "I assumed you were just being nice on Saturday night when you mentioned a job. You were feeling guilty I was wearing an apron instead of a tie."

"I didn't see any apron."

She conceded a small smile. "You know what I mean. I wasn't going to come today, but I just wanted to say thanks anyway. It was a nice gesture, but you don't owe me anything, let alone a job. And—" She took a deep breath as if bracing herself. "—we didn't start off on the best foot, so I wanted to apologize." Blue eyes speared him, nearly knocking his breath away. "I'm hoping we can have a do-over. A fresh start. For our parents' sake."

He loved her.

She was perfection.

He stared at her big eyes and strong features. That mouth. His heart thumped harder and faster. The world seemed to crash all around, leaving only Tempest.

She stood, her expression downcast. "Well, think on it. I guess I'll see you in a couple weeks at your mom's." She turned to leave.

He leapt to his feet, his pulse frantic. He darted

around his desk and slipped his hand over hers. She twisted to face him. She left her fingers in his.

"You forgive me for lying about my name?"

"Yes."

His grin stretched his cheeks and expanded his chest. "And I was serious about a job here. You're smart and have great work experience. We'd be lucky to have you."

Her cheeks pinkened in a way that made his belly warm. She glanced through the glass doors. Dean snapped his attention back to his computer. She looked down at their touching palms. "Thank you, truly, and I'm sure it would be amazing to work here." She lifted her hand out of his, leaving him cold. "But I don't think it's a good idea."

"What? Why?" He wholeheartedly agreed. It was a terrible idea. But he didn't want her to leave.

Her lips parted, revealing the tips of her white teeth. "Because it's hard enough trying to figure out how to be your sister. I don't think I can handle working under you right now."

He couldn't help it. One brow rose.

"How professional." Her voice was flat, but her face flushed.

He leaned against his desk, failing to think of something clever and charming to say. Instead he stared at her while imagining her on her back across his desk. Her eyes darkened as she held his gaze.

"So is this off-limits?" His gaze dropped to her mouth before returning to her eyes.

She swallowed. She drew her arms around her ribs like a shield. "It's probably better this way. Less risk."

"Risk isn't always the enemy. It can open the door

to incredible gains."

She folded in on herself a little more. "Who knows what could happen to us in the long term? Our parents are getting *married*. We're going to be family for the long haul. There would be no clean breaks, no escape."

He hated everything about that answer. His ribs squeezed his heart. "Okay."

****

It was Christmas Eve. Tempest hadn't talked to Leo since meeting him at his office, but she hadn't stopped thinking about him. She replayed their conversation over and over. He'd basically admitted to wanting more. And she'd rightfully put a stop to that. She'd been logical and calculated. She wasn't dictated by hormones. Blair had been no help. Blair's life—and love—motto was always, *go for it!*

Dinner tonight was with the blended family. She didn't like that word—*blended*. Like they were now a smoothie that was supposed to be pink but had too many ingredients, so it came out puce. Silvia had wanted to host again, but she'd gotten sick and was only now feeling better. Tempest thought her dad should host, but Leo had beaten him to the baton. So that's how Tempest, wearing a short plaid dress with black tights, ended up standing with Jo's family at Leo's front entry. Zena welcomed them inside. The house was still perfect, clean and bright, and tonight, smelling like fajitas. They'd all agreed—it was Jo's doing—that they'd skip the holiday gift exchange. They'd leave that for next year when they all knew each other better and there would be less pressure. Tempest tried not to think about the sweet torture of doing this again next year. And the year after. Tempest had brought a nice bottle of wine and a box of truffles for the host. When Leo appeared, she handed them over instead of sharing a hug.

"You guys look like a matching couple." Jo's gaze traveled from Tempest's green and red tartan dress to Leo's plaid sweater.

He paled and didn't respond.

"Thanks for having us," Tempest said.

"Come on in." He guided them down the hall past the office and formal sitting and into the main room. Vintage ornaments decorated a tall, skinny Christmas tree.

"That's gorgeous." Jo stepped closer to study an intricate red truck ornament. "Did you do this tree?"

"Not at all." Leo turned toward the kitchen. "And I might have had a little help with dinner from Joe T. Garcia."

"I love that," Benji said, his hungry gaze drifting toward the food.

Garlic, cumin, and lime scented the air. Tempest salivated at the lineup of to-go containers with rice, beans, guacamole, and enchiladas. Dad was already there with Silvia. He beamed from ear to ear. Tempest decided she'd suffer though a thousand family dinners with Leo if her dad was this happy. He kissed his daughters and patted his grandchildren's heads.

"Food's not getting any hotter." Leo looked to his mom. "Do we stand on ceremony here, or can we act like family and eat?"

Silvia stood from her seat at the dining table and smiled at the people gathered. "Thank you for having us all over, Leo. Zena, will you say grace?"

After the blessing, Tempest helped Hannah dish

her plate. She sat at the corner of the table with her niece, her focus entirely on keeping the little girl's rice and chicken off the floor. The meal went a hundred times better than Thanksgiving, and both parents had a look of delighted gratification as they watched their offspring intermingle. After dinner, Silvia spread crafts on the table for the children. She sat with them, showing them how to make magazine-worthy snowmen ornaments. Hunter wasn't interested, but after a hiss and a whispered threat from Jo, he didn't try to get up from the table again.

The adults moved to the sitting area. The only space left was on the couch, next to Leo. Tempest decided to find the bathroom instead. She glided down the hall, keeping her heels from clicking on the marble tile. She pretended she didn't see the guest bathroom, moving on to peek behind the door at the end.

His bedroom had pale gray walls. The king bed was made up with dark linens. A plush low couch sat at the foot of it. The nightstand on the near side had a lamp and four books stacked up, two biographies, a science fiction, and a thriller. The far nightstand had a photo of Leo and Zena with a good-looking older man standing between. His dad, probably. A mini bronze statue of a fox stood on the tall dresser. Nothing else. It was the opposite of Blair's cluttered private space. Leo's room should have felt austere and cold, but it didn't. It felt like a place completely devoted to that big bed there in the center. The duvet invited her over with the promise of a feathery embrace. She peeked down the hall. No one coming. The party in the kitchen seemed far away, a different dimension.

She slipped off her pumps and tiptoed to the bed.

She ran a hand over the puffy euro sham. Her pulse soared. If she pulled back the covers, he might notice later. Far too risky. But she couldn't stop herself from climbing up and lying on top of his bed. She picked his side, by the books, where she imagined his body weighing down the mattress every night. The bed was firm, holding her up, but not putting any unwelcome pressure on her joints. Her fingers played over the soft linen. This was what a bed should feel like. This was what money could buy.

She shifted her legs, her dress hiking up as her tights slid over the cool cloud of fabric. She looked up at the white ceiling and giggled. She had no idea what had possessed her, but this was a delightful rush.

The door swung inward on silent hinges. She froze, body pinned to the bed. The door opened wider, and Leo stepped into his bedroom.

He looked down at the carpet, barely stopping himself from tripping on her red heels, and then he looked up and saw her. His gaze traveled the length of her legs, covered with only thin nylon.

His jaw dropped. He swallowed. "What are you doing?" His voice was hoarse and uneven.

Heat rushed up her body and over her face. Horrors. She must look like she was lying in wait for him, propositioning him at a family party in the most blatant of ways. Well, naked would have been more brazen. What must he think after the last thing she'd said to him was they could never be together? *Crap*. She had not intended to be a terrible person tonight.

Careful to keep her thighs together, she swung her legs over the side and stood. "I was just seeing if your bed is as comfortable as it looks." She leaned over and smoothed out the wrinkles on the duvet, popping her bum up and arching her spine just a touch as she bent forward. She wasn't usually a tease, but she was embarrassed and reaching for any shred of power, even if it was underhanded. And now she was intentionally being a terrible person. Finally she straightened up and turned to face him with a frown. She put her fists on her hips.

He stuffed his hands in his jean pockets, his expression unreadable. "And was it?"

"More, actually. Congratulations on a supremely successful sleeping situation."

His brows rose. "Thank you?"

She nodded. "You're welcome." Chin up and features cold, she walked forward, picked up her shoes, and waltzed out.

****

She'd been lying on his bed. *On his bed.* What the blazing hell? Her already cruelly short dress had been hiked up to wazoo. Why was she wearing that to a family party anyway? And then to slide off his bed just to bend over it. He was never going to get that image out of his brain. What was she trying to do to him? At least she'd had the decency to look surprised to see him show up. Although it was *his* room. She was the invader here. And she'd caught him without his shields up.

He sat on the edge of his bed. The heat of her body lingered on his duvet, tickling his fingers. He folded forward, hands on knees, heart pumping. He inhaled, then hissed out all the air again when he caught a whiff of her jasmine scent. Panting through his mouth, he went down the list of the basic program codes he knew for python before he was steady enough to stand up straight. But emotions still surged.

Well, *Stormie*. Two could play this game.

He peed, just to prove to himself he was relaxed enough to do so. After washing his hands, he brushed his teeth to get off the fajita flavor and put on lip balm. Feeling ready for battle, he strode into the family room. Tempest sat in his spot on the couch, talking to Benji. She didn't look at Leo when he entered. Fine, then. Leo angled toward the kitchen where Mom worked with the kids on crafts. Hunter, his face screwed up in anger, leaned over his little sister's shoulder and scribbled with a blue marker on Hannah's snowflake drawing.

"Hey!" She whirled, scissors up and fire in her eyes.

Leo leapt. His hand wrapped her wrist, pulling the blades away from Hunter's nose.

"He ruined my thing," Hannah said.

"She ruined mine first," Hunter said.

"I did not."

"You did too. And you spilled the glitter on me on purpose." He motioned to the glistening silver down his navy shirt, like the sky on a clear night.

Mom reached her hands toward the children, panic growing on her face.

"Hannah," Leo said, "why don't you come with me? I have something to show you."

In a flash, excitement replaced her annoyance.

"I want to come to," Hunter said.

"You can both come if you promise not to fight."

"We promise," they both said in eager unison.

His mom gave Leo a grateful look as she stood to clean up the explosion of paper shavings.

Leo glanced at Jo, but she was talking to Zena, her body angled away from her children in the kitchen. He led his unknowing accomplices down the hall and into the room with his Steinway. He pulled out the familiar tufted seat and sat down. He flexed his fingers. His mom had put him in piano lessons after he beat leukemia. She'd heard music was good for healing anxiety. He'd taken to it like a fish to water. Music theory had flowed into his analytical brain and taken up residence. He loved the rules, the precision, how a string of simple notes together could make something powerful, a lot like computer code. He also loved the flexibility music allowed for creativity and personality.

Rules could be broken.

Few people ever heard him play. Piano was his fortress of solitude. His secret world. But today Tempest had made him feel reckless and bold. And mad. It was time to pull out the big guns.

"Don't be shy. Come up here where you can see." Leo motioned Hunter and Hannah to stand one on either side of him. "Do you play the piano?"

They shook their heads.

"How about a little game? I'll play a song, and the first to recognize it wins."

Hannah looked unsure, but Hunter nodded.

Leo played "Mary Had a Little Lamb" first to put the girl at ease, but still Hunter yelled it out in a rush before Hannah had time to open her mouth. Hunter also got "Star Wars," "The Eensy Weensy Spider," "Up on the Housetop," and "Jingle Bells."

Hannah stood on Leo's left with her short arms folded and a scowl on her face. Leo leaned over and whispered in her ear, "Silent Night." He'd only played the first two notes before she yelled out the answer. Leo laughed; Hunter did not. Leo decided he'd had enough of this game and enough of a warm-up. Next, he played a jazz piece. The kids didn't know what to say, but they both smiled. Only a gremlin could stop itself from being happy in the face of such peppy beats and fast fingers. Leo rarely had to use sheet music after playing a song more than a couple of times. The music stayed in his mind and hands like a familiar map. He could *see* exactly where to go next.

"That's cool." Hunter's hips started to move.

"I want to learn to do that." Hannah poked a finger out and struck a low D in the middle of his song. Leo tried not to cringe.

When he finished, he twisted his wrists and swiveled his gaze between the two. "No one knows that one?"

"Never heard it," Hunter said, voice defensive.

Leo chuckled. Footsteps sounded in the hall, but he refused to look up. He played a short modulation of "Away in a Manger"; it was Christmas after all. Hunter guessed it near the end, but Leo didn't stop playing until he'd finished the song. He knew the audience he'd hoped for had gathered. When he looked over his shoulder, Mom, Christopher, Benji, and Jo with her baby sat in the room's four chairs. Tempest stood, arms folded, against the archway leading into the room, like she didn't quite want to get too close to the fire but couldn't help being drawn in to his music. Just as he'd hoped.

"You are amazing." Jo's voice was a warm gush.

"I love hearing you play." Mom held a hand to her heart.

"Well, I didn't mean to interrupt conversation or anything with my plunking," Leo lied. "I can stop."

"Please don't," Jo said, her voice pleading.

Leo, with a wave of gratification, swiveled back to the keys and closed his eyes for one breath before he opened them and set his fingers. A soft, slow start, a building of volume and tension, a sweep of twinkling fingers as he moved through one of his favorite Chopin pieces. And because he loved it, he knew he played it like a real musician. He carried the song in his heart. He played from his soul. The room was silent but for the storm of his music.

When he finished, he turned with a sheepish slant of his shoulders, fighting an embarrassed flush of heat to his face. He might have gotten more carried away than he intended. He couldn't believe he'd just exposed himself like that to so many. Jo had actual tears in her eyes.

Tempest hadn't moved from the wall, but she stared at him, dewy-eyed and looking more than a little pissed, her jaw clenched as if she were braced for a fight.

Leo grinned, his gaze holding hers.

She scowled.

Benji's and Christopher's clapping broke the spell. Leo chuckled. He stood from the seat and accepted their compliments with a dismissive wave.

"That would be perfect for the wedding," Jo said.

Christopher's eyes brightened with hope. "Would you?"

"No. I don't play in public."

"But it's your mom's wedding, and everyone will just die over it," Jo said.

157

Leo opened his mouth to deny her more emphatically, but Benji stepped up to his wife and touched her elbow. "He doesn't want to, honey." A hint of iron hardened his voice, as if he were also reminding her that she was married and maybe she should stop swooning. She had the decency to school her face into indifference.

Mom swept forward and kissed Leo's cheek. "That was such a treat for me. Thank you."

"Speaking of treats, I think it's time for dessert." Leo shooed the group back toward the hall.

Tempest turned, padding into his kitchen without saying a word.

Mom served the sheet cake she made every Christmas Eve. The kids took their pieces to the table, but the adults stayed standing around the island.

"Here you go, Tempest." Mom held out an overly large piece to Tempest, who had managed not to look at Leo once, even though only three feet of marble countertop separated them.

Tempest hesitated before accepting the plate with a gracious smile. She took one bite and said, "This is amazing, Silvia. Wow."

At least she was being nice to his mom.

Mom beamed. "Thank you, dear. We like it. It's my grandmother's recipe."

Tempest set the plate down and looked up at Leo. He leaned back at the force of her blue gaze. Like a coward.

"Could I please have some water?"

"Of course." He jerked toward his drink fridge. "And what can I get everyone else?"

"The cake is good with milk," Silvia said.

"Is it good with beer?" Benji asked.

Everyone laughed, and as Leo passed out drinks, he forced his shoulders to relax. He used the excuse of cleaning up dessert to keep busy. Tempest cleared the plates. Probably because she hadn't eaten more than three bites of the dense chocolate cake, and she didn't want his mom to notice.

Jo gathered her children and told them it was time to go. Tempest readied to leave with them. Leo tried not to show his relief. The entire party walked to the door. Tempest gave out her civilized thank yous, but Jo gushed her compliments.

"This was the best night. I'm so happy we'll be family. Dad is so lucky to have found you. I feel like we're all so blessed right now."

She hugged his mom, and that made Benji step forward and embrace his new *family* too. It turned into a receiving line of hugs. Mom pulled Tempest forward into one of her suffocating arm holds and passed her off to Zena. Leo's pulse rose as the inevitable drew closer. And then Tempest was there, standing in front of him, clearly debating what to do. He couldn't not hug her. That would be noticed. He was skilled at the quick, pat-on-the-shoulder, no-chest-touching hug, he'd just preformed it like a champ on Jo, Benji, and Christopher, but to hell with that now. It was Christmas. And he wanted to hold her, if even just for one second.

He slid his arms around her waist. Her eyes flared in surprise as he drew her forward. She wrapped her arms around his shoulders as her warmth and softness pressed all down his front. The scent of jasmine and female curled up his nose. Her velvety cheek brushed his. Her body shifted under his hands, and that feeling of *ahhh* flowed through his body.

Shitteroni. This was a terrible idea.

He jumped back in a hurry, checking if anyone had seen that hug. Mom was helping button Hannah's coat. Zena was already walking back toward the kitchen. Christopher was chatting with Benji and Jo about tomorrow's plans. No one was looking at them.

Safe.

He looked at Tempest, her red mouth, slightly parted, her dilated eyes. Nope, not safe at all.

"Well, Merry Christmas," he said.

"See you in a few days."

"I can't wait."

****

"He plays the piano," Tempest told Blair for the hundredth time since dinner three days ago. "No. He doesn't just play the piano. He makes love to the piano." She threw the hiking shirt back onto the store rack. "You should have seen his fingers caress the keys."

Blair giggled.

Tempest scowled. She knew she was weak for bringing it up again and more than a little annoying. Like Blair wanted to hear about this again. But Tempest couldn't stop thinking about it. If it hadn't been so sexy, she would have been majorly bugged—he was already a genius billionaire. Did he also have to be a sneaky good musician? It was cosmically unfair. She'd dreamed about Leo again last night. He'd given her a private concert, wearing nothing but dress pants and a bowtie. She'd gotten all hot and melty in the dream like she had in real life. But in her fantasy when he'd turned from the keys, instead of grinning like an arrogant prick, he'd looked at her like she was a goddess to be ravished. And that's exactly what he'd done.

She picked up a guide to wildflowers from the table and started fanning her suddenly steaming face and neck.

"I still think guitarists are hotter than pianists," Blair said.

"You wouldn't say that if you'd seen him."

"Yes, I still would. But that's because I'm not blind with love."

"I'm not blind." Tempest ignored the love part.

"He's balding."

Tempest pursed her lips. "That's harsh. It's just a little thinning."

"He's a clean freak."

"Hey." Tempest's defenses flared. "I did not use the word freak, and I think that trait goes in the positive column anyway."

Blair rolled her eyes. "It would get annoying so fast. I'd never feel like I could relax."

Tempest decided not to say that Blair could do with a little less relaxing when it came to housework. "Is there anything you do like about him?"

Blair smiled. "His money." Her lips turned down. "But otherwise, nothing right now. He hurt you and didn't fix it when I told him to, so he's on my shit list."

"As long as he stays off your to-do list."

"Aw. But just think if I married him, we could be sisters for reals."

"Stop it."

Blair seemed to sense that Tempest really couldn't handle going down this tunnel right now, even in jest. "Besides, I'm more into artists than musicians."

"Starving artists." The man she'd gone out with last night certainly wasn't cashing in on his *abstract uncycled sculptures*. Blair had made him dinner, and he'd eaten three full plates.

"He wasn't hungry when I finished with him."

"Hungry for more Blair."

"Yeah." Blair leaned over the pile of T-shirts and high-fived Tempest.

An REI sales associate approached. "Can I help you find anything?"

Blair said, "Yes, my friend is going camping with a man she's in love with. What do you have in the way of seductive hiking pants? We want him to want to take them off."

Tempest wasn't sure whose cheeks were redder, hers or the young man who couldn't have been older than twenty-three. He gaped like a suffocating fish.

"I'm so sorry," Tempest said. "That was highly inappropriate." She glared at Blair who wasn't sorry. She turned back to the young outdoorsman, keeping her face as polite and professional as possible. "But if you are willing to still help me, I'm looking for something appropriate to wear to spend a day in the woods near San Diego."

He relaxed, keeping his sole focus on Tempest. "What time of year?"

"In two days."

"Let's check the weather forecast, then." He pulled his phone of out his pocket.

Tempest smiled. Her type of guy.

Blair picked up gray pants and unfolded them. She frowned at the large pant width and cargo pockets. "Can't she just wear yoga pants? She looks great in those."

The man glanced up briefly before returning attention to his phone. "They are comfortable, which is important, but the thing about cotton is when you sweat, the moisture is absorbed by the fabric and stays next to your skin. And with the tight-knit leggings, it can take forever to dry. It's worse if it rains or there's a stream crossing. If the temperature drops, you're cold and wet."

Blair rolled her eyes and moved on to examine the next stack of khaki.

"All right. Here's San Diego. Low chance of precipitation, but it could drop into the forties at night." He held up the screen for Tempest to see. Like she hadn't already checked.

He moved over the tables and racks like a bee scouting pollen. Carrying a pile of dirt-colored clothes, he led the women to the dressing rooms and held the door to the largest stall open. Blair waltzed in and sat on the bench, ready to be entertained. He laid out the clothes for Tempest and turned to leave. "If you're interested in boots, I can meet you over at shoes when you're ready."

"That would be great," Tempest said. "Thanks."

He tilted his face toward the carpet and pointed to the top pair of pants. "Those tend to look the most flattering on...young women." With that he darted out.

Blair and Tempest were left staring at each other and trying not to giggle. Blair failed. Surely that poor man had not escaped the sound of her bubbling mirth.

Tempest tugged off her stiff jeans and picked up the thin nylon, not sure whether she wanted to look good for Leo or not. She should be doing everything she could to douse this fire. Oh, who was she kidding? She wasn't going on a trip with Leo armored with anything but her best effort. She buttoned the pants at the waist. They were slim-cut but comfortable. The green fabric was light and flexible. It held tight around the hips but didn't squeeze her thighs or calves. Who knew REI was the place to buy good pants? How many colors did these come in? She turned in front of the mirror, assessing.

"Oh, yes," Blair said. "Your ass is perfect in those. That Boy Scout deserves a raise."

Chapter Nine
The Camping Trip

No one had camping gear. Not Christopher. Not Jo's family. Not Tempest. Zena, Mom, and Leo weren't any better. Leo didn't have so much as a hiking backpack. Instead of realizing that meant no one wanted to camp, Mom had bought tents and all the stuff the guy at Camping World told her she needed for spending the night in the woods. When speaking to Christopher and his daughters, Mom had made it seem like she already had all the gear sitting in her storage room. Mom kept telling Leo and Zena that this was the start of a fun new tradition and they'd use the new camping stuff every year, as if saying it would make it true. He didn't correct her. Anything to make his mom happy.

Usually Leo arrived at the private aviation terminal of the airport, valeted his car, walked onto his plane, and took off within minutes. Today he arrived a whole half hour before he'd told the pilots to be ready. His collar seemed to be trying to choke him. His blood pressure rose as he walked through the automatic doors, eyes scanning for a tall brunette. He was spending New Year's with Tempest. No, he couldn't think like that. This was a weekend trip with Mom's fiancé and his soon-to-be family.

He strode through the now familiar entry, nodding

hello to Cindy at reception. She pointed to the waiting room, and he changed course with a flicker of trepidation. He had wanted to be the first one to the airport to make sure everything went smoothly. He opened the door to see Jo and Benji waiting with their kids. Benji was holding the baby and watching TV, but Jo perched on the edge of her chair, her gaze darting nervously over Hunter and Hannah, who were in various stages of climbing the couch and coffee table.

"Good morning," Leo said. "I hope you haven't been here long."

The children squealed and ran over, taking up positions at his sides like miniature bouncy escorts.

Benji stood, moved the baby to his left arm, and held out a friendly hand. "I told Jo we had time, but she didn't quite understand that we really didn't need to worry about security lines or being left behind."

Jo frowned at her husband. "You've never been on a private plane before either."

Leo smiled at Jo. "Extra time for snacks." He opened a fridge. "Fruit cup? Something to drink? Candy? There are some sandwiches in here, but they don't look fresh. We'll have better ones on the plane if you can wait."

The children's attention went into a higher gear. Hunter ran behind Leo to grab Hannah's arm. "They have root beer in glass bottles."

"Only one," Jo said.

If that kid had more than one bottle of root beer, he'd be so keyed up he could probably run all the way to California before the sugar wore off. Leo lifted the chilled bottle and popped the cap. With only a hint of reluctance, he set it in the small, eager hands. "Help yourselves to anything. I'm just going to check on the flight."

"Thank you so much." Jo dipped her head as if in a slight bow.

Maybe the chartered flight was not a good idea after all. Leo lingered by reception, chatting with Cindy about her husband's cancer but mostly avoiding going back into the lobby with his new travel mates.

Mom and Christopher appeared a conservative ten minutes early. Leo greeted them and sent them to the waiting room. Leo was still standing near reception when Tempest arrived exactly at the set time he'd told the group to meet.

"Hello," she said.

She wore hiking pants that hugged her hips like a hot hippie, super tread boots, and a safari shirt unbuttoned at the collar. The only person here who looked ready to go into nature. Her tight shoulders told him not to try and hug her.

"Everyone's in the lounge," he said. "We're just waiting on Zena."

"Thank you for doing this. I'm sorry we're taking advantage."

"Not at all." He meant it. He realized right then and there that he'd do anything for her.

She tucked a chunk of hair off her face and behind her ear.

She was still wearing his sapphire earrings. They were the perfect color for her, making the blue in her eyes bluer. He wanted to kiss the spot below the earring. See what noise she made if he nibbled on her ear. The memory of her breathless moan when they'd kissed two months ago hit him like a laser beam, burning down his core. He forced a teasing grin. "Anything to support the parents, right?"

Tempest didn't answer. She turned toward the doors as Zena walked in, pulling a bag much too large for a weekend. Tempest let Zena hug her.

"That's all of us," Leo said. "Plane's ready. Go ahead and head out to the tarmac, and I'll grab the others."

Zena and Tempest chatted by the stairs while a worker stowed their bags underneath the jet. Leo handed his over and led the way on board. He sat in his favorite seat, the one on the left facing forward.

"This airplane is nice," Hunter said in awe, stopping inside the door so his mother stumbled into him. She nudged him forward.

"It's really small," Hannah said.

"What seat is mine?" Hunter surveyed the cream leather choices.

Jo looked to Leo. Leo stared back. Was he supposed to assign seats? No, thanks. Four big loungers faced each other near the front, and five smaller seats were in the back. Hunter sat in the spot across from Leo like a small emperor in his throne.

Fortunately, Mom came through the door and took charge. "I thought you'd like your family there." She pointed toward the back. "With the bench and the seats facing it. Room for all of you. And there's one more spot there." Mom glanced sidelong at Tempest, a worried and apologetic look on her face.

Should he trade her? Leo had work to do, and he shouldn't have to sit next to the kids. Leo could see the sense in Tempest being the one to sit with her own sister. But the seat configuration looked like first class and coach. *Us and them.* It wasn't like that. This private plane was a bad idea. Of course, Leo was not flying commercial, no way. All those crowds and lines and people. So many germs and shared air.

"That's perfect for me." Tempest slid past Leo and moved to the back.

He swallowed disappointment as Zena settled in the seat across from him. Mom and Christopher took up the other two plush recliners.

The pilot welcomed them, and after take-off, the co-pilot passed out the trays of sandwiches, sliced fruit, and cookies.

Flights were usually a good time for him to work, but between the baby's intermittent cries and Christopher deciding this was a good opportunity to get to know his soon-to-be stepchildren, Leo's laptop didn't come out of its case.

They rented two SUVs at the San Diego airport. Leo drove one, Benji the other. The Prestons needed all their seats in one, so Christopher and Tempest went with Leo. Leo thought it was Tempest's turn to sit up front with him, but he didn't say anything. Zena, as navigator, helped herself to shotgun. As Leo exited the airport, Zena pulled up her map and gave him directions. She'd called an old boyfriend before the trip to get the exact coordinates of a secluded little spot he loved and recommended outside the city.

Benji's car followed Leo's. Leo tried not to glance at Tempest in his rearview mirror but caught himself doing it every time he checked. He knew what she was doing better than Benji trailing him. She sat directly behind him and mostly looked out the window, but the few times she caught him peeking at her, her gaze seemed to trap him in the glass. He found he couldn't honestly be sorry they were here together.

One hour and twenty-four minutes later, not including the stop at Target for firewood and food supplies, they pulled off the side of a dirt road in Capitan Grande Reservation.

"Just there." Zena waggled a black lacquered fingernail toward a clearing on the right. She looked over the wilderness and chuckled. "Let's get this party started."

****

Tempest looked out the window. What were they going to do here in the woods for twenty-four hours?

It was pretty. Blue sky, warm sun, nature. But. But. She felt like a contestant on one of those survivor episodes. People liked to watch them so they could enjoy not being out there with children and stepfamilies and no toilet. An entertaining notion to think about while on one's couch, but not something to actually experience. Even still, Tempest couldn't wait to get out of the car. She'd sat in the back with Dad and Silvia. Silvia, not Mom. The two had held hands, and Tempest hadn't missed her dad rubbing his thumb over the woman's thigh. She was caught between wanting to vomit, cry, and scream. Yes, she was happy for them. No, she didn't want to see any of their love manifestations. Yes, she missed Mom, and this felt like a betrayal. No, she didn't want Dad to be sad and alone anymore.

Between the mushy couple on her right and Leo up front, the only safe place to look had been out the window.

"I don't have service." Zena tapped her phone with

a frown. "Zero bars. I told Jake I'd text him when we found the place."

"He's not invited," Silvia said.

"I know that, Mother."

Leo parked, and Benji pulled his car behind. The ten of them walked around like journalists over a crime scene, setting their feet carefully and keeping their noses slightly turned up. Ten yards into the forest of skinny trees, a clearing opened up. They all gathered in the middle of the dry grass and looked at each other with expectant faces.

"Well, lovely," Silvia said. Her red lipstick and tight jeans looked garishly out of place with the peeling tree bark and buzzing insects. "This looks like a nice place to set up. Who'll help me with the tents?"

"I will," Hunter said. He and his sister were the only ones with eager eyes and skipping steps.

"Come on, then, captain," Silvia said.

Everyone followed them to the cars. Jo put the passenger seat of her car all the way reclined and lay down with her sleeping baby. She put a shirt over her face and checked out. Tempest meandered over to where Leo unloaded the trunk of his car. He pulled three tent bags out and set them on the ground. He looked back into the car, rummaging but not finding another tent. He turned, his gaze drifting over Tempest before landing on Silvia.

"Is this it?" He asked his mom.

Three tents? How was that going to work?

"Yes. Two doubles and a four man."

Every face turned to her. Fortunately Jo was too far away to hear. Silvia bristled. "Christopher and I will take one. With the little children, I thought the four man would be enough for the Preston family."

"That leaves me, Leo, and Tempest." Zena voiced what Tempest was thinking.

Silvia's cheeks paled as she looked over the tight faces of the three single adult children. "I might have miscounted." When no one responded, she forced a bright smile. "Good thing y'all are trim. I'm sure they base those measurements off big people. It'll be good sibling bonding."

"You're kidding me," Zena said, again taking the words out of Tempest's mouth.

"Did you miscount sleeping bags too?" Leo asked, his voice pinched.

Silvia's shoulders curled in, making her suddenly appear small and fragile. Her eyes went big like a puppy. "The guy said it was so warm we wouldn't need sleeping bags. He said it made a lot more sense to use blankets." Silvia padded to the luggage and unzipped a large duffel full of fleeces. Her nervous mouth turned up. "And I got the thicker mats for people to be comfortable."

Like that made it all better.

Clearly Silvia didn't already have a storage room full of camping stuff. Was this her first time sleeping outside? Tempest certainly hadn't done it more than a handful of times. And not in fifteen years. Dread chilled her blood as she looked over the bag of fleece. She pictured the three of them crammed in a two-man tent, Zena wedged between her and Leo. Sharing blankets. This night was going to suck. At least Blair would love hearing the recounting of this fiasco when Tempest got home, if she made it out of here alive.

Leo took a deep breath—a yoga-cleansing-bad-juju

breath if Tempest had ever heard one—and with a resigned set of his shoulders, he picked up the bags and carried the tents ten yards to the clearing. Dad, Benji, and his two older kids jumped to help.

Zena and Silvia seemed to be having a silent conversation, which involved lots of tense staring. Tempest wandered toward the men. It seemed the safer option. She stopped at the edge of the clearing in the shadow of one of the varieties of wider trees. The men hadn't noticed her yet, and she hesitated to join, feeling suddenly like she didn't belong with this group either.

"I asked my llama if he wanted to go camping," Hunter said. "He said alpaca tent."

"Hunter!" Leo whooped. "My man."

Benji gave his kid a fist bump. "Coming in hot with the llama jokes."

Hunter beamed. Hannah looked annoyed she hadn't shared the joke first.

"Wanna go camping?" Benji asked, pulling the supplies from the biggest bag. He held up one of the rods. " 'Cause I'm pitching a tent right now."

"Nice." Leo chuckled. He handed Dad one of the two matching two-man tents.

So each of the men was in charge of pitching their own tent tonight. Tempest smiled at herself but didn't venture to share her thought. She didn't feel she had the right *equipment* to participate in this joke game. She smiled again. She was on a roll.

Dad dumped the contents of his duffle on the ground and peeled tags and plastic off the never-been-used tent. He picked up a pole. The top connection snapped together, but he couldn't get the bottom fold to straighten. He ran a hand through his hair and shook the misbehaving rod in frustration.

"That looks *in tents* over there, Christopher," Leo said.

Benji gave Leo a silly grin and a thumbs-up. "Punny."

Dad looked up, his brows tight with frustration. "Why do they have to make it so hard?"

"How else are you going to pitch a tent?" Leo pinched his mouth, but the grin won out, pulling his cheeks up.

"I guess you're right." Dad's focus remained on the gear. "It doesn't make sense to store the poles fully extended. But mine won't go straight."

Benji, squatting near the ground, chewed on his knuckle, his body silently shaking. He tilted his reddening face away from the older man. Tempest, standing near the trees, had her own lips clamped against the rising laughter.

Dad looked at Benji, brow raised in question. Benji finally turned to face his father-in-law, and a wave of laughter broke through his defenses.

Dad's face fell. "I get it. That's very funny." His voice dripped with sarcasm.

"I won't tell Silvia," Benji said, barely getting the words out over his giggles.

"I do not have a problem with my rod!" Dad shook the folded-over stick in Benji's direction.

Benji, clutching his side, keeled over out of his crouch and fell onto his butt.

"Looks like you can't get it up," Hunter said, his face innocent and concerned.

As the clearing erupted into a volcano of spewing laughter, Tempest slipped back to the car. Those men had definitely never been camping before. Still chuckling, she rummaged in her bag for the insect repellant. She sprayed her exposed skin, only her wrists, hands, and head, before wandering off to find a nice place to pee. It took a while. Even though the bushes here looked way less bug infested than the local wild preserves back in Texas, she surveyed every patch of grass carefully before exposing her tender underparts. By the time she returned to the group, three tents stood in a row. Those smaller ones were definitely two-person tents. She would be sleeping in the car.

"Who's ready for a hike?" Dad asked.

Why not? What else did they have to do around here? "I'm in," Tempest said. "Let me grab my hat."

"The baby's still napping with Jo," Benji said. "So it's just me and the older kids."

Five and seven years old hardly seemed older.

"And all of us." Silvia sent sharp stares to her two adult children.

Leo put a water bottle in each pocket before he came and stood by Hunter. Zena replaced her sandals with sneakers and put on big sunglasses before joining.

"Where are we going?" Hunter asked.

"On an adventure." Dad squinted at the surrounding dunes. "But hopefully it takes us up to the top of that hill." His lips curled down as he looked to Tempest and Benji. "Pay attention so we don't get lost."

"I knew I should have invited Jake," Zena said.

Dad surveyed the thick undergrowth and twisting trees between them and the hill he'd picked out. "But let's start down this road." It went not at all in the same direction he'd pointed. "And see if we come to a path."

"Good idea," Tempest said. Getting lost out here with no cell service was not in this weekend's agenda. And she wasn't prepared for bushwhacking.

They started out slow. Tempest walked near the front of the group. If she couldn't see Leo, maybe she could pretend he wasn't here. Didn't have a freshly shaved face. Hadn't flown them all out on a gorgeous jet where the pilots had called him Mr. Allred.

They walked in silence except for the chatter of the children.

"Watch out for snakes," Benji said to Hunter, who'd taken a stick and traipsed into thick undergrowth.

Tempest started devoting a portion of her attention to snakes.

"What kinds are here?" Hunter moved closer to his dad.

"The only poisonous ones I know of around here are rattlers," Benji said. "But you know about those."

Hunter rehashed the story about the time they'd found one in Texas. Then he shared a story about a water moccasin in the neighborhood lake. Hannah added a story about chiggers. And another about a brown recluse.

"I think maybe that's enough stories for this camping trip." Zena had her arms pinned close to her chest as she walked. "Maybe we tell more when we're headed out in the cars tomorrow."

Leo chuckled. "This is why we're camping in California. Nothing dangerous here."

"That's not exactly true." Dad held up a finger.

"Maybe let's talk about that later too," Leo said.

Tempest looked over her shoulder as Leo put a

comforting arm around Zena.

Dang, why did he have to be so thoughtful?

"So." Benji turned to Zena. "You used to live down here?"

"In Carlsbad. I'd just graduated from college and was getting serious with Jake. I got a job in the area so we could see if we could make it work. It didn't in the end." Her lips turned sad below her big sunglasses.

"Still a beautiful place." Benji looked like he'd put his foot in a hole.

"Yeah. I loved living here. He taught me how to surf. I'm still not very good, but..."

"Better than the rest of us, I'm sure." Benji's shoulders loosened.

"I couldn't really tell you why we broke up. We were just fighting about the dumb stuff. We were both stubborn and short-tempered. But we're still sort of friends. He told me about this camping spot."

"Not sure he was doing us a favor," Leo muttered.

Tempest bit her lips to keep from chuckling.

"He's still single." Zena pushed her glasses higher up her nose.

"I'll keep that in mind," Benji said.

Leo frowned at his sister. "Please don't tell me you're going to see him. That breakup tore you to pieces."

"I've grown up since then." Zena motioned to her body. "And as you can see, I'm still in one piece."

"You still fall in love too easily." Leo's voice was as soft as a breeze.

Her retort came out sharp. "Better than refusing to ever fall in love."

Everyone stopped walking. Leo stiffened. His gaze

flashed to Tempest. The look was short, but it cut her to the core. *Never loved?* Good thing she hadn't let herself get in any deeper with Leo. But she had the almost overwhelming desire to comfort him now. His shoulders had curled in, and he looked tensed up against a blow, trapped by a gang closing in. She wanted to hold him and kiss the sadness from his face.

Leo straightened suddenly and strode out in front. Zena rushed to catch up, her muffled apologies filtering back to the Swan family trailing behind.

The road did not turn up the mountain; it ran straight through the low valley. They enjoyed a continuous view of bushes, bugs, and branches. Hunter complained about being hungry.

Hannah tripped. She yelped as she landed over a fallen log. She rolled to a sitting position, her lips quivering as she looked over her scraped palms. Her knee oozed blood. Her legging had ripped, the front shin getting increasingly soaked by the red dripping down.

Benji knelt at her side and peeled back the torn black cotton over her knee.

"Don't touch it!" she screamed, lashing out at her father.

"I need to get the dirt out, honey."

She cried louder.

Benji flinched against the shrill sound. "It's going to be fine." His voice was hard. "You're *fine*."

"Hey, tough little lady." Leo crouched at her feet, the bloody leg between them. "You took that fall so well." He pulled a water from his pocket, unscrewed the lid, and handed it over.

She had to stop yelling to drink. After a guzzle, she

handed it back, sniffled, then clutched her thigh with a grimace.

"I have some doctor stuff back at the camp. We can get it all cleaned up, and you can even pick out the bandage."

She eyed him warily.

"I have a box with glow-in-the-dark bandages." He lowered his voice and leaned in. "And I'll show you where the secret stash of gummy bears is. It's only for emergencies, but I think we could use some for this."

She brightened like a light.

"But my brave soldier is going to have to be strong on the march back to base camp." He held out his palm, and Tempest's heart might have melted all the way through when Hannah's dirty, scratched up, bloody little hand slipped into Leo's.

"Thanks, Uncle Leo."

And just like that, Tempest's heart froze back to stone.

****

Leo could not believe he was the only one who'd brought a first aid kit. What kind of parents took three children camping without bandages and allergy medicine, at the least? After Leo finished helping Benji clean and fix up Hannah, he rubbed in a third application of hand sanitizer and tried not to think about the smear of her blood on his sleeve. After ALL, acute lymphocytic leukemia, nearly killed him at age nine, he'd had a hard time believing the doctors when they told him he could relax his germophobia after years of having a compromised immune system. True, he hadn't been sick, not even a cold, for seven years, but was that a result of his now apparently strong immune system or his energetic handwashing schedule? He didn't think it was worth the risk to find out. He was not paranoid. He was cautious. And it was totally normal to want a shower after a walk in the woods.

He knew nature, trees, rocks, and worms and such, weren't generally disease ridden. He'd mostly gotten over that particular anxiety. Some sun-sanitized dirt on his skin no longer made him crazy. And so he would leave the bloody shirt on for the rest of the day just to prove he wasn't afraid of bodily fluids anymore. Blood was the hardest for him to overcome. It was so powerful and personal and vivid. But he was stronger now. He wasn't a frightened child. He wouldn't even notice the rusty red stain.

The children had joined their mother setting up folding chairs by a firepit. Good, fire killed all the germs. Maybe he could accidentally burn his shirt.

His duffel bag called to him from the backseat of the car. He had four clean shirts in there. Four. He didn't need that many for tomorrow. Children carried all sorts of diseases. Giving in, he walked around the side of the car. The Ford Explorer shielded him from the group. Careful not to touch the blood, he peeled off his shirt and stuffed it in the trash bag his mom had tied to the side view mirror. He breathed deeply, smelling fresh loam. *Ah.* Much better. He sanitized his hands and wrists one more time, and then he found a navy long-sleeve tee in his bag. He turned at the sound of footsteps. Tempest stopped by the back wheel, her focus snapping to his bare chest.

"Um." She looked up at his eyes. "Uh."

A slow grin spread over his face at her mumbling. She wasn't quite as cold as she pretended.

She looked at his mouth, a frown forming on her lips, before her gaze dropped to his belly once more, like she just couldn't help herself.

His smile grew.

She looked at the dirt. "Your mom wanted me to ask you to bring over the cooler bags with dinner. They're getting the fire going." She whirled around. Her shoulder hit the side of the car in her fluster. She stopped. Tilting her chin, she looked sideways up at him. "Thanks for helping Hannah. That was really cool of you." She strode away.

Satisfaction slipped over him like the feel of his freshly laundered shirt.

****

When the initial pit fire burned to embers, they cooked dinner over the hot coals: pineapple slices, bratwurst, and s'mores. Everything tasted better than it should have. After all the food had been cleaned up, the scraps and garbage shoved in a cooler bag and put in the car to discourage foraging creatures, they added logs to the fire. The adults sat in a semicircle upwind, sipping drinks and staring at the flames, while the kids ran around scaring off wildlife. The sun had long since set when Jo and Benji finally decided to force their children into their tent. When the Prestons migrated away from the burning embers, Christopher and Mom carried the conversation, talking about their favorite places to go and favorite things to eat and favorite books. Hadn't they already had all these conversations? Zena chimed in sometimes, but Tempest mostly stared at the fire, the flickering golden light dancing over the angles of her face and throat.

"Well, honey." Christopher stood from the folding

chair and stretched his legs. "I'm spent. I can't hang with these young kids anymore."

Mom got to her feet and took Christopher's hand. She looked over at the three left around the fire. "Y'all got what you need? I'm sorry about the tent. I thought it would be bigger."

"That's what she said." Leo glanced at Tempest in time to catch her fleeting chuckle.

"What?" Mom frowned.

"We're fine," Zena said.

"I'm so glad we're all here together." Mom looked to each of them in turn. "Thank you."

"You're welcome," Leo said.

"Good night." Firelight gilded the smile Tempest gave his mother.

Mom and Christopher shuffled to their tent. The only sound in the clearing for a long time was Jo's loud whispers telling her kids to hush, Christopher peeing not at all far from camp, the sound of nylon shifting, then Mom and Christopher helping each other get comfortable. Christopher put his sweatshirt under her sore hip. How sweet. When the sound of lips smacking started up, Zena growled.

"Those walls are *thin*." Zena's voice cut through the air.

The kissing stopped.

Tempest buried her nose and mouth in her sweatshirt and giggled.

Zena snorted, her shoulders seeming to relax for the first time in hours. She poked at the dying fire with a stick, cracking open the charred wood. "Should I put another log on?"

Tempest glanced at Leo, her eyes glittery through

the clear smoke. "Nothing else to do."

"Ain't that the truth," Zena said.

Leo got another two pieces from the pile they'd bought on their way into camp. Felt a little ridiculous buying firewood for five bucks a bundle when they were now sitting in a forest. He set the logs on the crackling embers.

A few yards away, Jo and baby Harrison left the tent. She had a blanket over her shoulder and her lips pinched tight. She didn't say a word as she climbed into their car and closed the door.

At least he didn't have a baby to take care of tonight.

Leo watched flame devour wood, listened to crickets and rustling leaves, and felt the contrasting kiss of hot smoke and cool breeze on his skin.

After long minutes, Zena broke the spell. "It is mesmerizing." Her pale eyes reflected orange and gold.

"Hours of entertainment," Leo said. "Caveman style."

Zena coughed when the wind shifted, sending a plume of gray into her face. She waved at the offensive cloud. "I wonder how often they got high from burning different stuff." She leaned back in her chair and stuck her hands in her hoodie pockets. "Probably discovered all sorts of drugs by accident."

"Maybe that's why they worshiped the Earth as their god," he said.

Zena grinned. Tempest watched the flames dance.

"Ancient man did discover an impressive number of medicinal herbs." Leo picked up a round stone and rolled it in his palm.

"Exactly what I'm talking about. Low tech

geniuses."

He laughed. "They also were into human sacrifice."

"Can we really knock it until we've tried it?" Zena coughed as another round of fumes punched into her face.

"I think it's time for you to stop smoking and go to bed." He shifted on the fallen log. He'd been sitting too long, and his lower back hurt. A knot in the wood was digging into his butt.

Zena looked up at the stars. "I know you hear this all the time, but I am not sleeping with you."

"It's just sleep."

"Is that what you tell all the ladies?"

He rolled his eyes, careful not to look at Tempest.

"You're a fully grown man, even if you are my brother. What if you forget who I am and try to cuddle? Or get morning wood?"

He glanced sidelong at Tempest as she looked up from the embers. Their gazes locked, but he couldn't read her expression. Her eyes were like melted stars in the darkness. At least she couldn't see the heat rising to his cheeks. She was coming in that tent with them too. This was so weird. "We're camping. How can I not pitch a tent?"

Zena shook her head and put a hand between her brows. "I cannot take another stupid camping joke."

"Too *in tents* for you?"

She hissed at him.

"I'll sleep in the car to give you guys more room," Tempest said.

Zena stood. "That's kind of you to offer, but I've already claimed it."

"You can't do that." Leo's pulse doubled.

"Watch me." Zena turned to Tempest. "Good night, sis."

Tempest blinked glittering eyes at Zena. Her mouth made an O shape, but nothing came out.

What just happened? He wanted to sleep with Tempest. Oh, did he ever, but not like this, with no bathroom, no space and comfy mattress, and nothing but thin nylon and twenty feet separating them from their "parents." And it wasn't sleeping he had in mind in this fantasy.

Zena marched to the car. He leapt to his feet and followed, fear pounding through his blood. Zena pulled open the back door of the Ford. The car light flooded the jumble of bags and blankets. He wedged his body in close to hers as she shifted his duffel off the seat.

"You expect me to sleep in that tent with just Tempest?" he whispered.

She tugged her purse over. "You said brother and sister sleeping together is no big deal."

"She's *not* my sister."

She looked over her shoulder at the woman sitting like a statue by the cold fire. She pulled a face. "What's your deal? It's just a few hours' sleep. She's not ugly or gross. It's not like you haven't had boy-girl sleepovers before." She winked. "Stop being dramatic."

"I'll sleep in the car. You should be the one to sleep in the tent with Tempest."

"You're being sexist."

"I am not."

"They why should I be the one to sleep with her if it's not because I'm a girl too?" She stopped looking through her purse and turned her intense gaze, red from the smoke, on him.

Dammit. She was going into Zena-debate mode. He didn't stand a chance to win this argument now.

"I don't want to sleep with some random woman out on the dirt," she said. "I hate camping. And since this whole trip is *your* idea—"

He flinched.

"You get to share the tent with the stepsister." She turned back to her purse, her shoulders set. Conversation over.

Leo exhaled in defeat. His heart beat erratically as he found his toiletries, a flashlight, and a bottle of water. He stomped off into the woods. His nerves were still on fire when he returned. Tempest was spitting out toothpaste by the car, and Zena already lay rolled up across the backseat with her eye mask and noise-canceling headphones on. Tempest put her stuff away. She shivered in her sweatshirt. Without sun or fire, the temperature was dropping quickly. Tempest shut the trunk. The lights went out. She was a silhouette in the moonlight. Like they were in a dreamscape, they walked side by side to the tent. For something so small it seemed to loom like a mountain. He unzipped the opening and held back the flap for her. She smelled of woodsmoke as she crouched next to him.

"I can't believe this is happening," she whispered as she crawled inside.

He couldn't either. He exhaled. Once. Twice. This was not real. He just hadn't decided if he was living in a dream or a nightmare.

Chapter Ten
The Two-Man Tent

Tempest lay on the thin air-filled pad, hugging her ribs and blinking at darkness. Silvia had been thoughtful enough to provide small pillows. That was something nice. Leo zipped the tent closed. Sealing them in together. She was in the middle of nowhere in a tent with Leonard Allred. He crawled forward.

"Sorry," he muttered as his hand fumbled over her leg, feeling for his space.

Desire awakened at his touch, at the darkness they shared like a secret. She pressed into the tent side to give him more room, but she had no space to give. He slumped to the ground next to her, the smell of campfire gusting up. His shoulder rested against hers. After lying on his delightful bed, she hadn't imagined her first night sleeping with him to be on rocky ground. She wasn't supposed to be dreaming of any nights with him. Especially not when he was right there, sharing these intimate shadows with her. The night chill had sunk through to her bones, and she wanted to curl into his warmth.

"We stink," she said.

"That's you."

"You stink too." Her voice rose slightly.

"Nah. It's roses over here." He shifted, his knuckles brushing across her thigh as he unfolded the fleece and spread it over the two of them.

"One blanket." Her voice came out a little hoarse.

"Zena took the other one."

"Who do you think your mom forgot about when she was counting?"

He didn't answer. Which was answer enough, not that it wasn't obvious from the moment Silvia stuck Tempest on the jump seat in the plane as an afterthought.

"I should have just not come. She wouldn't have noticed." She didn't mean for the hurt to come through in her tone, but it did hurt. Christopher didn't have a whole bunch of children for Silvia to remember. Only two daughters. One. Two. She thought of her mom at that moment, and a pang of grief slashed through.

"Shh." Leo rolled on his side, facing her. "That's not true."

His hand came up and touched her jaw. He gently coaxed her to face him. Her body readily obeyed, curling toward him. She couldn't see his expression, but she could feel his closeness. His fingers slipped into her hair. His breath smelled of mint.

"Forgive an old lady's mistake."

She wanted him to kiss it better, but Silvia's insult still melted away under his touch.

"You would have been missed." His voice was low. His hand had shifted to cup the base of her neck.

Her body awakened. Her breath hitched. Her lower back arched, betraying her desire. *Kiss me like last time.* Her bottom lip curled between her teeth. She clamped her legs together. He had gone very still, but his breathing was too fast. They had all night confined in here together. But what would happen if they did kiss?

Where would it lead? They couldn't make noise with only these cloth barriers between them and their "parents." What if someone came over? Talk about risk! And what about the morning when they remembered they were supposed to be brother and sister now? Sweat and smoke slicked her skin. She would have to stay in here with him no matter what happened, good or bad. She'd peed twice now without toilet paper. Oh, gross. And she wouldn't have a bathroom to visit later to wash up either. His hand slipped forward and down, his fingers trailing sparks over her neck. His thumb traced her jaw. *Nope.* She rolled away from him, and he lifted his hand. Her tender skin prickled, wanting him back. She pulled the blanket up to her face, rubbing the fleece over her cheek.

"Did you go camping growing up?" she asked.

He shifted onto his back with a resigned exhale. "My best friend's dad took me once with their family."

"That's cool of them. How old were you?"

"Nine."

"You didn't get invited back?" Her voice was teasing.

"No." The word dropped like a stone.

She swallowed.

"I got diagnosed with acute lymphocytic leukemia shortly after the trip, and I wasn't up for much for a while after that."

Horror struck. Was he sick now? She tried to think if she'd said anything in the past that might have been offensive. "Leukemia? Like cancer?"

"Yes. It was horrible. It almost killed me, but it didn't. Obviously. And it's the kind that doesn't come back. I'm fine now."

The tightness in her chest gave way. She shifted a tiny bit closer to him, embarrassed at how relieved she was. "Good." The word was heavy with sincerity.

He chuckled.

She elbowed him, heat rising to her face.

"I get a little weird about germs sometimes. I was a total loser in high school. Wouldn't touch anyone. Always carried hand sanitizer and cleaning wipes. I wiped down every desk I sat in. Every class period."

"Whoa." That explained why he was a thorough and consistent hand washer, and she could eat off the floors of his house.

"I spent a lot of nights and weekends on my computer."

"Well, that paid off."

"Yes, it did. Not such a loser now." He said it with such arrogance she elbowed him again. He grabbed her elbow and was slow to let it go. "I've gotten a lot better in the last decade with the germophobia too."

"How often does the cleaner come to your house?" She had really been wanting to know.

He chuckled. "Will you judge me if I say five times a week?"

"Yes." She smiled, but it was dark, so she quickly added, "But why not? It makes you happy, and it gives that person a job, and your house is amazing."

"Thanks." The word came out so quiet and grateful and sincere that she almost gave in to the desire to kiss him. With one half body roll, she'd be on top of him. And in another half second...

She changed the subject. "You haven't been camping since age nine?"

"Not sleeping in a tent. I went hiking often when I lived in Northern California. And we took a trip out to Yosemite and up through the redwoods, but we stayed in hotels."

"That's the way to do it."

"You're not loving this setup?"

"I didn't mean it like that," she lied. She rubbed her cold feet together. She should have brought wool socks, and her one sweatshirt wasn't enough. In her defense, she thought she'd have a sleeping bag.

Heavy silence struck, and she struggled with what to say. Blair would have known what to say, how to blow over any awkwardness. Tempest's lips curled up. "What do you want to bet I can guess what you like to eat for breakfast on workdays?"

"All right. Weird bet. But okay."

"What's the wager?" Blair usually came up with those.

"I'll share my body heat with you if you get it right. And if you're wrong, you have to warm me up."

"Naked?"

He choked, coughing and laughing all at once.

She bristled, her face burning. "It was unclear. I didn't know if you were imagining those survival shows or something."

"I am now."

"And it wasn't even a real wager."

"I'm *really* cold. And you're shaking."

"You're not much of a gambler, are you?"

"It depends on the risk. And I'm not about to risk hypothermia tonight because my mom thought a blanket would suffice on December thirtieth, in the *northern* hemisphere."

She didn't want to argue that. "You have a Protein Lover's smoothie."

He chuckled. "Wrong."

"Ugh! I mean a Love Your Grains bowl."

"Right, but too late."

"I should have known Dean would pick the smoothie, not you."

"I'll take that as a compliment. Now, come here." He lifted his arm. "Warm me up and tell me how you turned into such a stalker."

She rolled under his wing. "He was in front of me in line at the juice shop once."

"Creepy good memory."

"It was a weird moment." And she only remembered because she'd thought Dean was Leo, the man on whose chest she now rested her head. She really didn't want to talk about that false start right now. She recoiled at how stalkerish she had acted. What would have happened if she met Leo for the first time at the meet-the-stepfamily Thanksgiving dinner? His hand stroked down her back. Would she still feel this same spark at his touch? *Oh, sweet mama.* "This feels so good."

"Yeah," he whispered.

She coughed on a laugh. Her body flushed with embarrassment and boldness. Had she said that out loud? And he'd agreed?

"I'll probably be missing this setup when I'm sleeping alone in a plush bed tomorrow," he said.

"Liar." But pleasure tingled down her spine. She slipped her arm across his trim waist. His free hand found hers, and he held her hand over his pounding heart.

She snuggled closer. She could enjoy this tonight. Just this one time.

****

Leo woke to the sound of a baby crying and a dead arm. He and Tempest were spooning, and he'd augmented her small pillow with his bicep. He reluctantly lifted his other hand off the curve of her hip. Sunlight through the tent cast a creamy filter over her sleeping form. He could get used to waking up to this vision. They'd stayed awake most of the night, talking and cuddling. He'd been hoping more time with her would make these feelings pass. That's what usually happened with women—at least so far that's what had always happened. But now that he knew her better, he liked her—wanted her even more. Her body pressed against his had been sweet torture. And she'd kept moving to "get comfortable and warm," she'd said. So many positions. She felt good from every angle.

He gently moved his arm from under her head and sat up. He closed his eyes on the sudden headache. Maybe they'd slept all of two hours? Maybe. This was the worst part of camping—the morning—when all he wanted was a shower, a toilet, and a hot breakfast. And he wouldn't get any of those.

Sneaky as a raccoon, he crawled out of the tent and put on the boots he'd left by the door. The sun hung low to the east and had done nothing to expel the cold. Benji and Jo and their kids were over by their car, looking destroyed. Zena was a lumpy log across the back seat of the Ford, and he saw no sign of Christopher or Mom. He trudged over to the Preston family.

"Who wants to come with me to find breakfast?"

His tongue felt like a cotton ball.

"Yes." Jo bounced the fussing baby.

"Maybe we can find a McDonald's with a play place," Benji said, already herding his children toward the Honda CRV they'd rented.

"I want a kid's meal." Hannah gave her father a commanding look before getting into the backseat.

"I want seventeen coffees," Jo said.

Leo retrieved his toiletries and wallet from the other car. Zena remained as lifeless as a rock even when he shut the door next to her head. He joined the Prestons.

"You sit up front." Jo held up Harrison. "I want to be in the back with him."

Another day Leo might have put up a fight. This morning, he got in the front seat. He needed a toilet. How far were they from civilization?

"How was your night?" Jo asked.

He thought of Tempest's body curled into his, the softness of her breast when she'd leaned on his arm. The heat of her thighs against him. "You had three kids with you. I feel like I can't complain."

Jo laughed without mirth. "I like your mom, and I'm on board with this wedding, but I'm never doing *that* again."

"Fair enough," Leo said.

"It helped when the baby and I moved to the car."

Benji hit a rock, and the car bounced.

Leo should have peed before he got on this ride.

"I saw Zena had the same idea as I," Jo said. "But I thought you would have slept in the car. Leave the two-man tent to the women. That was hilarious, by the way. Silvia forgot about Tempest." Her laugh was full of pity and amusement—the sound of a big sister poking fun at a little sister.

"She didn't *forget* her." Leo's defenses rose against his will.

Jo snorted at the obvious lie.

Benji looked over at Leo, a suggestive arc to his brows. "Wait. It was just you and Tempest in that tiny tent?"

"It was no big deal." Leo broke eye contact and looked out at the trees.

"It's not like anything would have happened," Jo said.

Wait. What did *that* mean? She'd said it with such certainty. Was he supposed to be offended right now?

"Jo's right, right?" Benji sped up as the dirt road mercifully ended and merged with smooth asphalt.

"Yes," Leo lied.

"I'm hungry," Hunter said.

"I know, baby," Jo said. "Food is coming."

Fifteen minutes later cell service returned, and in another seventeen, the golden arches came into view. A cheer went up in the car.

"I hate this place." Benji's lip curled. "But it looks like heaven right now."

Leo took note of the donut shop next door. He'd found out last night Tempest usually had an overnight oatmeal cup or scrambled eggs with sautéed greens for breakfast. Pretty much the opposite of fried and frosted circle cakes.

Benji parked. They all went straight to the bathrooms. Thirty minutes later Leo, Benji, Jo, and baby Harrison sat in a booth and watched the two children run circles around the play place. Leo hadn't gotten food. Only the black coffee. He didn't usually drink coffee, but nothing about this trip was usual.

"Did you see the parents this morning?" Leo felt weird saying *the parents* like they were true siblings, but it was easier than making a big thing about *my* mom and *your* dad.

"I did," Jo said. "I was feeding Harrison and watching the sunrise when they got up. They both looked a little stiff." She chuckled. "They took some snacks and drinks and went for a walk."

Sleeping on the hard ground would not have been good on Mom's hip. Even Leo's healthy joints were complaining this morning. "Hopefully they don't get lost. I don't want to hunt down a couple of tin soldiers today."

Jo smiled generously at his poor attempt at a joke. "They were going to stick to the road."

Benji stood. "Maybe we should head back before they start to wonder if we actually bailed."

Jo's face fell as she looked over at her happy children.

"There's an acai bowl place a mile from here," Leo said. "Maybe I can run over and get something there for the others. The kids can play a little longer."

Jo relaxed against the booth, snuggling the baby into her ample softness. "Perfect."

"I'll come with you," Benji said, looking mighty eager for the fifteen-minute reprieve.

****

Everyone was awake and exuding boredom when they returned. Tempest, looking better than she had any right to look, sat in the car with Zena, who had raccoon makeup smudges under her eyes. Mom and Christopher

196

were folding blankets and fussing with all the crap a camping trip required. High maintenance, low yield.

The women climbed out of the car and walked over, their gazes roving over the bags and cups Leo and Benji carried. Zena kissed Benji on the nose when he handed her a still-hot coffee.

"Oh," he said, looking startled.

"You are a gem." Zena batted her fake eyelashes.

Leo handed Tempest an acai bowl.

"Thank you," she said.

He leaned in, offering her his cheek, now rough with stubble.

She sent him an incredulous look but leaned forward and pressed soft lips to the tender skin below his eye. "You are a gem too."

He nodded but didn't trust himself to speak. That had not ended up as lighthearted as he intended. He strode toward the parents who were looking at the tents like they were quantum physics problems. "There's hot coffee and smoothie bowls in the car. Let me finish this up."

"Thank you, son." Mom walked up to him. Her eyes were bloodshot and her face a tad pale. She lowered her voice. "Can we check in early to the Fairmont?"

"I already called. They said they can have one room ready in an hour. We'll have to wait on the rest, but we can use the pool and other amenities while we wait."

She squeezed his forearm. "Let's get the hell out of here."

****

They'd been at the Fairmont pool for two hours,

197

but Tempest couldn't seem to relax. After showering, she'd soaked in the hot tub long enough to remove all traces of their little excursion into the wilderness, but she couldn't so easily wash away the night with Leo. They'd talked. Oh, they'd talked for hours.

He liked fishing and wandering through bookstores. She liked meditating before bed and lesser-known sci-fi movies. They both did not like baking or watching movies in public theaters. Or eating dessert for breakfast. He had zero friends from high school—not a surprise after the story about him wiping down his desk every class—but dozens of people from high school starting acting like they were buddies when his company went big time. People were lame. She had told him about her job search and was surprised to find that she didn't resent him anymore for Red Rocco. She'd admitted that it was nice to step back and reevaluate her life plans.

Maybe it was time for something new. Dare she say it…something with an ounce of risk? Not in the relationship department, though. They'd been way too familiar last night, and not familial enough. She could almost still feel his hands on her back, on her waist, his hips warming hers. She picked up the laminated pool menu and fanned her face.

Jo sat on the lounge chair to her right, baby Harrison asleep between her calves. Zena napped on Tempest's left, out of the shade of the umbrella. Tempest had debated what swimsuit to bring. This was a family vacation. She'd opted for bottoms that covered her butt and a top that looked more like a sports bra than a sexy bra. Zena went for a shimmering blue string bikini with Brazilian cut bottoms. Jo, wearing a postpartum-appropriate one-piece, scowled every time Zena got in her field of vision. Leo was still playing with Benji and the kids in the pool. He really was that good with children. He'd be an incredible parent one day. Much better than Tempest. Kids didn't come naturally to her. Did he notice that even her niece and nephew already preferred him to her? She was glad for her sunglasses. No one could tell how often her focus tracked him around the pool.

"He's a handsome guy, isn't he?" Jo said.

Tempest whipped her head around. "What? Who?"

"Leo." Jo tilted her head to where he stood in the shallow area, holding a small football above his head, his abs rippling with the movement.

Yeah. Tempest was into him. "His hair is thinning." She cringed inwardly at her mean cowardliness.

"Picky, picky. You can't have perfection."

"You do." Benji was great, but Tempest said it to change the subject.

"I do love my man's thick head of hair." Jo moved her focus to the man blowing bubbles for Hannah like a hippopotamus. Jo leaned back into her lounger and tucked her hands behind her head. "This place is nice. I could get use to *this* kind of vacation."

Zena's phone alarm buzzed. She sat up with a groggy groan. "I'm headed to the spa now, ladies."

"Have fun," Jo said with only a touch of jealousy.

"See y'all at dinner."

"Why did I ever have kids?" Jo said as she watched Zena strut away.

Tempest gazed at the sleeping cherub. "Because look at him."

Jo's face tilted down, and her whole body relaxed as her mouth curved into a smile. "He is the sweetest. I'm totally smitten." She ran a finger down a round cheek, and the baby's lips twitched up on reflex.

"He is the cutest thing ever."

"Who are we swooning over?"

Tempest looked up to find Leo drying off by her feet. He fluffed his hair so it stuck up like chick feathers.

"You, of course," Jo said.

He winked at her. "Just checking." He flopped onto Zena's lounger. "Oh, that sun feels good. I forgot how nice California winters can be." He closed his eyes and didn't move again.

"Did you guys sleep at all last night?" Jo focused on his inert form.

He flinched but didn't open his eyes. Tempest flushed hot.

"Dad and Silvia still haven't emerged from their 'nap.' " Jo did air quotes over the word nap. The one bedroom ready to check into early had become theirs.

"Gross. I don't want to think about what they're doing…ever," Tempest said. "New topic."

"Well, slightly related note. It's New Year's Eve tonight. I don't think I'm even going to make it to kiss Benji at midnight. We'll have three kids in our room. Not to mention that it will feel like two a.m. our time. But if we don't *kiss*." She emphasized the word. "You know what I actually mean when I say kiss."

Tempest chuckled, remembering when Benji declared he and Jo never just kissed anymore. What would be the point of that? "I always know what you mean."

"Well, it's bad luck if we start the new year off not *together*. If you know—"

"I *know*," Tempest said. "And you can stop complaining. At least you have someone here to *kiss*."

She glanced down at Leo. His eyes were closed, but his breathing was too shallow and uneven for sleep.

"I'm scoping for you." Jo's sharp gaze scanned the pool. "There's real potential here. Check out checkered shorts at two o'clock."

Tempest looked across the pool. "I'm pretty sure that woman next to him is not his sister."

"All right. But I don't see a ring on her finger. So..."

Tempest rolled her eyes.

"I saw the hotel is doing a special at the bar tonight," Jo said. "I think you might get lucky."

Leo sat up. "I'm going to see if my room is ready."

"Will you text me if ours is ready too?" Jo asked. "I think these kids need some downtime, or they will turn into monsters before dinner."

"I will do that." He picked up his phone, put on his Red Rocco baseball cap, and walked away.

No, tonight Tempest was definitely not getting lucky.

****

They ate dinner at the hotel. After the meal, an awkward moment hit where everyone stood in the lobby and seemed to wonder what to do. Zena broke first.

"Are we done with family stuff now?" She looked to Mom.

Leo's mom nodded with reluctance.

"Okay." She pulled her phone from her purse. "I'm

201

headed off to see a friend."

"Who?" Mom asked.

"Just an old friend." Zena wore a low-cut tank top under her jacket and had a lot of makeup on.

Definitely Jake, Leo thought, but he said, "You're ditching us?"

"I don't want to spend New Year's Eve with my brother." She looked at Tempest and Jo. "No offense."

Jo shrugged. "None taken."

"I don't blame you." Tempest glanced at Leo. "I don't want to spend it with my brother either."

"I'm not your brother." His tone came out cold and sharp.

"Leo!" Mom's voice was scolding, as if what he'd said were rude.

Zena's brows creased as she reached for Tempest. "I'd invite you to come with me, but it's not that kind of hang out."

"Oh, no. It's fine." Tempest held up her hands in emphasis.

Mom's lips turned down. "Zena, are you meeting Jake?"

She kissed her mom's cheek. "Don't worry about me."

"I always worry."

"And don't wait up." Zena turned to Tempest. "Don't bolt me out of our room when you go to bed." She waltzed out the front doors.

Another beat of tension hit.

"Thank you for dinner," Jo said to Mom. "And for a lovely weekend. I think I'll take my kids on up if that's okay."

Mom looked relieved. "Of course. Have a great

night."

"I'm heading up too," Leo said, while his mom and Christopher kissed the children. "Good night everyone." He strode away without waiting for a reply. He went to his room and promptly put the comforter on the floor—they couldn't get those things properly clean—and pulled back the sheet. He took off his shoes and lay down. And then he thought of Tempest. He was really into her. And he had not only been rejected, he'd basically been forbidden from dating her. This sucked. She had been funny last night and clever and a little bit odd. She was organized and fastidious, but soft and peaceful too. The thing that really killed him was that he could have sworn she was into him too. Humans didn't cuddle like that with someone they weren't attracted to. They just didn't.

He lay still for a long time, alternating between cursing and praising Tempest as he drifted in and out of slumber. His phone read eleven p.m. when he finally rolled up to a sitting position. He refused to be alone in his hotel room at the start of the new year. He couldn't be that pathetic. He brushed his teeth and hair and put on a fresh button-down shirt.

He found the bar easily—loud music, loud lights, loud people. They'd pushed the tables to the side and set up a small dancing floor in the middle of the restaurant. He worked his way through the crowd to the bar. Okay, some cute women here. He caught the eye of a petite blond. She winked at him. He smiled, his mood brightening. Tempest was a no-go. Time to move along. Fine. He took his time walking over, gathering courage. He really hated "the approach." He stepped up to the bar next to the stranger. When he glanced over, she was smiling at him. She didn't look anything like Tempest, with her long wispy hair and button eyes.

"So did you accomplish everything you wanted to this year?" He cringed at his lame pickup line.

She tossed him a coy half smile. "I'd thought so until you walked in."

Wow. Too brazen. He gave himself a little pep talk. He could do this. She was cute and obviously willing. What more could he want? He didn't allow himself to answer that.

When he didn't say anything, she chuckled. "How about we start with a drink?"

"Yes. Drinks." Nerves flaring, he leaned over the counter to try and get the bartender's attention.

And that's when he saw *her*.

Sitting at the end of the bar, her back to the wall, her chair turned so she could watch the room. Best seat in the house. A man stood at her elbow, talking to her, but she wasn't looking at the stranger. She'd found Leo, her gaze dark and steady on him. He froze as if zapped. The dim light and uneven shadows gave her an otherworldly look, like smoke and fire incarnate. She'd changed into a black dress that showed almost the entire length of her golden thigh as she perched cross-legged. Why did she even bring that dress on this family trip? His thoughts battled. Turn around and face the flirty blond or go over and get denied by Tempest? A chance at a New Year's kiss or no chance? A lady he didn't know or a woman he shouldn't like? Safe or stupid?

The man put his hand on the bar in front of Tempest, blocking Leo's view of her as he leaned closer, whispering something in her ear.

"Excuse me. Have a great night," Leo said to the woman who'd suddenly become dull.

Tempest's leech straightened up, giving Leo an unobstructed line to his target. He stalked down the length of the bar, raging with the unfamiliar desire to be both predatorial and territorial. Tempest watched him the whole way, her eyes like candle flames in the dim.

"There you are, Stormie," he said with a charming smile. He enjoyed the irritation that tightened the stranger's face.

"Hello, Arty." Deadpan. Not a flicker of emotion.

If he kissed her right now, he'd get a reaction.

The man looked between the two of them. He was tall and dark, but he had big ears. Even still, the man was probably handsome, in an annoying sort of way. "Are you two here together?"

"No." Leo pulled out the stool next to Tempest and sat down. Picking up the menu wedged between a tiny succulent and a saltshaker, he read over the list of appetizers. He wasn't hungry. At least not for food. He grinned at the menu when Big Ears finally tried talking to Tempest again.

"So you said you're from Dallas. I go there sometimes for work."

She didn't follow up and ask him about his job. Leo overcame the temptation to peek at her. Was she looking at him, or was he imagining her focus burning him up?

"Do you come out here a lot?" Big Ears asked.

"No," she said.

The bartender walked over and nodded at Leo. "How's it going?"

"I'm not the one working on New Year's."

The young man quirked his lips. "I'll know how bad you feel for me by the size of my tip."

"Oh. Bold move."

"No other way to live."

Leo couldn't help but look at Tempest then. She was watching the bartender. Yes. She'd heard it.

He ordered a soda with ice.

"Bold move." The bartender picked up a glass from the shelf. He turned to Tempest. "Want a refill?"

She pushed her empty drink forward but shook her head.

Big Ears drained his glass and set it on the counter. "Want to check out the dancing?"

"No," she said.

Leo laughed. He tried to cover it with his knuckles, but he was still chuckling when Big Ears slunk away in shame.

"Such manners." Leo spoke to the soda in his hand before taking a sip.

"I've been drinking," she said. "I don't like saying please and thank you when I'm nice and loose."

He cocked an eyebrow and glanced at her sidelong. Shit, she was hot. "How loose?"

Eyes dilated, she leaned forward and put her lips on his ear, sending a shock down his spine. "Not loose enough to tangle with you."

"I think we might need that refill after all." He managed a teasing tone, but his hands shook as he set down his glass.

She stood, the silky black dress draping over her curves. "What an appalling suggestion from our dear brother, Leonard."

He flinched, clutching his soda like a lifeline. He

drank as if he could douse the fire growing in his belly. The carbonation fizzled his throat. Hissing, he set down the drink. She leaned forward, the scent of jasmine assaulting him like an enemy invader. She picked up his glass and took a swig.

"Oh, that's straight syrup."

He didn't share drinks as a general rule. But tonight he wanted to put his lips exactly where hers had been and drink deep. "Have more. You could still use sweetening up."

She giggled and leaned forward, the softness of her breast pressing into his shoulder. She was not wearing a bra.

"You're killing me," he said.

"I'm sorry." She straightened up and pouted her lips.

It was too damn much. "I'm going to kiss you."

Her eyes went wide, and she put her fingers over his mouth. He kissed them, tasting a trace of gin. She giggled as she lifted her fingers. He put his hands on her hips, drawing her closer.

"No, wait. It's not midnight." She looked around. "What time is it?"

He checked his smartwatch. "Eleven forty-six."

"We have to wait." She slipped her hands around his neck. "And we have to be outside under the fireworks."

"Yes, ma'am." He left a twenty on the counter. No time to wait for the bartender to return.

With Tempest under his arm and his heart pounding like a racing rhino, he led the way behind the hotel. She wasn't drunk enough that he should feel bad about this, right? They'd kissed before. He knew he was too in love to stop now. Which was probably the biggest reason he shouldn't do this. But he was going to get to kiss her again. He was so freaking excited he might dance right out of his skin. When they hit sand, Tempest folded over. She leaned against him for balance, her dress riding higher as she took off her strappy sandals. The walkway light illuminated her foot tattoo.

Leo squinted and bent over, his arm still tight around her waist. "You enlarge my steps under me. And my feet have not slipped," he read. "What does that mean?"

She shrugged. "It's a Bible verse about God directing our path. But I've slipped a lot since I got it, so…" She giggled as she twisted out of his hands and stumbled onto the beach.

He chuckled. He'd never seen giggly Tempest. She was adorable.

Sandals in hand, she ran, kicking up sand as she went. He followed, slower. He didn't want to take his sneakers off. He'd have to hold them, and he wanted his hands free to hold her. And he probably shouldn't run; he didn't need his pulse any higher than it already was.

He caught up with her a few yards down the beach, close to the moonlit surf. She'd stopped next to another couple. A wave of cold crushed over him as recognition hit. Mom and Christopher. The long string of curses pinging through his brain did not help him feel better. He trudged over.

"Leo, honey, hi," Mom said.

"Are you cold?" Christopher asked his daughter, looking over her bare arms and legs. "Do you want my jacket?"

"No. The breeze feels good." She sounded stone sober now. Had she been playing it up a little for him? Because she wanted him too and thought she needed an excuse?

"Lucky we ran into you," Mom said. "Now we can welcome the new year together as a new family."

They were rescued from having to reply to that buzzkill by voices yelling along the beach. "Ten, nine, eight..." Christopher and his mom picked up the chant. They turned to each other, eyes starry and expectant. Leo felt a bit like vomiting. "Three, two..." Tempest turned sad eyes on Leo. "One."

Fireworks exploded across the sky. Green, red, and yellow reflected off the ocean. All along the sand, couples came together. Christopher drew Mom into his embrace and kissed her.

Leo and Tempest stood there, staring at each other like the sorriest idiots in the world.

Chapter Eleven
The New Job

Tempest parked her car in her typical spot—the one in the corner of the lot, farthest from the building she was quickly coming to despise. She'd taken a job as a market research analyst with Komler Insurance the first week of January, a month ago. And she hated it. The small cubicle with no windows. The way her boss's breath reeked of fish and coffee. The way they shifted meeting schedules constantly with no warning or apology. The size of her paycheck. The lack of connection she felt with her coworkers.

She hadn't talked or texted or emailed or communicated in any way with Leo since his plane touched down in Dallas on January first. Maybe that dead zone was affecting her ability to integrate into this new work environment. She just didn't care if Komler Insurance succeeded or failed. They couldn't read her apathy in the reports—those were done well—but she worked like a robot. She had all her walls up, and it was killing her slowly. She sighed as she shifted her car into park and turned off the engine.

"Another day, another dime." She lifted her leather work tote and marched into the brown building.

"Good morning, Ms. Swan," the office receptionist said.

She frowned at him as she strode past. "Hi."

He wasn't much younger than she and called everyone else in the office by their first name. The worst part was she knew he used her last name because he didn't like her first name. She found her cubicle, hung up her coat, and sat down. She had put exactly zero decorations or personal touches on her desk. If this company asked her to clear out her desk, she could laugh in their faces because it was already done. The woman who worked one cubicle up appeared at the opening to Tempest's tiny space. Sherla's office looked like she might have moved in, complete with photo montages and a full-service tea station.

"Happy anniversary," Sherla said.

"What?"

"You've worked here one month." She clapped small pudgy hands and brought them to her chest.

Tempest was not in the mood for whatever what happening right now, but she forced a half smile. "Oh. Thanks."

"We celebrate the occasion around here." Round eyes popped out with eagerness.

"Why? Is it rare?"

Sherla giggled. "You are so funny."

Tempest hadn't meant it at as a joke. She plugged her laptop into her work monitor.

"One month is the perfect amount of time for new folks to get integrated and trained and start to feel like this is home."

This felt nothing like home.

"And I hate having people feel like they aren't family around here." Sherla said it with a slightly accusing tone.

"Thank you for the warm welcome." Tempest

pointedly turned to her screen.

"I started the tradition to celebrate this important milestone. Got permission all the way at the top." She motioned to Tempest. "Come on."

Dread trickled into Tempest as she looked up at the beaming woman. That's when she realized the office had gone quiet.

"Up, up." She reached for Tempest.

Tempest stood quickly so Sherla wouldn't touch her, but she put her hands on Tempest's elbow anyway. Tempest went around the far side of her chair so Sherla would be forced to remove her fingers.

"I'll follow you."

Sherla's excitement bated at the blandness of Tempest's tone. She turned, and Tempest followed the wide swinging hips toward the breakroom. Tempest had work to do. Her mind was poised to get it done. She'd worked out hard this morning. She'd pushed herself in her yoga practice these last few weeks, willing her body to be strong enough to overcome her heart. Her muscles were warm and tired, and she just wanted to sit down and look at the stupid data. She walked into the lounge and froze as the office staff let out a cheer.

"To our newest member...now an old familiar." Her boss's voice boomed, and he saluted her with his coffee mug. "We're so glad you're here."

She needed to find a new job. Pronto. "Thank you."

He moved to the side, revealing a cake sitting on the table, one lone candle on top.

"To one great month and the hope of many more," people said in unison. They'd done this before. And that meant Tempest would have to do it in the future.

Should she quit right this second?

"Hurry, the wax is melting down," a voice said.

"Make a wish." Sherla's eyes glimmered.

Well, that was easy. Tempest wished she were anywhere but here right now. She strode up and puffed out the tiny flame.

Clapping and cheers.

A man lifted a knife to cut into the sheet cake, and that's when Tempest noticed the design on top of it. A stormy ocean. The picture was hideous. Blair would have done something cool with the idea. As Tempest stared at the blackish-blue swirls, she couldn't help but feel like that tiny toy boat stuck in the churning frosting of towering waves.

"It's a tempest for our Tempest," someone said.

"Yes," Tempest said, voice flat. "I see the sea."

A laughing male voice said, "She sells seashells by the seashore."

Tempest pulled her phone from her pocket. "Before you cut into it, do you mind if I take a picture? This is all so nice."

Sherla beamed.

"Gather around, but I want to see that cake," Tempest said.

"You need to be in it."

"No, no." Tempest snapped the picture, cutting off most of the people but getting a good image of the mess of grays and blues.

She passed around thank yous, wondering if she could finally slip back to her desk and get to work, when horror of horrors, a man handed her a massive corner piece.

Nope. It was nine eleven in the morning, but even

if it were five p.m., Tempest wouldn't want to eat this brick of grocery store cake. She already felt plenty sick inside.

"This is so nice of y'all. Thanks so much." The room went quiet as she set the piece of cake down on the table. "Please excuse me, but I'm allergic to blue food dye."

Sherla looked stricken.

Her boss looked suspicious.

"And eggs."

Another beat of silence.

"Please eat y'all." Her armpits were getting hot.

"I'll have her slice," a man said, breaking the tension.

"Yes, see," Tempest said. "That's perfect."

****

After work, Tempest sat at the kitchen counter, shoulders slumped, eating an arugula pesto pita pizza, watching Blair sing as she washed eclair batter out of a pastry bag.

"You're my cherry pie. My greatest lie. You're my diamond heart, though it's been years apart... I'll never forget, never, no, never, no, never give up on you..."

Blair looked so happy, singing off-key and sliding across the floor in her stocking feet while she did her work. That's what life was about. Tempest needed to find something that made *her* hum while she scrubbed. Nothing came to mind. Except Blair. Her best friend always put her in a good mood. What would she do when she no longer got to come home to Blair?

Tempest pulled up this morning's photo on her phone and passed it across the counter. Blair leaned over and looked.

Her song ended abruptly. "Whhaaattt is that?"

"My one-month anniversary, Tempest-the-tempest, I-work-in-hell cake."

Blair snorted. She dropped her dish towel and picked up the phone. "Did someone put goldfish in the sea?"

"They were made out of gummies."

"I mean, it's fascinating." She zoomed in on the cake. "Who knew frosting could look so unappetizing?"

"They meant it to be sweet and welcoming, and I feel like a terrible person for despising the gesture. It didn't help they served it first thing in the morning." Tempest finished the last of her glass of water. "And now they hate me for not eating it."

"You know." Blair's bottom lip curled in, her face focused. "It's not a bad idea. It's the execution that's off." She glanced over at her plate of lovely eclairs. "Storms and weather and earthy things are a super-rad idea to put with dessert."

"Your frosting looks like fluffy clouds. Except this time, I mean that in the good way."

Blair set down the phone and walked over to her tray.

"Also, when are you going to offer me one?"

They were for Blair's monthly baking club, but she always set aside one of her creations for Tempest. This was why Tempest never wasted her calories on subpar treats.

"Just a minute." Blair pulled out a mixing bowl and slid her pot back over the stove. She melted white chocolate and mixed in a drop of yellow coloring. She pulled a stencil from a cupboard, then poured the chocolate into the lightning bolt molds.

"How do you even have that form?"

"You know I have no self-control when I go to the kitchen supply store." She put the tray in the freezer.

Tempest took her plate to the sink and started on Blair's dishes. By the time she closed the dishwasher and dried her hands, Blair had finished her eclairs. She handed Tempest one on a tiny porcelain plate. Blair had an eclectic collection of mismatched china she'd collected over the years from flea markets. This plate was navy with tiny gold stars. The perfect backdrop for a pastry overflowing with fluffy vanilla custard. Blair had stuck the lightning bolts into the clouds of frosting. Whimsical and mouthwatering.

"A storm fit for my Stormie."

Tempest pulled a face, but inside she swelled with warmth at Blair's kind gesture. "Thank you. It's adorable." She took a big bite, savoring the perfection. She made the appropriate and thoroughly genuine moan of pleasure.

Blair watched, her brown eyes glowing with satisfaction.

"You're really good at this." Tempest licked custard off her finger.

"I know."

"No. You're really good at this."

Blair twisted her wide lips into a cocky grin. "Good enough for baking club?"

"Good enough to sell."

Blair's smile faltered. "Someday I hope to find out if that's true."

Tempest took another bite.

"Thanks for helping me clean up. I'm headed out. I'll be back late."

Tempest didn't respond, her thoughts caught up in an analytical storm of what if…

****

Leo sat at brunch with his mom and sister. Daisies and fresh herbs in pink glass tumblers dotted the table. His silverware had dainty swirl flourishes on the handles.

"The New Year's trip with the family went so well," Mom said.

He did not agree, but Zena beamed. Jake had been out to Dallas the last two weekends in a row. She was exuding lovey happiness in the most disgusting way. He found it hard to be around her.

"And the more Christopher and I talk about this wedding, the more we want to do a destination with only our family. At our age, with our history, it seems like the best way."

"Love that idea." Zena popped a strawberry in her mouth. "Where are we thinking? Oh, Tuscany?"

Mom shook her head. "I'm craving beach."

Zena's eyes lit up as she nodded.

Leo didn't say anything, too busy deciding if having to see Tempest again for all the wedding stuff would be better here or there. It wasn't going to be easy anywhere. He hadn't seen her in over a month, since California, and he was still hung up on her. He'd only met her for the first time seventy-six days before that. After such a short relationship, if he could even call it that, how was he thinking about her when he went to bed at night and in the morning when he woke up horny? She roamed his mind as if she owned the place, bothering him when he had a quiet moment at work or while swimming laps.

She'd clearly moved on. Not a single text. And she'd been so cold to him on New Year's Day after the kiss that did not happen. It was like he'd been invisible on the flight home.

"We found a resort in Cabo. They had an opening for February fourteenth, so we booked it."

Leo's fork lowered, coming to rest on the scalloped china plate. His jaw unhinged as her statement sank in.

"For next year," Zena said, voice high-pitched.

"No. This year." Mom had the decency to look guilty.

Christmas. Then New Year's. And now this? Were no holidays sacred?

They were in a public place, the only reason he wasn't throwing his chair against the wall. Also, he didn't do that sort of thing—angry or not. But he imagined taking the white wooden thing and smashing it into kindling, then lighting it on fire. Maybe this whole girly restaurant would go up. Maybe he'd go to hell with it. And then, at least, he wouldn't be having this conversation.

"I know it's last minute," Mom said.

"It's next weekend." Zena's eyes turned cold as sapphires.

At least she was mad too. "You do realize that is *Valentine's* Day?" he asked.

Mom's eyes went dewy. "Yes. Isn't it romantic?"

Zena caved faster than an avalanche. "Yes." She sighed. "And think of all the years together where you get to celebrate your anniversary on the day of love."

"That's what I think," Mom said. "And Christopher's the romantic type."

Leo hated Valentine's Day as a general rule, and

one week wasn't enough time for him to mentally prepare to see Tempest again. The remembered feel of her lips whispering against his ear had him gritting his teeth. The image of a tiny black dress and golden thighs was branded into his brain.

"I was going to go to San Diego, but I'll just invite Jake to Mexico instead."

Mom didn't appear like she wanted that at all, but she said, "That's fine." She looked to her son with pleading eyes. "Does it mess up your plans?"

Heaven knew he didn't have any hot dates on the calendar. "No, Mother. It will be great."

He might as well get this over with. A few days in Mexico and then he shouldn't have to see Tempest again until Mom's Fourth of July BBQ, unless he could figure out how to skip that too.

****

Jo was pissed about the bridesmaid's dress. "You can see my butt fat through the fabric!" She twisted to get a better look in the trifold mirror in the department store.

Tempest stood next to her sister, trying on the same pale pink gown. High neckline in front, but swooping very low in back. The fabric had no stretch or give. It was designed to fit a tall, trim figure. It flattered Tempest nicely.

"What is the other option?" Jo asked the store clerk hovering nearby.

The woman's eyes went wide. "This is what Silvia Steele picked out for the three daughters to wear. She just said this one."

Jo scowled at the way the fabric puckered around her waist. "And I'm still nursing! Did she not think about these ladies?" She cupped her huge breasts. "No way am I going braless for the wedding with nothing but a pink tissue of coverage for support." She hadn't even been willing to take her bra off for the fitting, and the cream strap cut straight across her exposed back.

"We'll be in Mexico. No one will see." Tempest grimaced. A postpartum mother and this unforgiving dress were not a good combo.

"I'll see myself! And what about the photographs? There's no way in hell I'm wearing this." Jo turned to the attendant. "I'm going to need you to find me something else."

The young woman nodded with a slight bow, the way she might have to a stern school principal. She darted out of the changing area.

"If you switch, it'll just be me and Zena matching," Tempest said.

"I don't give a shit."

"Okay." Time to step back before Jo really lost it.

Tempest quickly changed into her jeans. Jo didn't need to see that dress on Tempest any longer than necessary. Jo tried on every pink option in the store and nixed them all. While they waited for the harried sales associate to search every corner of the massive store for something acceptable, Jo stuffed her bra with tissues to soak up her leaking milk.

"I didn't think this would take so long. I should have brought Harrison. My poor baby needs to eat."

Tempest was getting hungry too, and she was not sorry the baby wasn't here to slow things down even more. She resisted the urge to check her watch.

"Pretty cool we get to go to Cabo," Jo said. "It's so romantic."

Tempest's stomach twisted.

"I need more beach in my life." Jo let out a wistful sigh. "This marriage is the best thing that ever happened to us. Think of all the amazing things we'll get to tag along for. A billionaire brother-in-law." She giggled. "Well done, Dad."

The saleswoman appeared with another armful of pastel garments, saving Tempest from having to pretend to agree with Jo. This marriage was the worst. Tempest closed her eyes and leaned back in the tufted chair. Why did Mom have to die? And of all the other women in the universe, why did Dad have to fall in love with Leo's mother?

Eighty-nine minutes and fourteen million dresses later, Jo picked a flowing, flattering piece that fell to her calves and draped loosely over her body.

"Thank you," Tempest whispered to the heavens as she stood and shook out her stiff joints.

"I've put them on Ms. Steele's bill." The associate handed them each their tissue-wrapped dresses in familiar brown bags. "Goodbye." She said it with such finality that Tempest chuckled.

The sisters strode toward the exit.

"Good," Jo said as they stepped into the chilly afternoon. "I feel good."

Tempest had a headache.

They would see what Silvia was really like when Jo showed up in that blue dress. Maybe she'd call off the wedding. Then Tempest could date Leo without any complications. But Dad would be so sad.

Jo looked down at her phone. "Oh crap. The babysitter has been trying to call me, and I am so late. I'll see you Thursday at the airport." She darted toward her minivan.

Two days. In two days, Tempest would be getting back on Leo's private plane. She was going to a beach resort with Leo. At least this trip couldn't go any worse than the last.

****

Leo triple-checked his garment bag. He had everything he needed for a wedding in Mexico, yet he felt completely unprepared. He was spending Valentine's Day with Tempest Swan. But not really *with* her. How the hell was this happening to him? Oh, he hated this holiday. He'd loathed it ever since high school when all the cute people had flower grams delivered to their desks during class, the coolest getting dozens and the losers getting none. Obviously he was the latter. What kind of society supported such a terrible idea? It made the lonely kids in school feel worse about themselves and overinflated the popular kids' already massive egos. Toxic and destructive. Why was the world so stupid sometimes?

He loaded his bag into his Aston Martin. Anxiety and the engine power of approximately five hundred and three horses sped his drive. At the airport, he valeted his car, passed his bag off to the attendant, and climbed into his jet. He was the first one here, and he did not go back outside to wait for the others. He pulled out his laptop and connected to the internet. He had a long list of work to do. He put on his noise-cancelling headphones and got to it.

When the rest of the wedding party arrived, he tugged down his headphones and welcomed them all with a smile. "Come in. Help yourselves to the snacks. Nice to see y'all again. Wow, Jo, Harrison's gotten so big." He nodded to Tempest, one hundred percent ignoring the reaction seeing her caused to his heart. The conversation blockers went back over his ears. She sat behind him again. Good, easier to pretend she wasn't here, that she didn't look like heaven in her tight blue jeans with her curling dark hair. He didn't look up for the duration of the two-hour flight.

Leo didn't pack away his computer until after they'd landed and taxied. He kept his back to her as they deplaned. Hannah slipped her hand in his as they walked into the hot fug of the Cabo San Lucas Airport. She looked up at him, the foreign smells and unfamiliar faces clearly making her nervous. He sent the little girl a genuine smile, grateful for the anchoring feel of her small fingers.

"Don't let go of her," Jo said at Leo's side. Her forehead already glistened in the heat. She tightened the strap of the baby carrier on her chest.

"I've got her." Leo tugged Hannah closer to his side.

"Thank you." Jo hitched a duffle onto her shoulder.

"You mean *gracias*," Hunter said from where he walked holding Benji's hand.

Leo gave the boy an appreciative head nod. "*De nada.*"

"What does that mean?" Hannah asked.

"It means you're welcome," Leo said.

Hannah muttered the words over and over to herself as they worked their way through passport control. She held his hand tighter as they entered the crowded lobby. He exhaled with relief when he saw the two men holding signs that read *Christopher Swan.*

He looked over his shoulder, his gaze catching on

Tempest. She'd taken off her sweater, revealing a ribbed tank top and lean arms. What was he going to say? Oh yeah. "Our drivers are here."

"Thank goodness," Mom muttered, fanning her face with a brochure.

"*Hola*, Mr. Swan," the first man said. "Everyone is here?"

Leo nodded to him and turned, still holding fast to Hannah. "Mom. You and Christopher go in the first car. Take Tempest and Zena with you."

Tempest opened her mouth.

"You should come with us too," Silvia said.

"I'll go with the Prestons. I know where we're going and can make sure they don't have any trouble." He glanced down at Hannah. "Besides, we're in this together."

She beamed, softening his aching heart just a little.

Jo sent him a look of utter adoration. Being helpful was the lesser reason for doing this, but he was still happy to stay with these kids. He could feel Tempest's focus on him, but he didn't look her way. He spoke to the second driver. "Lead the way. *Estamos listos.*"

He sat in the back row of the van with Hunter, looking out the window and enjoying the boy's delighted discourse on the differences between Cabo, Mexico and Plano, Texas. Not all that different, it turned out. They practiced all the important Spanish phrases they might need like: *dónde está el baño* and *quiero muchos tacos* and *habla usted Inglés*?

Mom and Christopher had rented two houses next door to each other. Christopher and his daughters in one, Leo's family in the other. Mom's sister, Aunt Penelope, would arrive soon from Miami. She would bunk with Mom until tomorrow, when, after the wedding, Christopher and Mom would move to a romantic suite at a resort nearby. *Gag.* Then all the kids would be left to enjoy another two days together, along with Aunt Penelope and the other half-dozen family members that made the short invitation list, before everyone would finally be allowed to return to the land of the free. Mom assumed that once people had made the trip down to the beach that they would want those extra days to relax and enjoy the sunshine and spending time together as a new family.

Why would she think that?

Chapter Twelve
The Night Before

Tempest sat at the end of the table, facing the ocean. Moonlight flickered over the lapping waves. She breathed in warm oxygen and salt. The soft breeze kissed her bare arms and danced with her thin dress. The long table had been set up on a carpet on the edge of the sand. Candles lit the many dishes of fish tacos, fresh guacamole, jicama salads, and mango salsas. A server set a tray of steaming churros with chocolate dipping sauce next to her mimosa. This was paradise.

But it felt like hell.

Silvia had directed Leo to sit by Tempest, but he'd abrasively maneuvered himself to the other end of the table. He'd claimed he needed to catch up with his cousin George. They apparently hadn't seen each other in *weeks*. Maybe it wouldn't have been so offensive if he had the decency to come up with a good excuse. But that wasn't true. It would have hurt no matter what. Tempest wanted to sit with Leo. She'd been looking forward to this time with him, this excuse to be together when they couldn't *be* together. And he was avoiding her. Disappointment weighed her down like a lead blanket.

The seat across from Tempest was empty now that Hannah had run down the beach to hunt for seashells. Benji, on her left, was talking to Leo's Aunt Penelope about fishing in Miami. Tempest didn't even try to participate in the conversation. Zena and her boyfriend were on her right. She couldn't bear to look at them; they were mushier than the guacamole.

Leo was ignoring her. So that's how it was going to be. It wouldn't hurt as badly if he weren't being so relaxed and kind to everyone else. The contrast was pure cruelty.

She exhaled. Okay. Putting distance between them was a good idea. She could deal with this. After this mandatory trip, she would only see him on holidays, at the most. Over time, maybe those get-togethers would diminish. She could start traveling over Christmas. Or more likely, he would. This weekend was the worst of it. His coldness was easier to handle than his charm. If she kept telling herself that, would it start to be true? He'd been impossible to resist on New Year's Eve. The way he'd found her in the bar. He'd waltzed in and eclipsed the man who'd been working so hard to flirt with her. She imagined his hands on her waist. His lips on her fingers. She leaned forward and glanced down the table at Leo. He seemed riveted by something Jo was saying, her sister's smile bigger than the moon. The hole in Tempest's belly yawned wider. She couldn't take it anymore. If it weren't her own father's wedding, she would've faked sick and left.

Dad stood, clinking a knife against his wine glass. He smoothed his graying hair back with a nervous hand. "Humor an old man, would you? I have a quick toast." As the table quieted, he smiled down at Silvia. He put a hand on her shoulder. He didn't speak for a moment, and when he did, his voice came out hoarse with emotion. "I'll never forget the day I first saw you.

I rounded that grocery aisle, sidestepping the pyramid of crackers and dip."

"And there you were." Silvia's gaze locked on Dad.

"And there you were." A pause as they stared at each other.

Tempest pushed away the thought of her mother. When was it going to stop feeling a little like they were all cheating on Mom?

"I asked if you knew were the ketchup was." Dad chuckled. "You said no."

"You didn't even need ketchup," Silvia said.

"I don't know why that was the first thing that came to mind. I think I reverted to a twelve-year-old boy."

Silvia's sister, Penelope, snorted.

"I moved right on past you." Dad looked up at the rest of the table. "I'd completely forgotten at that point what I'd stopped at the store for. It wasn't my usual route, but I'd come into Dallas for a lunch and needed to pick up something on my way home."

"Probably a bag of almonds and a gingersnap," Silvia said.

He chuckled. "You know me so well." He leaned down and kissed her brow.

Tempest's heart squeezed at the sweetness of it, at her dad's total joy. He turned his focus on the table. He grinned at Tempest. She smiled back, her eyes heating.

"I never did get it because I couldn't stop thinking about the blond on aisle twelve. I stalked her, contriving to pass her another three times, still with nothing in my basket. And then she checked out. I watched her from two aisles down, faking like I was looking at a magazine. She smiled to the clerk. Said thank you. And then she walked out those double doors." He looked back down at Silvia, his eyes watery and soft. "She was so beautiful. So kind. Radiant. And I was rooted to those dirty tiles. I couldn't do it. Just walk up to a woman. I'd hadn't done anything like that for forty years. It was too scary. Too hard. She would turn me away faster than a rotten pear."

Silvia glowed.

"On the borderline of having a heart attack, I dropped my empty basket and darted outside. I tried to look cool as I jogged around the parking lot, my mind already torn to bits with regret. She was just closing her trunk when I finally found her. I was awkward, and I might have stuttered."

"Only a little," Silvia said.

Everyone chuckled.

"But she, with her generous heart, gave me a chance anyway."

"And when he took me to dinner the next day," Silvia said, "he didn't stutter once."

More polite chuckles.

Dad held out his glass. "Having the courage to talk to you before you slipped away—it's the best risk I've even taken."

Tempest looked at Leo as those words sank deep into her soul. Candlelight lit his face, intensifying the angles and shadows. His gaze found hers for one heart-stopping moment before flicking away, leaving her unmoored.

"The reward is all mine," Silvia said.

"I love you." Dad tugged her to her feet and kissed her.

Benji whistled, and Jo hooted. Tempest had gone quiet as her father's words broke through her meager defenses. He'd given voice to her truth. And her fears.

When the beaming couple broke apart, they all drank to love. Tempest drained her glass.

"And to both of you." Dad looked to Leo and Zena. "I've always wanted more children. I hope we can grow to be a *real* family."

Zena smiled up at him. Leo looked frozen. Tempest felt as if a grenade exploded in her chest.

Dad sat down, but the conversation stayed on a recap of their whirlwind romance. Their love and joy gushed over the table, and Tempest couldn't stop herself from being very glad for them.

The group didn't leave the beach until the kids were practically falling asleep standing up. The rest of the small wedding party went to their rooms at the adjacent hotel. The Swan and Allred families separated on the street in front of the two rental houses. Dad and Silvia were spending their last night with their own kids. Something was said about it being unlucky for the bride and groom to sleep together the night before the wedding. Dad and Silvia kissed, *again*. Tempest was looking forward to this wedding being over so she didn't have to watch all the public displays of affection anymore. When would they get to the regular old-married-couple stage?

"See you in the morning, darling," Dad said to Silvia.

"Bye, y'all." Zena waved with the arm that wasn't glued around Jake's waist.

"Night," Jo said. Benji had already taken Harrison inside.

Dad draped his arm over Tempest's shoulders and turned toward the house with his daughters. He went straight to bed. He'd had enough to drink that even nerves wouldn't keep him up. Lucky.

"Want to watch a movie with me and Benji after we get the kids in bed?" Jo asked.

"Maybe tomorrow night," Tempest said. "I'm turning in." *Turning in? Who talked like that?* "It was a long week at work, and I'm tired."

"Lame."

"I know."

"Kinda weird about the wedding." Jo didn't move from her stance by the couch. She held strappy heeled sandals in her hand. She might have been stalling so Benji had to put the kids to bed without her.

"She's nothing like Mom."

Jo shook her head. "No."

It was weird. It felt like a betrayal to the woman who'd given thirty-seven years of her life to Dad. But Mom was gone, and she wasn't coming back. "Dad seems truly happy," Tempest said.

"I hope she doesn't break his heart."

Tempest nodded. That was for sure.

"And I have to say, he chose very well," Jo said. "I mean we could have been stuck with total weirdos. Benji and I are stoked about family vacations with Leo and Zena." She looked around the rental. It was nicer and bigger than her home in Plano. "I could get use to this."

Tempest chuckled. "I think you already have." She leaned over and hugged Jo. "Love you, sis. See you in the morning."

Jo pulled back at Tempest's tone. "You okay? Is

this wedding bumming you out because Dad's getting married before you?"

Tempest blinked at Jo. She hadn't considered that. Dad was on marriage two before she'd started on one. She didn't want to start worrying about that now, but Jo had planted the seed. Was it the truth? Was her pain less about Leo and more about her loneliness?

Jo pursed her lips in pity. "I'm sorry, sweetie. That sucks." She ran a familiar hand over Tempest's shoulder and down her arm. Jo squeezed her fingers.

Heat flared behind Tempest's eyes. She nearly broke down and told Jo everything. She was in freaking *love* with her new *brother*. And he wouldn't even look at her. But in the end, she just gave Jo another hug, taking strength from her sister's attention.

"I'll see you in the morning." She walked to her room and closed the door. She sat on the chair. She perched on the bed. She paced in circles, then stared out the window at darkness. The clouds moved, and a million stars twinkled into existence. A hysterical laugh cackled up her throat as she made her decision.

—*I'm going all in.*— Shooting off the text to Blair, she tossed her phone on her bag.

She brushed her teeth, refreshed her eye makeup, and added a layer of deodorant. Dad's words keep ringing through her mind. *Courage.* Her heart fluttered and spun. She cracked the door open. Dad's room was quiet. Jo and Benji were in the bathroom, brushing Hunter's teeth and convincing Hannah to just go pee one more time. Tempest closed her bedroom door and tiptoed out the front. On the street between the homes, she stopped. She panted as if she'd sprinted half a mile.

What was she doing? She should turn right back

around and watch that movie with Jo. But she didn't want to do that. She wanted to talk to Leo. She wanted to do more than talk. She wanted to take a risk. She wanted to chase this feeling in her belly. She wanted the reward.

The lights were on in every window of the Allred's house that she could see. How long were they going to stay up? It was already ten. She was kidding herself if she thought they were the kind of people to go to sleep right now. Penelope had been quite energetic on the golf-cart ride back to the houses. Tempest was not interested in any more conversations with her. Or any of the females.

The best two bedrooms were in the back, with ocean views. Would Leo have one of those? He was the older brother. Penelope was sleeping with her sister, Silvia, for one last night. Tempest skirted the house to the left, careful of the sharp succulents. She peered in the side window. Zena and Jake mixed drinks in the kitchen. Leo sat on the couch, looking at his laptop. *Ugh.* Tempest had no plan, but it already wasn't a good one. Silvia came out of a bedroom wearing a silk robe. Tempest could cross that bedroom off the list. Penelope cheered at her sister and held out a glass. Tempest slunk around the back side of the house. She paused by the patio door. Leo was still on the couch engrossed in the blue screen.

Go home, Tempest.

She imagined walking back to her lonely room, getting into pajamas, lying in bed, and staring at the ceiling. The zing in her nerves refused to follow that path. Keeping to the shadows, she darted across the patio. The curtains were drawn in the next windows.

She skirted the air conditioning unit, stopping at the next glass pane. The room was dark. This was a terrible idea. She was going to have to knock on the front door. What would her excuse be for doing that? Nothing excusable came to mind. Nope. The front door approach wasn't going to happen. She wasn't that brave. She'd had her adventure. She'd tried to see him. It wasn't going to work. Better to get over it right now.

She kept up the internal pep talk as she moved around a little wall, expecting to come to the front of the house. Instead, she happened upon an outdoor shower. Feeling like a complete creeper, she walked through the shower and stopped at the door. Through the glass she could see the bathroom counter, but the room was too dark for her to tell whose stuff was laid out. Probably Zena's room.

The light flicked on. She flinched against the sudden brightness. Standing in the doorway to the bathroom, Leo turned away from the switch. He jumped when his gaze landed on the glass door. He yelped and reared back, his hand coming to his chest.

Tempest grinned.

He blinked at her.

She waved.

His brow furrowed as he walked forward and unlocked the door, pulling it open. He was breathing fast. "You scared the shit out of me."

"I'm glad that's not literal."

He chuckled before seeming to remember himself and then scowled. "What are you doing here?" He looked behind her at the empty outdoor shower. "Is everything okay?"

"Yes. Well, mostly. I just felt like you were

ignoring me."

"I mostly was."

"Well, I didn't like it, so I decided to be the bigger person and come over and say hi." She cringed inwardly. Going on the offensive had not been her game plan.

"By creeping around my bathroom door."

"I didn't want to have drinks with the bridal party."

"I can't blame you there." He folded his arms. He wore a cream linen shirt, unbuttoned at the collar, and gray shorts. His hair was no longer combed and styled but sticking up in all directions. Standing by his toiletries arranged in a neat row, he studied her.

She went still under his gaze. After a stretch of humiliating silence, she asked, "Are you going to invite me in?"

He hesitated.

Her pulse soared. Fear trickled through her veins. He was going to turn her away. This was why she hated risk. Reward was great and all, but she could not handle the loss. The dark churn of anxiety and failure welled in her belly. She should not have come.

She took a step back at the same time he unfolded his arms and said, "I hope I don't regret this." He motioned her in.

She could barely breathe. Run away or walk forward? Looking at his pale eyes, she knew she'd already jumped. She could do nothing now but fall and see where she landed.

She took off her sandals, now muddy from her adventure, and left them outside. As she stepped on a plush mat, he moved close to shut and lock the door. His chest was inches from hers. She almost wrapped her arms around him and proclaimed her love right there in the bathroom. She bit her tongue and slipped away, padding into his bedroom.

"I came in here to pee. Which I still need to do." He shut the bathroom door so hard she jumped.

The door to the main room was cracked open, high voices ringing through. Tempest glided over and closed the door all the way. Her heart pounded. The king bed dominated the space. He'd taken off the quilt and dropped it on the floor. The sheets were pulled back on one side, and the pillow crumpled where he must have rested his head earlier. Desire rose though her body. She turned on a dim lamp, sat on the little couch, and crossed her legs, letting her dress ride up on her thigh a bit extra.

The sink turned off, and Leo strode out. He eyed her, glimpsing her exposed leg, before taking up the seat across the tea table from the couch. Close enough to talk quietly, but they would not be touching. Disappointment sank through her bones.

They sat in silence. She picked at a loose thread on the hem of her dress. He stared at the diamond shapes on the rug. This was too hard. Love wasn't supposed to be like this. *He* wasn't supposed to be like this. She'd taken a risk by coming over here so at least she could go home proud of herself and knowing it was never meant to be. Even as she thought the words, a heaviness spread over her chest. She stood. She took a step toward the bathroom. He stood.

She turned to him, surprised to see distress on his face. "Thanks for having me over."

"Um."

"I'm sorry I bothered you tonight."

"You didn't. I'm glad you came over. I'm sorry I've been standoffish. It's just…" His voice faded.

She smiled at his nervousness. So he wasn't unfeeling.

He looked down at her mouth and frowned. "Okay. So we'll talk like normal step-people."

Her lips drooped.

"How's Blair?"

"Great. She's still catering and dreaming of owning her own pastry shop. How's Dean?"

"Worse for having met Blair."

Tempest chuckled, a tiny thing that wouldn't escape the walls of the room.

"Are you seeing anyone?" Leo looked down at his hands.

Her pulse rose. "No. You?" She braced for the answer.

"No."

Hope broke through the gloom like the first rays of dawn.

He lifted his gray eyes. "Did you find a job?"

"Yes."

"Do you like it?"

"No."

His face crumpled as if stricken with a blow. Silence pulsed. He looked down at the tea table. "Seems like the parents are really happy."

"Yes."

"It's pretty lucky they got to find love like that." He looked right at her, his gaze piercing.

Her pulse was a foghorn in her ears. *Do it. Don't think about what you have to lose. Think about the beautiful man before you.* She sucked in a breath and stepped closer. "I've been thinking about how my dad said he didn't want to live with the regret of not taking a risk on Silvia."

Leo's breath hitched as she put a hand on his shirt, on the buttons under the open collar.

"Living safe hasn't done me any favors." She swallowed, heat racing over her face. Her nerves buzzed. "So I'm just going to say it."

His irises dilated.

"I'm in love with you."

His lips parted.

"I want to be with you."

He wasn't breathing, but his heart raced beneath her fingertips.

She tilted her face, bringing their mouths within inches. "What do you think? Am I worth the risk?"

His hands found her waist and slid over her lower back. He drew her against his body. "You're worth everything."

She moaned as his mouth closed over hers. He started slow, his lips soft, his hands sliding up her sides, over her ribs. He tasted of heat and cinnamon. Her blood warmed as it had that night at the party, but now no costumes or other people got in the way. Instead of a beard, his face felt like smooth marble. She opened her eyes just wide enough to find the buttons on his shirt, her deft fingers making quick work of them. She slid his shirt off, his shoulders and chest hot beneath her hands. He shuddered, and his tiny nipples went hard.

He cupped her neck, guiding her focus back to his dark eyes, his flushed lips. "I love you."

Her whole body seemed to melt into a smile.

This time when he drew her chin up, his hungry

mouth crushed against hers. He kissed her as if he were a drowning man and she were air. His teeth chewed at her lower lip. Her knees weakened. His breathing turned heavy. Her hands wrapped the muscles of his arms as she tilted her head back, exposing tender skin. He kissed along her jaw, at the base of her ear. As his tongue trailed down her neck, a dam burst, and fire flooded her body. Everywhere he touched, her nerves ignited. His palm found her thigh and slid up, over her hip, her ribs, her bra. She lifted her arms, and he tugged the dress over her head. As his gaze drank her up, he uttered a string of curses that had her flushing from her toes to her nose. Hands on her waist, he drew her against him, their skin meeting in a soft whisper. He kissed her slowly. So slowly her fingers dug into his back muscles to keep from exploding. His exploring hands left smoldering fires along her skin. As one they shuffled toward the bed until her legs bumped the mattress, and together they fell.

****

A shrill voice cut through the pleasant haze weighing down his limbs.

"She's gone!"

Who was that screaming? Leo opened his eyes and couldn't stop his smile at seeing Tempest curled at his side. He slid closer, put his arm around her waist, and kissed her bare shoulder.

"And this is Mexico." The upset woman seemed to be getting closer to his bedroom door. "Do you think a human trafficker stole her in the night?"

Jo. That was Jo. *Oh, shit.*

"No." Mom's quiet voice was muffled by the wall. "I'm sure she's fine. Maybe she went for a run."

"She hates running." Jo's tone turned sharp.

Tempest woke with a start, huge blue eyes turning to him.

"She didn't sleep in her bed last night. Her phone is in her bag. She left everything. It's like she was abducted by aliens. Or the cartel." Jo sounded like she was about to burst into tears. "Is she a sex slave now?" She sobbed. "She must have been taken last night. *Hours* ago."

Tempest pulled the sheet up to her nose. Naked. They were both naked. Her eyes turned panicky as she blinked up at Leo.

What time was it? Sunlight seared through the narrow slits in the drapes. He'd slept so well with her, like it was the most normal thing in the world. Once they'd gone to sleep that was—they had stayed up very late.

The sheet was thin, no blanket over top. Leo could see the swells of her body and the sudden pop of her nipples when his gaze raked down her. The worried female voices drew closer to the door. He considered rolling on top of her to hide her body, but that might not be the best idea right now.

"Leo?" Mom's voice penetrated the closed door.

He sat partially up, keeping his chest covered, and held his pillow over the thin sheet not hiding his pitched tent. He grabbed another pillow and rested it on top of Tempest's torso. She stayed lying down, her eyes brimming with a mixture of horror and threatening laughter as she turned her focus toward the rotating doorknob.

Mom didn't wait for his response before she swung the bedroom door open. He probably should have checked that it was locked last night. His mind had been on other, more pressing matters.

Dressed for the wedding, in gowns and makeup, Mom, Zena, and Jo stepped into his room. They froze as their gazes soaked up the scene, each face shifting into different emotions. Mom, shock and horror. Zena, amusement. Jo moved quickly from relief to confusion.

"She's here." Leo said it as if he were the hero who'd rescued the princess. He grinned. "And there was no slavery involved." He couldn't help the edge of arrogance that laced his voice.

Tempest grunted out a laugh. Only the top half of her head was visible peeking out of the sheet.

Wearing a simple white dress, Mom stumbled in and plopped down on a chair. "My children are fornicating."

Jo was still as stone, staring at her sister.

Zena, looking unruffled and highly entertained, picked up a magazine and starting fanning Mom with it. "They are not related."

"No, you're right," Mom said, her gaze unfocused as she thought. "They aren't related yet. We won't get married, and then it will be okay."

Before Leo could object, Christopher walked into the room. His gaze went to his bride first, and his wholesome face turned down with worry at her stricken figure. He glanced up, saw Leo and Tempest in the bed, and reeled back, his jaw slack and his eyes popping.

"But you're gay," Jo finally said, her voice breaking free of the freeze.

Everyone in the room turned to Jo and looked at her as if she were an imbecile.

"Nope." Zena's voice was dry, but her lips turned

up in delight. "Just incestuous."

"Get out of my room!" Leo felt the disadvantage of being naked in bed but had had enough of the judgment. He sat up all the way, and the sheet fell down to his waist. He regretted the move when everyone's attention went to his bare chest.

"How long has this been happening?" Mom asked.

"Just once, last night," Leo said. "Well, three times." He glanced at Tempest. She pulled the sheet higher over her reddening face.

Christopher put a hand on his belly. "I think I might vomit."

"It's just wedding nerves," Jo said.

"This is not what I had it mind when I said I wanted you to get along with Christopher's daughters," Mom said.

"What are we going to do?" Christopher looked at Leo's mom, his face conflicted.

"You're all going to get out," Leo said, glad for the commanding ring of his voice. "We will be ready for the wedding in thirty minutes. And you two *are* getting married. Tempest and I are dating, and y'all can get on board or not. But we are not blood related, and we will not be calling each other brother and sister. Ever. Now get out."

Each person had to look over the couple cowering in bed once more before shuffling out. Zena winked at him before closing the door.

Leo turned to Tempest.

She sent him a wicked smile. "Looked like the shower is big enough for both of us."

They weren't ready in thirty minutes as promised, but they smiled all through the wedding.

Chapter Thirteen
The Bakery

Tempest perched on the counter stool in her kitchen. She stood. She walked around the house, straightening the books on the shelf, refolding the bathroom towels. Blair still hadn't come home from work. Tempest's heart tried to jump out of her rib cage. She'd been riding on adrenaline since she gave her two-week notice at work this morning. She, Tempest Grace Swan, had *quit.* In truth, she'd been flying high since she snuck into Leo's room in Mexico a glorious nine days ago. They'd spent every available moment together since. She'd had no idea what real love could do to a person. She couldn't believe she was capable of such happiness.

If she'd learned anything from it, besides how much she craved Leo, it was that she had to take the risk. She had to venture out into darkness to see the stars. And she wanted stars.

Footsteps sounded outside. She squeaked and returned to her seat at the kitchen counter. She picked up her lukewarm tea and took a sip as Blair walked in.

"Hey, Stormie."

"What's up, Big Stick?" Tempest rolled her smile between her teeth and willed her face to appear nonchalant. "How was work?"

"I'm so over it."

Tempest suffered another jolt of excitement.

"Some asshole flipped my tray of shrimp cocktail over when I was walking past."

So that explained the red sauce splattering her clothes. "Sorry, babe."

Blair dropped her purse and shoes on the floor by the door and tiptoed to the kitchen.

Tempest motioned with her chin. "The kettle is still hot if you want a cup."

Blair grabbed a mug and poured the steamy liquid. She leaned against the counter with a tired sigh. "I didn't expect to see you. I thought you'd already be over at Leo's by now." Blair glanced at the oven clock, which read 8:11 p.m.

"I wanted to see you tonight."

"Trouble in paradise?" Concern flashed over Blair's face.

"No. He's perfect. It's perfect. We are so in love it's disgusting."

"Did you want to see me for any other reason than to make me jealous? And a little nauseous?"

Tempest blew on pretend steam from her cold tea to hide her desire to grin. "Do you have a name yet for your bakery?"

Blair sipped and scowled. "Don't bring that up tonight." She inhaled, her nose close to the hot tea. "I'm too depressed for dreams."

Tempest's voice was bland, uninterested when she said, "How much money do you have saved?"

"Eight grand. It's not enough." She dropped a napkin into the trash drawer and kicked it closed. "I'll never have enough."

It was more than Tempest had hoped for. She

couldn't quite suppress her bubbling emotions when she spoke again. "I bet if we add my fifty-three thousand, we'll have enough to get started."

Blair stared. She set the mug down. She held Tempest's gaze. Her dark eyes filled with tears. She licked her pinkie and stuck it out. "I'll take that bet."

****

Leo pulled up to Sticks and Storms, as he'd done nearly every day after work since the pastry shop opened last summer. They'd done an impressive job. Tempest was a wiz at the business end—Leo's COO acted as their consultant, which helped. And Blair Stickley had surprised him. That little tiger was at the bakery every morning before the sun.

He skirted the dozen people waiting in line, peeking over shoulders to see the day's offerings. Bacon scones were still available. He loved and hated Blair for introducing them to him four months ago. And as always, a glass case was stocked full of sky-and-forest-inspired treats such as pine-tree chocolate-dipped pretzels, pecan cloud clusters, blizzards of coconut, and grizzly bear gingerbreads. He let himself through the door that said *Employees Only* and slipped into the back office. Tempest's gaze flickered to him and then back to her computer, but she lifted her chin, inviting him to kiss her while she typed. He didn't go for the quick peck, not today. He cupped the base of her skull, tilted her head back, and let her have it.

When he released her, her lips were flushed crimson, and her eyes were melted sky. Her hands had gone limp on the keyboard.

"Uh," she whispered.

"Get back to work."

"What's work?" She leaned up toward him, her lips parting in welcome, but he forced himself to step back.

She scowled.

He grinned.

"I'll be done in five minutes. I just need to finish payroll. Then you're going to finish what you started, tease."

He shrugged noncommittally, but his veins throbbed. "Take your time. I'll be over with the discards." He sauntered out and went to the back of the kitchen where he found the tray of rejects. He picked up a piece of broken bacon scone, but he couldn't taste it over the anxiety tearing him apart. He'd triple-checked his plans for tonight. Everything needed to be perfect.

Blair sashayed in, her curls wrapped in a bright green handkerchief. Flour dusted her apron.

"You're here late," he said.

She usually left after the lunch rush. Even when she ended then, with her sunrise start, it was a long day for her.

He lifted his treat. "Thank you for this."

"I got busy with Valentine's orders. Nothing says I love you like pink chocolate."

Silvia and Christopher and the rest of humanity had firm claim on Valentine's Day, but today, February thirteenth, belonged to Leo and Tempest. His pulse rose as he lifted the tiny box from his pocket. "What about this?" He popped the lid, revealing the bulging diamond ring nestled inside.

Blair's hand flew to her heart, and her eyes softened as she swooned. "Now *that* is an engagement ring."

"I hope that's Tempest's reaction too." Nerves

sparked. He'd never been happier than he was with Tempest. They were so deep in this he didn't know where he ended and she began. She was his everything. But asking to be her husband felt like stepping off a cliff. He'd never been more scared, even when he thought he might die at ten years old. Tonight he was going to risk it all, offer up his pounding heart to her, because he needed all of her, not just now, but for the rest of his life.

Blair's gaze was riveted to the sparkle. "Boy, can I marry you instead?"

"Maybe Tempest will say no." He forced a teasing grin to cover his nerves.

"I wouldn't bet on it." She held out an open palm.

He handed her the box. "Don't touch it. No smudges."

She held the precious stone right in front of her nose. It reflected every color of the rainbow on her chocolatey eyes. He had already spent hours staring at the flawless diamond, building courage, waiting for today and the perfect date he had planned.

"Well, *that* is gorgeous."

He whirled at the familiar voice, his heart dropping out of his body. "Shit."

Tempest's brows rose at his hissed curse. "What? If you didn't want me to catch you proposing to my best friend, maybe you should not have done it at my work." Fortunately, she didn't look angry. She bit her lip.

Blair's wide-eyed gaze tracked in slow motion from the incriminating evidence in her hand to the woman who'd snuck up on them. Blair hadn't moved anything but her eyes, making no sound, as if that would make her invisible.

Leo lifted the box, snapped it closed, and stuffed it in his pocket. "Nothing to see here."

"Boo. I want to see it." Tempest folded her arms and looked stoic, but he'd seen her fingers tremble before she hid them under her arms.

"You have to wait." His heart was going to break his ribs.

"Why?" Her jaw tightened below eyes that turned glossy with emotion.

This wasn't how it was supposed to go, but how could he leave her looking so vulnerable? "I still have to ask your father for permission to marry you." He blurted it out, then laughed at his own joke, but the sound came out rough with nerves. Tears threatened behind his eyes. "Seriously, though. I have it all planned."

Her whole body softened, and she reached out. "This is perfect. I don't need helicopter rides or candlelight or a famous singer serenading us." Her lips curved up. "Actually, I still want to do all the fancy stuff you planned, but I just *need* you." She took a step toward him. "And with my best friend here watching"—Blair was holding up her phone, documenting—"it saves me from having to tell her everything later." Tempest slid her arms around his neck. "But you are not going to keep me in suspense about what that ring is for unless you want me to consider changing my answer."

"I'm sorry I ruined it." His face was inches from hers now.

"Just shut up and tell me how much you love me."

His shaking hands found her waist. His voice

quivered like a flicked doorstop spring. "I love you."

She nodded. "Tell me more."

He laughed, and his shoulders loosened. "You're my favorite stalker. I'm so glad you creeped on my house and fell at my feet."

She pursed her lips. He kissed her pucker.

"You're the best sister ever." He grinned, adrenaline rushing through his veins. "And you let me do you."

"Is this seriously what you had planned?" She wiggled backward out of his embrace.

Turning grave, he knelt on both knees. Through drips of sugar and flour, he scooted forward, ignoring the pain in his kneecaps, until he was flush against her legs. He gripped the backs of her thighs and tilted his head to look up.

"Please." The heat of tears flickered to life behind his eyes. "I will die without you." His heart came out with the words.

Her legs went soft in his hands, and her weight hit his chest before she managed to balance upright again. Her palms found the nape of his neck, and she cradled his head as he gazed up at his goddess.

"I don't know how to tell you how much I love you, because there are no words for what consumes me," he whispered.

Blair let out a massive, "Awwwww."

"Shut up, B. I'm pretending you're not here," Tempest said without looking over. Her glittering eyes stayed hot on his.

He took a steadying breath. "Will you marry me, Tempest? Will you never, ever, *ever* leave me? Even when the rest of my hair goes?"

"I love your balding head."

He leaned back and pulled the box from his pocket. He opened it and held it up in offering. "Say yes."

Her smile was like an April morning. She was so beautiful. Her hair had grown to her shoulders, and she'd taken to wearing it straight, sharpening the angle of her jaw. And those eyes, almond shaped with blue irises the size of the sky and just as enchanting. And below her face…he felt a flush just thinking about her smooth skin, long legs, and soft curves.

He lifted the ring from its silk pillow. "Will you travel around the world with me, cuddle with me while we watch movies, let me play the piano for you, and have my babies?" He flipped the ring back and forth in his fingertips so it sparkled like a supernova.

Her face went soft as she traced his jaw. She wasn't looking at the diamond. She was looking at him as if he were the treasure. A tear slid down his cheek. She leaned over and kissed it away. Her lips moved to his. He tasted salt. It was the kind of slow, heavy kiss that melted his muscles.

"Yes, please," she whispered against his mouth. "Yes to all of it and everything else."

He scrambled to stand, careless of the pastry mess on his shins. He slid the huge rock on her long, slender finger.

"It really is gorgeous. Too nice for me…but I'm keeping it."

"That's what I say about you." He brought her mouth to his again. Her shifting lips sent sparks down his body. She opened to him, her hands sliding up his back, and his blood went white hot. "Can we consummate this engagement in here?"

"Hell no," Blair said, striding up.

They broke apart, but Leo kept his arm around Tempest's waist as they turned toward their friend.

Blair tucked her phone into her pocket. "First of all, congratulations. Second of all, that was weirdly adorable. And third, y'all are making me insanely jealous, so get out of my kitchen."

Tempest turned her face to him. Her lips were crushed rose petals, and her eyes bubbled with happiness.

Risking his heart was nothing compared to this reward.

A word about the author...

Mary Beesley believes humans are born to create, and promotes creativity in all its beautiful forms. She's learning calligraphy and watercolor. She loves exploring our magnificent planet and finding all the best places to eat around the world. But nothing beats coming home and sharing a pot of slow-simmered soup and homemade sourdough with friends and family. If she's not in her writing chair, you'll probably find her hiking in the Utah mountains with her husband and four children.

~*~

Visit Mary online at:
https://www.marybeesley.com
or on Instagram and Twitter @maryrbeesley